Quest 1

A Woman's Adventure in Europe
Bavarian Cross

An adventure novel
by BRETT HARRIMAN

Brett Harriman — Travel Publishing, July 2019.

Copyright © 2019 Brett Harriman. All rights reserved.

No part of this book may be reproduced, stored in a retrieval system, or transmitted by any means — electronic, mechanical, photocopying, recording or otherwise — without written permission from the author.

ISBN: 978-1-5488277-6-2

Printed in the United States of America.

Edited by the delightful and proficient Laura M. Peach from Colorado and Jazzy J. from Washington, D.C. Without there valueable input, their'd bee alota mustakes.

All maps hand-drawn by © Brett Harriman.

Pictures used throughout the interior of this book were taken by © Brett Harriman, unless otherwise noted. Pictures on the front and back cover of this novel were taken by © Brett Harriman.

Cover created by © Brett Harriman.

NEWS FLASH: This novel has its very own tour package. Really! Experience the adventures of Sydney Endicott and her "Quest for the Bavarian Cross" with the novel's author, Brett Harriman.
Tour departs this year September 14, 2019, in Frankfurt, Germany.
Space is limited. Will you join the "Quest" with Brett?
(Go to BrettHarriman.com for latest tours & dates.)

NOTE FROM SYDNEY ENDICOTT: Please pass this book on to a fellow adventurer. Let's get this novel into as many homes and hands across the country as possible.

EDITOR'S NOTE: Please share Sydney's quest by reviewing this novel on *Amazon* or elsewhere. As a small publisher, we get pumped about the little things. That's why positive support and word-of-mouth from our readers means the world to us. Thanks in advance!

All comments, suggestions, or whatever it is you want to get off your chest, e-mail: Brett@BrettHarriman.com

Quest for the Bavarian Cross

A WOMAN'S ADVENTURE IN EUROPE

Contents

Chapter 1: *I Need a Break (Diplomaville, USA)* ... **1**
    Part II: Thursday morning — the exam ... **9**
    Part III: Friday morning ... **10**
    Part IV: Sunday afternoon ... **13**
    Part V: Happy Monday ... **15**
    Part VI: Tuesday, last period ... **16**
    Part VII: Wednesday morning ... **19**
    Part VIII: Thanksgiving ... **19**
    Part IX: D-Day ... **20**
    Part X: Bon voyage ... **24**

Chapter 2: *A New Beginning (Chiemsee, Germany)* ... **27**
    Part II: The Waldheim ... **29**
    Part III: Chambermaid Extraordinaire ... **33**
    Part IV: The e-mail ... **33**
    Part V: The hallway pick-up ... **34**

Chapter 3: *Jesse's Tour (Salzburg & The Sound of Music)* ... **39**

Chapter 4: *My First Youth Hostel (Salzburg, Austria)* ... **63**

Chapter 5: *Look, But Don't Touch (Baden-Baden, Ger.)* ... **77**

Chapter 6: *An Alpine Village (Berchtesgaden, Germany)* ... **103**

Chapter 7: *The Letter (Munich, Germany)* ... **127**

Chapter 8: *Bulwarks and Mysteries (Rothenburg, Ger.)* ... **165**

Travel Europe with Brett ... **190**

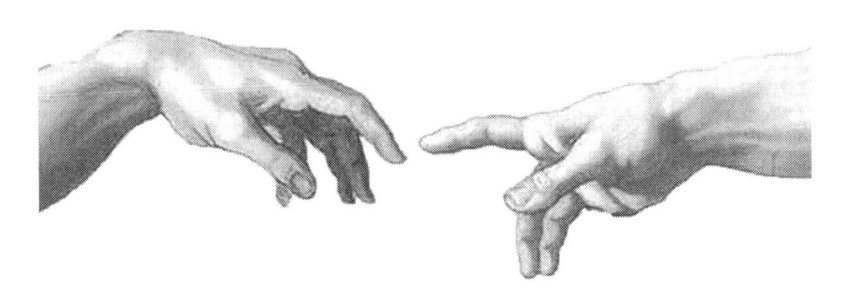

I can't believe what a year it's been for a girl like me. One afternoon, on the way back from the student union, I experienced an overwhelming feeling as if a giant finger broke through the clouds and pointed at me. For what, I could only imagine. But like all good celestial encounters, I found myself on an aircraft bound for a faraway place. If serendipity has a home, let its roots flourish in my travels. If I only do this once, the time is now!

I Need a Break

Chapter 1: PART I

I must have been the last person to board because it seemed like the plane began moving before I even fastened my seat belt. There was no turning back, now.

I stared out the window and watched the tarmac race by while our plane soared down the runway and powerfully lifted off. The earth dropped away beneath me. Below were the territories of a nation; its diverse ranges and multicolored topography led to the rippling blue expanse of the Atlantic Ocean. We cut through the clouds, then the sun came beaming through my window. It was magnificent.

Our flight attendant patiently navigated the narrow aisle with her mobile cart while offering an assortment of beverages. When she approached me I asked for my usual with a perky smile. "Hot cocoa, please."

"Sorry," she replied. "We only have hot tea and coffee."

My smile wilted. I politely thanked her, but declined.

Some 20 minutes later the flight attendant rolled by again, this time she handed us each a white tray wrapped in foil. It was lunch: chicken with peas, carrots, and a mini container of vanilla pudding. What little appetite I had dissipated at the airport when leaving Mom and Dad. Nonetheless, I knew it was to be a flight of endurance and I'd better consume what nutrients I could.

The cabin darkened and the small video screen fixed into the seat in front of me came to life. It was like having my own personal television, which displayed a selection of on-demand movies. One such feature film was titled *On My Own*. How appropriate.

I wasn't in the mood for a movie anyway, thus I ripped open the thin plastic bag containing my complimentary pillow and slung it against the window to comfort my head while I pondered home and the future. It was hard to fathom that the time had come and I was actually en route, covering half the globe on a journey no one in my family had ever undertaken. My conclusions repetitively traveled in one direction; home was 13 months away and the future held new adventures.

Our captain's voice interrupted my thoughts to announce the possibility of strong turbulence ahead. I buckled my seat belt as instructed and braced for a jarring ride. I missed home more than ever.

∞

Four months earlier, mid-November, Diplomaville, USA

For a fleeting moment, I thought if I banged my head hard enough against the wall I could knock myself unconscious and have the perfect excuse for missing the exam. However, having enough guts to wallop myself that hard was certainly not in my gene pool. So I opened my psych book to Chapter One, *Introduction to Social Psychology*, which might as well have read: Don't Even Bother!

The psych exam would cover the first 10 chapters. So far, I had read the cover of the book and managed to scribble two pages of notes during the handful of lectures I'd attended.

My psychology class was 50 agonizing minutes three days a week with the most long-winded, self-important, pointy-headed, beady-eyed, anal-retentive, height-challenged, and badly dressed professor that I'd ever had the distinct displeasure of encountering in a classroom. It was going to take a mountain of motivation to get over this hump and, inevitably, a miracle to survive the mid-term exams. My pending collegiate failure seemed more real every day, and unless compelled I wouldn't give my troubles to a howler monkey in heat.

The exam would begin at 8 a.m. tomorrow. It was now 7:37, Wednesday night.

"Sydney! Miss Sydney Endicott, are you in there?" I heard a piercing voice followed by a rap on my door and the slight nasal tones of my vivacious cohort, Heather. She was a bubbly redhead from Long Island who lived down the hallway in our dormitory and specialized in running with her sorority from one fraternity party to another while putting an enormous amount of energy into trying to get me to rush her house. Unfortunately for her, I couldn't hurdle the thought of branding my clothes and advertising the fact that I was paying a few hundred bucks a semester

I Need a Break

CHAPTER 1

for the privilege of going to private parties. I'd just as soon acquire my own booze and deal with the idiots at large.

"Yeah. Come in."

Heather stepped into the room and immediately her perfume hit me like a freight train, jostling my senses. "Whew! Smells like you've got something on the line tonight."

"Yeah, I'm off to *The Jungle* with a few sisters. I think some of the guys from the football team will be there. Wanna tag along?"

"No thanks, but I appreciate the invite."

I just wasn't up to it with all the academic pressure piling up on me. Plus, hanging with a group of jocks whose primary topics of conversation consisted of football and which girls they screwed last was not my idea of fun. Besides, I was positive that my respiratory system couldn't handle all the perfume and after-shave.

"Whatcha doin'?" Heather asked while bopping across the room and glancing curiously at the textbooks in front of me.

"Psych exam, tomorrow morning."

"And you're only on Chapter One!?" She said, frowning. "Don't ya think you're starting the semester a little late?"

"Please, don't remind me." If she only knew how badly I was really doing, but I didn't want to bother her with my problems. Reclining in my chair, I could only feign pleasantness. "Have fun tonight."

Heather shrugged and walked back to the door. "Ya know, life would be a whole lot easier if you'd either commit to school or commit to breaking the news to your folks that you're not committing."

Heather wasn't much better at studying than me, but she was a buckle-down-when-you-have-to kind of a girl. Her major was fashion design, which presented a slightly different academic perspective from liberal arts. Nonetheless, I was failing my classes and Heather wasn't.

"I don't know what's gotten into you lately, Sydney, but your dejection is creeping down the hallway and into the rooms of a few girls who are close to gagging...including me!" With that thought, she exited the room and pointedly slammed the door.

It was the middle of my sophomore year, and if I didn't shape up, my future would entail dragging home a handful of Fs for the Christmas holidays. Needless to say, Mom and Dad were going to flip out.

It was time to get serious and regain my scholastic worth. I put on some background music and made a cup of noodles before sitting down at my desk. Generally, I studied with a cup of hot cocoa and the TV tuned to "The Simpsons" or something as wacky. The time I spent in high school absorbing unhinged network programming led to some academic accolades and admission to a decent university. Unfortunately, my academic success failed to follow me to its hallowed halls.

Sweeping the hair from my eyes, I stared down at the first page of the first chapter for the very first time all semester. Outside a low-pressure system had consumed the city and rain began softly tapping against the window left of my desk. The tempo was a pleasant accompaniment to "Closing Time" by Semisonic.

A bout of lethargy struck me like a sedative. I put the book down while glancing at the clock. It was time to hop online and get my brain cooking again.

I'm not among those Internet enthusiasts who spill their guts to cyberstrangers or indulge in all-night sexual fantasies with aging, overweight, unhappily married men pretending to look like Chris Hemsworth. If I were to crave such a fantasy world, I would hardly rush to one that used a keyboard as its primary mode of transportation.

I had found something more interesting and certainly more intriguing: Puzzles. Not just any puzzles, not like jigsaws or anything. These were more like mysteries.

My first real-life mystery was assigned as a development study in psychology class. The course syllabus certainly had required reading, but one also had to volunteer for three lab experiments. So far, the only exercise I'd been involved in was a real mindbender. We all read the same convoluted story about a man who allegedly murdered his wife and hid the body in a nearby forest. By taking apart the story, we were to decide where the body was buried and whether the husband was guilty. The experiment was essentially about group thinking and establishing the pecking order in social situations. I thought the project was engaging, but the other students didn't share my enthusiasm. So most of the talking and all of the reasoning was left to me. The grad assistant never told us whether our conclusions were right or wrong, which was frustrating. Nevertheless, the whole idea of wading through the plot for clues and putting the puzzle together was captivating. The one hour we worked on it zipped by like a New York minute. A week later, I bumped into the grad assistant who ran the experiment and I asked him where he'd gotten the story. That's when he mentioned the puzzle Web site.

The site featured brainteasers, intriguing quests, and any story with a twist. Most interesting was the subtopic, Searches for Lost Relics.

Some of the guys hooked on the site regularly held treasure-hunt parties and cyber-geek get-togethers, which I backpedaled from as quickly as possible. A few mysteries, however, leapt out like a 3-D docudrama.

I Need a Break

That's how I came across ShoSho12. We'd been chatting about relics stolen from noble landlords in Europe when he referred to a mystery involving his German ancestors, a lost crucifix, and a dead monarch. I read his story eagerly.

In the 19th century there was this king who had a ton of money, the love of the people, and a penchant for building castles. King Ludwig II of Bavaria constructed a number of storybook castles all over southern Germany, filling each with fanciful works of art and precious trinkets. The king suspiciously drowned in a lake the depth of a kiddie pool, but not before he allegedly doled out his treasures to charitable groups and personal acquaintances.

One lucky recipient was the son of a wine merchant from a village near Chiemsee, a lake in Bavaria, who on his 10th birthday received a jeweled crucifix made of gold. The boy's family was indeed touched by the king's generosity; however, they were penniless and immediately made plans to sell it. A jeweler in the region took one look at the crucifix and just about coughed up a cat. He was so awestruck by the relic that he gave the wine merchant all but the shirt off his back to purchase it. The wine merchant left delighted and much richer, while the jeweler rushed home with the cross to show his wife. She was impressed for sure, but not to the extent of handing over all their money. After a losing argument with his wife, the jeweler set out to get their cash back before the couple starved to death.

The jeweler traveled all night to reach the wine merchant's house, only to find out the entire family packed up and left town. He had no choice but to turn around and head for Munich, where he intended to find another jeweler or anyone with money to purchase the crucifix. On his journey, four bandits robbed him. They took the crucifix, his horse, shoes and one gold tooth. They did, however, leave him alive — but stranded. As the jeweler began his long walk home, he realized that if the freezing temperatures of the Bavarian winter didn't kill him, his wife would. As fate would have it, the weather proved too overwhelming and he met his maker right there in the tranquil forest south of Munich. Toothless, barefoot, and flat broke.

The thieves sold the crucifix to a wealthy old woman in another small town near Chiemsee. Overjoyed, they set off to spend their ill-gained riches. Later that day the thieves themselves were robbed, dying in a shootout.

The old woman who had purchased the crucifix did so in the hope that her terminally ill husband would wear it around his neck to affirm his devotion to God. So heavy was the cross that it became impossible for her feeble husband to wear without collapsing from its weight. The old woman instead hung the sacred relic on the wall above his bed. The nail upon which it rested gave way and the crucifix came crashing down, killing the feeble man and making a mess of the sheets. Being superstitious, the old woman believed the relic to be a bad omen and consequently gave it to her manservant to pawn at the nearest jeweler.

Coincidentally, the jeweler was the widow of the man who originally purchased the crucifix from the wine merchant. Since that fateful event, she had become reliant on the charity of her brother and his intolerable wife to survive. Upon witnessing the rebirth of the cross, she went nuts speaking of its evils and thrashing the manservant with a wooden candlestick. Bruised and beaten, he hobbled back to his employer.

Upon his arrival, the manservant told the old woman the tale of the cursed crucifix. Shocked, she ordered him to take the relic somewhere and bury it. Aware of its value, he instead carried the king's opulent cross to his quarters and locked it away. A month later came news that Ludwig had tossed himself in a lake. The old woman's trusty manservant, concluding that the time was ripe to capitalize on the king's death, immediately grabbed the crucifix and headed into town to sell it. He never made it any farther than the end of the cobbled lane where his horse began bucking wildly out of control, unceremoniously throwing the manservant onto the road and crushing his neck. When the crucifix was discovered on his body, the old woman seized it, wrapped it in wool, and placed it in a steel lockbox. She wrote the tale of the cursed crucifix, set the pages inside and secretly took it to the shore of Chiemsee lake. She buried it deep within the soft earth, in view of King Ludwig's tribute to Versailles: Schloss Herrenchiemsee.

The old woman went to her grave without divulging its location, and the legend of the crucifix spread like wildfire. Many tried to find the king's treasure, but none succeeded. Some believed the crucifix would never be found, as Ludwig had reclaimed his gift from the earth.

The story was certainly fascinating, but if numerous fortune hunters had been sniffing the trails for so long wouldn't someone have stumbled upon it by now? There is only so much shoreline, and a hundred-plus years was plenty of time for every grain of sand to have been scrutinized once or twice. However, ShoSho12 reminded me that nobody ever found the Nazi gold, either. Maybe those people are darn good at hiding things. But what about the crucifix's alleged curse? For a treasure seeker, I suspect this would be offset by the spirit of the adventure and the proverbial pot of gold at the end of the rainbow.

Fantasyland devoured my time while reality stared me in the face. My psychology book remained open to the first page of the first chapter. One thought came to mind: Screw it! I could read all night and still fail the darned test.

After grabbing my jacket, I slipped into some comfortable shoes and headed out the door. There was no way, regardless of weather, that I was going to stay in the rest of the night with a book I wouldn't absorb even if I ate it. The student union seemed the logical place to seek a cup of hot chocolate, newspaper, and a distraction from my troubles.

Despite it being 11 p.m., the commons were full of people with their books, ill-fitting clothes and strange, unkempt hairdos. I blended in fine. Most were in the lounge area conversing in small groups, contrasting the few who were quietly studying. To be honest, if one truly wanted to study on a Wednesday night, would one really be here? Case in point: Me.

At the refreshment counter, I dumped a packet of cocoa into a cup, poured in hot water and a shot of milk, picked up the daily paper, and sat down at a table near the television tuned in to the Travel Channel for the 10 or so people eating overpriced gourmet soups and stale croissants.

Anxious, I opened the newspaper, turned straight to the Employment section and kept an eye out for the perfect job for me:

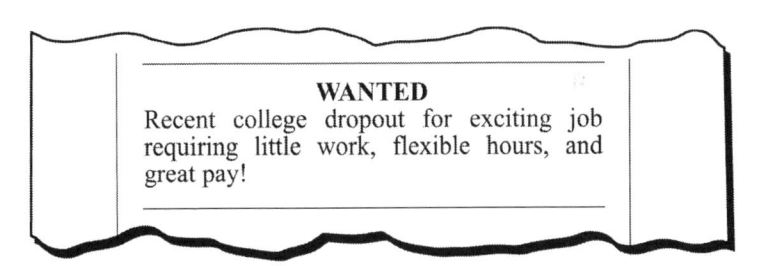

> **WANTED**
> Recent college dropout for exciting job requiring little work, flexible hours, and great pay!

Never found that one. At any rate, the fact that I wasn't exactly heading for *summa cum laude* made me think seriously about finding an alternative. Although, unearthing a job that would present such an enormous opportunity to justify dumping my college education would be tricky, at best.

I skimmed through some more advertisements. Most jobs required prior work experience, but how does one get experience if one cannot get a job to gain the experience?

Nevertheless, my vocational skills were definitely lacking, limited to a summer of scooping ice cream and blending smoothies. In high school, I didn't have to work much as I had reassured Mom and Dad that my invaluable study time after school would get me into a decent university.

Some two years later and I was no closer to finding my future than the night of high school graduation. I seemed to be living a rudderless existence, wasting vital discovery time sitting in class and telling professors what they wanted to hear, not to mention squandering more of my parents' money! Of course, my looming failure in psychology class, along with two or three other subjects, had brought the whole grim affair sharply into focus. Failing was undeniably my fault, but I honestly couldn't think of a single reason to be all that concerned. Well, except for the fact that my parents were likely to kick my butt onto the street without so much as an old clunker to live in. Albeit, homelessness held as little charm for me as finishing the semester.

I meticulously scanned every ad. One job stood out from the rest, practically leaping off the page and slapping me in the face!

GOVERNMENT JOBS AVAILABLE AT EUROPEAN RESORTS
We are looking for energetic people to fill hotel positions at our resorts in Garmisch and Chiemsee, Germany. Waiters/waitresses, kitchen workers, room attendants, desk clerks, and recreation assts. Will receive airfare, subsidized meals and housing, competitive pay and benefits.

I couldn't believe what I was reading: the opportunity to travel to Europe, earn money, and get away from school — all *without* my parents.

An epiphany struck; my eyes quickly re-scanned the job ad. The resorts were located in Garmisch and Chiemsee, Germany. Could this be the same Chiemsee where the king's crucifix was buried? Was going all that way to track down an old ancestral tale justification for dropping out of college?

I had to confess, traveling an ocean away to work for the U.S. government did sound more appealing than washing dishes at the local diner. At the very least, I could see Europe before settling down and becoming mired in life's obligatory car, rent, and insurance payments. I certainly couldn't tell Mom or Dad or any of my friends about the quest for a lost crucifix. They'd all think I was nuts!

Nonetheless, these were all assumptions. First, a few phone calls were necessary to see whether the ad was genuine. Like the old adage: If it sounds too good to be true, it probably is.

Chugging the rest of my cocoa, I tore the ad from the paper, stuffed it into my jeans pocket and practically ran out of the student union. Outside, the light rain had turned into gently falling flakes. No snow had accumulated in the streets or on the boughs of the trees, but if it continued, *hallelujah*...snow day!

Back at my desk, guilt made me skim over the unread chapters and useless notes for psychology class. Around 2 a.m. my eyes grew heavy and the text read like gobbledygook. It was going to be a long night.

Thursday morning — the exam
PART II

The alarm *screeeeeched* good morning in its usual maddening way — 7:30 came much too early. I must have passed out while "studying" because I woke with my face implanted between the pages of my psychology book. With any luck, I absorbed the required reading by osmosis.

Following a brisk shower, a frantic fumble through my clothes that had since piled up, and a glass of orange juice to wash down an unsavory piece of burnt toast, I grabbed my bag and landed a seat in the class auditorium by 8 a.m. I felt like I was dragging a piano behind me, but as usual I was denied the accompaniment.

Looking uninterested and lethargic, Professor Davis' grad assistants began passing out the exam booklets. I dreaded this test like no other. My fellow undergraduates appeared confident, sitting tall in their worn seats. They must have studied. When the professor finally announced that we could begin, I filled in the little circles so fast that I don't even remember reading the questions.

My mind drifted in a sea of emotional upheaval. The left half of my brain calculated the frightening consequences of academic failure and dropping out of school. My right hemisphere held me motionless below the ceiling of the Sistine Chapel in Rome, staring upwards in wonderment at Michelangelo's Creation of Adam.

Thirty minutes later, I oozed down the stairs and outside the building, knowing I'd failed the exam miserably but relieved that the ordeal was over. If I never do that again, it'll be too soon.

Who am I? What am I doing here? Where am I going? My hands rested deep within the pockets of my jeans and my head hung low as I stared at the asphalt beneath my feet. I must have kicked every stone from the auditorium to Jefferson Avenue, eventually arriving in front of the dorms. *Carpe diem*, I convinced myself, seize the day. I pulled the crumpled newspaper ad from my pocket and dialed the number listed.

I heard a steady drone: *b...e...e...p* — followed by silence then a second beep before a man answered. "Resort Europe, Human Resources, this is Jim. How may I help you?"

My voice countered some 5,000 miles away: "Is your ad for real?!"

He assured me that the ad was legitimate, there were positions available, and yes, the resort was indeed on Chiemsee lake. Additionally, they would give me a free plane ticket, partial reimbursement for extra baggage, discounted meals, and a roof over my head. All I had to do was fill out the application that he would e-mail. If accepted, the contract covered a 13-month period. Upon its completion they would fly me back home and into the loving arms of my parents. If I wished to stay longer, we could discuss the details later. He also told me that a majority of the workforce were young people about my age, many of whom take advantage of their days off to travel around Europe. Who could ask for more?

I gave him my e-mail address then ran over to the campus library as fast as possible, not caring about how uncool I looked. While waiting for a printer to become available, I reflected upon how desperate I was for a change in my life. Any change. Maybe this was it.

The buzzing of the printer roused me from my trance. I paid the cashier, sat at a table and filled out the application. It was pretty basic stuff, taking only 10 minutes to complete. The clock on the wall read 10:20 a.m. I knew Germany was several hours ahead of local time and I decided any further action could wait until tomorrow. By then, the results of the exam would be up and I'd have the ultimate reason to seek other options.

Friday morning
PART III

Friday came, and as suspected, I failed! Not just barely, I went down like a kamikaze pilot in the Pacific, scoring a mind-blowing 47 percent and officially qualifying for the most pathetic attempt to fake it through an exam. There was no point in showing up for classes on Monday. Why delay the inevitable. Nevertheless, I was determined to finish out the day's lectures, until I promptly fell asleep in American Literature minutes after arriving, which was a good enough reason to skip my afternoon classes and progress to the dorms for some much-needed rest.

The cup of hot cocoa I brought back from the student union made lounging on my cold couch a little easier to take. Abruptly, in the corner of the room, my flower vase began to tremble in synch with the rhythmic grunting penetrating the thin wall.

"Oh no, not again!" I huffed. Had I'd known that my neighbor, Cheryl, was in her room with Gene, hormone extraordinaire, I would've remained in class and slept there.

Anticipating the love connection to climax multiple times, I cranked the music up loud to drown out the irrepressible moaning.

My thoughts, challenged as they were, contemplated notifying Sho-Sho of my employment opportunity at Chiemsee. If I were to get the job, perhaps he would be willing to divulge information to a virtual stranger about a chunk of gold studded with jewels worth considerably more than either of us could earn in a lifetime. Yet, if I were afraid to ask, the consequences could mean that I spend more tedious hours trudging through the Chiemsee mud than necessary. I had nothing to lose. The worst that could happen was that he either ignores my query, or sues me if I were to get my hands on the crucifix first, which is assuming an awful lot.

I logged on to the chat room with the hope of catching ShoSho12. He wasn't online. The next best option was to type him a tactful e-mail.

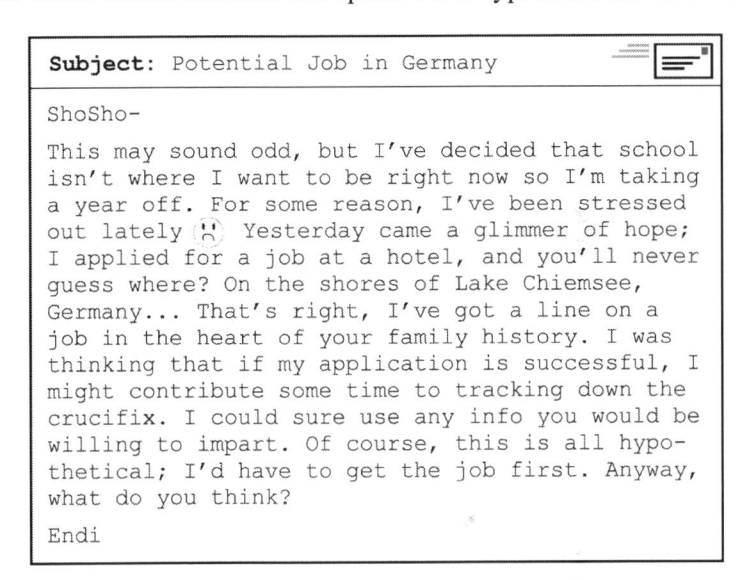

Subject: Potential Job in Germany

ShoSho-

This may sound odd, but I've decided that school isn't where I want to be right now so I'm taking a year off. For some reason, I've been stressed out lately :) Yesterday came a glimmer of hope; I applied for a job at a hotel, and you'll never guess where? On the shores of Lake Chiemsee, Germany... That's right, I've got a line on a job in the heart of your family history. I was thinking that if my application is successful, I might contribute some time to tracking down the crucifix. I could sure use any info you would be willing to impart. Of course, this is all hypothetical; I'd have to get the job first. Anyway, what do you think?

Endi

I clicked on "Send" and the e-mail whisked away. While I remained seated and fretting for no reason, someone knocked forcefully on my door.

"Come in." The door opened with a bang! I jumped in place and turned to see Cheryl standing in the doorway wearing a bathrobe, an angry expression, and very little else. If she was shooting for modesty by donning a sheer white robe, she missed the target by a long shot.

"Would you mind turning down that frigging music? It's making my walls shake it's so gawd-damned loud!"

Her arms were wrapped across her flat belly, just south of her equally flat chest, which was heaving with what she thought I would assume to be indignation. I knew for a fact that physical activity will also do the same thing to a young woman, and judging by the way the pictures on my wall had been swaying, I'd testify she had been pretty active in the next room. Needless to say, her screaming "Fuck me harder" might also have given it away.

"Why, Cheryl, you *are* capable of walking upright. Isn't that hard to do with a mattress strapped to your back?"

"Don't mess with me, Endicott!" Her eyes narrowed. "Turn down that music or I'll rip out the speakers myself."

I was not intimidated. For starters, I was too absorbed with crash-and-burn academia to be concerned with the exasperation of an egotistical, bottled-blonde tramp. Cheryl was no great personality, either, but extremely popular with a large number of guys on campus, from what I'd heard.

Composed, I walked over to her at the doorway. We stood a mere two feet apart; mascara ran down her cheeks. Despite Cheryl's petite 5-foot-1 frame, she meant business. I couldn't believe this mindless episode was even occurring, but it was — and she deserved a verbal plateful.

"Look, you foul-mouthed freak show... I turned up the music so I wouldn't have to listen to you and Gene trying to hump your way through my bedroom wall. Frankly, I don't care how big his dick is or how good it feels when he slaps you with it. What I do care about is having a little peace and quiet in my *own* room. So if you want me to turn the music down, you should take your stallion over to his room at the frat house. It's not like they haven't all seen you naked before!"

A slap was tickling the palm of her hand, so I quickly slammed the door closed before she could give it a shot.

The computer then caught my eye. The e-mail icon displayed the arrival of a new message. I bounced into my chair and double-clicked "Open." It was from ShoSho12.

Subject: Happy Travels!

Endi,

Congratulations! A job in Europe, WOW, lucky you! I don't mind at all if you search for the cross. But if you find it, just save me one of its brilliant gems. The only bit of info I have is my great-grandfather's name, Franz Bauer. He supposedly was the nephew of the servant. I think Bauer is a pretty common name in Germany, so it might not help too much. Tell you what, give me a month or so and I'll see what else I can find out. Happy travels!

Peace, ShoSho

Fortunately he was congenial about the whole idea. However, he didn't seem to know much. But at least his great-grandfather's name was somewhere to start.

Meanwhile, I was beginning to feel guilty about yelling at Cheryl and maybe minutely frightened that she might be eagerly waiting outside my door to mash my melon with something mammoth. Although, considering how much energy she exerted helping Gene unload some excess fluids, I'd say she couldn't stand out there for very long without falling over.

Sunday afternoon
PART IV

The weekend flew by as I spent most of it researching the Chiemsee region in hopes of submitting a successful application. With any luck I'll be convincing my parents that the government job is an opportunity of a lifetime, and that Nazis don't wander the hills of Germany anymore.

My parents, of course, would be against me going and therefore wouldn't offer me a whole lot in the way of financial assistance. Despite the discounted meals, I would still need some spending money in Germany, and I had very little of value that could be sold. The biggest ticket items were my hybrid bicycle and laptop computer with companion speakers. My parents gave them to me as gifts for college, and assuming they took the news of my imminent failure as I predicted, these were going to be the last donations I would receive this side of the grave.

Premonitions aside, I drew up a handful of flyers to advertise my things for sale. Heather and I spent the last hours of daylight traipsing all over campus tacking them to every bulletin board we could find. By the time we made it back to our dorm, I had almost persuaded her into being the proud new owner of my computer. But there's always that same lousy stumbling block for every college student — she didn't have the cash to spare.

She did, however, have more than enough friendly chitchat. "What are ya gonna tell your parents? Mine would die of a heart attack if I were to tell them I was dropping out of school. My dad didn't talk to me for three days when he discovered my major was fashion design. When he finally did speak to me, he said: 'HEATHER, if you design any of that queer bondage crap, I'll cut you off without a dime!' What a prince, huh?"

"At least you're still allowed to live. I'm thinking of telling my folks from the window of the bus as it pulls into the depot. That way my dad can't get a clean shot off in the transit rush."

Heather rolled her eyes. "As if your dad's actually gonna try to kill you. He'll probably give ya an earful and then try to scare you back to school."

"Yeah, they'll try everything to talk me out of my decision, but when Dad hears how badly I'm doing, he'll want to re-examine his financial contribution to my career pursuit."

"What, you're not doing well?" Heather's eyes widened. "You mean you're failing some classes? The girl who's always studying?" The sarcasm was dripping from her tongue, down her designer sweater and onto her leather shoes.

"Go ahead, milk it for what it's worth." I wondered if I should help her assemble the gallows. "I need some time to think and reassess my future. It's only for a year."

There are classes I like, for sure, but I just can't believe that half the crap I'm expected to learn is going to help at all. And some professors don't seem to give a damn whether you've learned anything useful or not. They just want to hear themselves talk. Anyway, my parents pressured me into college straight out of high school by relentlessly hounding me about getting a good education.

Heather accepted the fact that I needed some time off. She also took pity on my mom and dad, whom she had met on several occasions.

"You make your parents sound like such ogres," she asserted.

"Aww, I know, but this time they won't understand. Plus, I'm going home for Thanksgiving to drop this bomb on them. For the rest of my life, I'll be reminded that this was the holiday when I broke their hearts. Bet you a million dollars my mom will guilt me with tears, and there won't be any backup support. Except for the liquor cabinet. I guess I could always raid that."

Heather smiled. "That's where I'd go!" Her expression then changed to that of suggestion. "Listen, before ya leave for Thanksgiving vacation, let's all get together for one last hurrah...say, Tuesday?"

"Okay, deal. But please don't tell anyone about me quitting school or my plans to go to Europe."

Heather agreed. And on that note we parted ways. Job or no job, I was leaving college.

Happy Monday
PART V

The next morning I woke to outstanding news. Jim from Resort Europe called to tell me that I'd been selected for a position as a hotel room attendant and that my plane ticket would be waiting for me at the airport on the day of departure.

It was as if I'd won the lottery. I dropped the phone, danced to the window, and shouted at the top of my lungs to the whole campus: "I'M GOIN' TO EUROPE!" I had to fill my shoes with nickels to keep from floating into the air.

My voice echoed from building to building, raced across Campus Square, and returned through my window with such force that it swept my hair back.

Behind me, I heard a startled voice. "Syd, is everything okay?"

I swiveled to see my neighbor, Kayumi, standing in the doorway wearing a perplexed look.

"Everything's great!" I exclaimed.

"What's all the racket about?"

"Oh, nothing," I replied.

She shook her head and began to leave.

"Ah, Kayumi, before you go."

"Yes." She swung her body back around toward Sydney.

"Are you free for drinks tomorrow night?"

"I'm not doing anything special." She double blinked. "Why, what's up?"

"Just tell the girls to keep it free and be here at seven."

"Oookaay," she curiously replied before reiterating her concern. "Are you sure you're feeling all right?"

"I promise. I haven't felt better. See ya tomorrow night."

∞

The idea of cleaning rooms or scrubbing toilets as a hotel room attendant wasn't in the slightest bit alluring, but more unappealing was failing my classes and living in shame with Mom and Dad until finding a job I was qualified for — which probably would have been cleaning rooms or scrubbing toilets.

It's amazing how piggish people can be when they know some minimum-wage worker will come in the next morning to wipe up whatever mess they make. A cleaning lady once gave me the gimlet eye at a motel outside Lincoln, Nebraska. My grandfather had passed, bringing the extended family together to grieve and sort things out, which required a few motel rooms to accommodate everyone. That night my parents, brother, and a few relatives went to Grandma Maple's house for a family discussion concerning post-funeral expenses, while my older cousins and I elected to stay at the motel. It just so happened that we stumbled across a bottle of tequila in my uncle's suitcase and ended up consuming a few shots.

Somehow, during the course of the evening, I fell into the bathroom and vomited all over the towels and floor. The next morning the folks caught on when I staggered into their room, with bloodshot eyes and rotgut breath, to ask if I could use their shower. Mom and Dad were curiously drawn to the side of my face that I must have slept on because they recited the motel's logo from the fine impression left by the bath mat. They probably would have lectured me about underage drinking, but I told them it was an adverse effect from Grandfather's passing. That's when Mom broke down crying again and leaned into Dad's arms. I was off the hook for the time being, that is, until I went back to the vomit room just as the cleaning lady was exiting. She would have given me both barrels if that sort of behavior didn't mean getting fired with a jail sentence to boot. Job or no job, I don't think I would have cleaned that mess up. There had to be a restaurant nearby that was hiring.

My burning desire in life wasn't to gain membership into a club of hotel room attendants, but if that's what it took to escape college doomsday, that's what I was prepared to do. Europe was calling.

Tuesday, last period
PART VI

Closing the door on my collegiate curriculum channeled me through the administration office. I half expected someone to try to talk me out of it, but nobody so much as looked at me sideways. They really didn't appear to give a damn, except to be adamant that under no circumstances would my tuition be refunded. I jokingly told them that my parents wouldn't be so worried about the tuition, since my funeral would be costing a whole lot more. This statement managed to evoke a slightly arched eyebrow in return for my sarcasm. These people had heard all the sob stories before and didn't give two hoots either way. Unless I walked in with a noticeable limp and perhaps a lawyer, I doubted they would show me any signs of concern at all.

Aside from the administration formalities, my last eight hours at college went somewhat smoothly. I sold both the computer and bicycle, gave my ice chest to a freshman across the hall, and tossed my defective toaster oven, aka the Prince of Darkness, in the garbage. Lastly, I packed all my belongings into boxes and hauled them to the post office to mail home.

As we had arranged, Heather came by with the girls at seven for my farewell. Saying goodbye was more difficult than I had imagined it would be. In the past, we spent most of our time together goofing around, window shopping, or at happy hour. However, I broke the news of my departure while we were all stone sober and lounging on my sagging couch, which put me center stage to four befuddled faces.

"Well...aren't you girls going to say something?" I asked.

They sat in silence until Kayumi got up and left the room. This seemed to be a signal. The girls began whispering busily among themselves while ignoring my presence. A mild form of torture would have been more agreeable.

Kayumi suddenly returned to the room with a large box. A conspiracy appeared to be underway. Heather must have been the ringleader; she pivoted my direction and spoke first. "I'm sorry, Syd...but I already told the girls you were leaving. I wanted to make sure we got you a little something for your travels." She then handed me the box on behalf of the girls. "We hope you like it!"

I was mesmerized, as sure as a deer in headlights. Nonetheless, excitement got the better of me and I opened the box at blinding speed.

"Oh, girls, you shouldn't have! A backpack?"

"It's a travel pack," Kayumi responded. "You're now officially a backpacker!"

"A backpacker?"

"Yeah, that's what everyone's doin' now. It's the cheap and easy way to travel." Kayumi continued, animatedly. "Pack your belongings in here, zip it up, throw it on your back and presto, you're mobile."

"Great idea!" I said. "Beats the heck out of lugging around my two big suitcases."

I put the backpack down and turned to the girls. "Thank you so much. This is exactly what I needed, something to kickstart my destiny." They got up one by one for a hug. A few tears were shed, until I broke the spell by reminiscing about lighter times.

"Kayumi, remember last February at Heather's costume party, you came wearing that toga?"

"Oh please, Endicott, don't bring that up again!"

"Sorry, Kayumi, just thinking about your public appearance makes me laugh."

"What appearance?" teased Ann, my freshman-year roommate.

The girls edged closer to hear the story one more time. "It was after midnight when Kayumi finally gathered the courage to ask Brad, The Body, for a dance. On her way over to him she bumped into Dexter, who was dressed as a tree, and one of his branches tugged at her safety pin just enough to loosen Kayumi's toga, exposing her left breast. About a half hour later, after Kayumi had danced with Brad and all his buddies, Heather came over to hand her a drink and noticed the 'exposure.' Red as a beet, Kayumi ran off hastily and collided with Dexter again. This time the whole toga came loose, falling to the floor."

Kayumi, wasting no time, exacted her revenge. "Save your laughter, girls. What about you, Syd?"

"Wait. What?" Time to call an audible. "I have to pee!"

"Endicott, you sit your butt right back down!" The girls weren't game for any charades, certainly not Kayumi, who stared me down and demanded sportsman-like conduct. "Remember first semester of freshman year when you had that big date with Brandon?"

"All right girls, you got me," I announced while raising a white tissue in an act of surrender.

"Thought you might remember," Kayumi said, savoring the moment. "It was such a crack-up when Ann, Heather, and I walked into your room to wish you a nice evening and found you practicing the 'make out' with your pillow."

As if that wasn't embarrassing enough, the girls continued down memory lane. "More tongue Sydney.... Mmm, bet that fabric tastes yummy!"

The stories materialized in abundance. No one got off lightly. We then drove over to the Casa Bar for dollar beers, which increased the amusement considerably. We got so smashed that we all started to cry. At 2 a.m., we stumbled across the street to La Grande Tortilla for burritos as big as your foot. Thank goodness we had enough sense to stop Heather from driving her dad's old Buick back to the dorm, otherwise I'd possibly be breaking the news of my college departure to dear Mom and Dad from a hospital room.

I Need a Break 19

Wednesday morning, one sheet in the wind
PART VII

I hauled my overstuffed bag onto the half-empty Greyhound bus and dragged it to the rear where I collapsed head first into a seat. There were a handful of girls in the back laughing and joking as if the seven-hour party bus to Mardi Gras had just begun. Anticipating the scolding I was to face at home, exuberance didn't ring a bell. The onboard cheer was making me wish I had decided to save the $25 and walk instead. If it weren't for the bitter cold this time of year, I would have given it a shot.

Nevertheless, I was so exhausted from the goings-on of the past week that I slept through the party and woke as the bus pulled into its final destination: Home. I scanned the station for my parents to no avail.

The depot resembled an extended food court in a shopping mall. There were eight different fast-food counters running the length of the building, umpteen tables, two soda machines, and a decidedly clean bathroom that I was busting to use. It didn't look much like a bus station at all. Maybe that was the point, the town planners wanted to attract a better clientele by discouraging vagrants from setting up camp. Although, one would think the homeless would prefer to wake up to the smell of grilled burgers and fries than to cigarette smoke and urine like perhaps in the alleyway outside the shelter.

There they were, Sid and Dolores Endicott, my lovely parents bouncing with anticipation as I stepped off the bus. Mom squeezed the stuffing out of me while Dad wrestled the bag off my shoulder. "Your bag is so heavy, Dear." He glanced inside. "Books! Ah, you plan to study while you're home. That's my girl." Dad smiled and hugged my guilty soul even tighter. I felt something inside me slither off into a dark corner.

Thanksgiving
PART VIII

The day of our forefathers came and went with the usual gluttony and shameless lounging around the house. My parents and relatives pretended to watch football, but everyone was really waiting for their stomachs to recover from the shock of overeating. I thought about jumping in with both feet and announcing that I was leaving school, but they all looked so content. My proclamation meant shattering the evening, not only for my parents but also for my favorite aunt, uncle, and three cousins. Instead, I scooped another heap of whipped cream onto a piece of pumpkin pie and sat down to watch the football game, warm and secure at Father's side.

Before sliding between the sheets that night, I promised myself to face the music first thing in the morning. I knew it would be a long day ahead and therefore a rehearsed speech, or something semi-calculated, was necessary.

Lying restless in bed, I tossed and turned all night pondering the probabilities of zero hour.

D-Day
PART IX

I rolled out of bed and looked into the mirror. My reflection was no ally in the cataclysmic day that lay ahead. Leaning into the bathroom sink, I cupped my hands and threw cold water over my face. "Miss Sydney Endicott...it's time."

I marched downstairs with absent courage, straight to the kitchen where the voices of my parents echoed. "Dad." I announced.

Ignoring my tone, they countered with warm smiles and pleasantries. "Good morning, Sydney. Sleep well?"

"Mom." Be done with it, I thought.

"Yes, Dear."

A lump in my throat formed. "Uh.... Can I help you with breakfast?" What a wimp, the diminutive courage I managed to muster left me as quickly as it came.

Dad and my brother, Alexander, were hovering over Mom, snatching scraps of bacon and slurping coffee while she flipped the pancakes and hash browns.

Breakfast was outstanding as always, but I had little time to enjoy it. My stomach churned, kinked, and coiled at the thought of breaking the news. We sat at the table nursing our coffee and handing praise to the chef. I took a deep breath and thought it was now or never. "Mom... the food is delicious."

"Why, thank you, Darling." Mom always had that special way of letting her kids know they were loved. "It's such a treat to have you here with us again. We miss you so much, you know."

"I know, Mom, and a day at college wouldn't be the same if I didn't wonder what everybody was doing back home...especially lately."

"Oh, Honey." She reached over and stroked my hair with motherly

I Need a Break

love. "I made the hash browns exactly the way you like them."

"Mmm, I noticed. I love it when they are that extra bit crispy... I've decided to leave college!"

Bad timing prevailed. My hasty judgment coincided with Dad taking a sip of his coffee. It was time to get out of Dodge.

My stunned parents and confused brother sat quietly, seemingly in a state of shock at my announcement. Mom looked me in the eyes and began to speak slowly, as if to a mentally challenged child. "Honey. What are you saying? What ever do you mean? If you leave...what will you do?"

I allowed a scant smile to creep across my face as I tried to hide the terror I was beginning to feel. "Well, Mom, I'm just not getting anything out of it..."

Dad interrupted with an expected tirade. "Except an education! Let me tell you a secret, little girl, there's no career of any kind without a degree! Oh, I see now, you want to be a trash collector! Or is it a dishwasher? That's right, drop out of school. You can't even keep your room clean!"

Dad was clearly not amused. I could see the rest of his arguments bubbling in his head. He was gathering momentum and would blow sooner or later. As a means of survival, I had to hurry and cut him off before we were all caught in the blast.

"I don't have to be at college to learn something. I just feel like I'm wasting my time, and your money. I'm no closer to finding out what I want to do and it's been a year and a half. When Alex got out of high school, you gave him a year to decide his future. Just because I waited 18 months to ask, is it now too late for me to find out what I really want to do?"

I figured I was gambling there, but it was worth a shot. My brother, Alex, had set the precedent by taking a year off after high school and doing odd jobs. He bounced from one employer to another because working put the pinch on his big plans to party. Dad was so mad he just about had kittens. Alex eventually caved and enrolled in a community college and partied seldom. Things between Alex and Dad simmered down after that, but the whole debacle was a fairly sore subject around the house. Nonetheless, here I was nearly two years later and hitting Dad with similar trash. I was effectively taking college, wadding it up in front of him, and throwing it in the garbage.

Dad's rebuttal was exactly what I anticipated. "So you want to go from job to job for a year until you figure out what I already know...

which is that college is a necessity and no one will hire you without a degree! Do you think your mother and I wore old clothes for 20 years so you could thumb your nose at the education we worked our butts off to pay for? Do you?!"

Afraid to look him in the eyes, I stared into my orange juice and desperately continued my plea. "No, Dad. I'm not saying I'll never go to college, just not now. It's not the right time. I don't want to be merely spinning my wheels to find out years later I went for all the wrong reasons. I'm not planning on staying here living rent-free and running around with friends from high school... I've got a job."

I lifted my head to face everyone. Mom tried her best to fake a smile while Dad wore that suspicious look he gets when he thinks someone is trying to con him. Alex, on the other hand, resembled a 10-year-old boy doing his best to hold back an extreme case of the giggles. I suppose it was a nice change for him, watching someone else get the business end of Dad's fury.

"Doing what?" Mom asked, wanting me to tell her a fairy tale and make things all better. I could see she was looking for a lifeline. She didn't handle family conflict well, especially over the breakfast table.

"Well, Mom, Dad... I saw an ad for a job in hospitality."

"And doing exactly what, Sydney?!" my father barked. "I see you've managed to skirt that issue pretty well."

I shifted in my chair. "I'll be a room attendant at a hotel."

"Is that another way of saying... someone who cleans rooooms?"

"Yes, Dad." I swallowed my tongue.

"Are you telling me that you're dropping out of college to make beds and vacuum carpets in some hotel around here?!"

"No. The hotel is in Germany."

Suddenly, the room went silent — except for the hypnotic hum of the refrigerator. A brief calm before the storm.

"Germany...?" My father's eyebrows disappeared into his hairline as his voice boomed to a level that made his temple veins appear ready to burst. "GERMANY! Have you completely lost your mind?! You can't speak German! You've never been to Germany! Do you even know where the hell it is? Do you!? I'll tell you where it is.... It's a hell of a lot closer to the Middle East than it is to here! It's a hell of a lot more expensive than here, and it doesn't have your college education flapping in the wind! I... can't...believe...you'd pull a stunt like this!"

Dad got up and brought the coffee pot to the table before continuing. "Now you have two days to work out whatever it was that made you decide throwing away your future was a good idea. Then you're going back to school, and that, young lady...is final!" He poured coffee into his cup and filled Mom's to the brim.

Mom looked pale and shaken. I could see tears welling in her eyes. "Europe? That's such a long way from home, Honey."

"I know, Mom, but I've always dreamed of traveling to Europe. The hotel representative told me that plenty of people my age work there, and in their free time they travel all over the continent. I would get to see other countries like Italy, Austria, and France. I will be able to witness firsthand the various cultures and historical sites we learned about in school and travel documentaries. That alone is an education. Neither of you have been there, so please don't deny me the opportunity."

I looked at Dad, who had already left the discussion and was trying to concentrate on the newspaper. Although, he couldn't have been concentrating too hard as it was upside down. Reaching across the table, I pulled the paper away from his face. "Daddy, when Alex and I were kids you loved to tell us about Grandpa's heroic actions on D-Day, and how America helped to mount the greatest amphibious invasion force in the history of the world. You would name the beaches where the Allied soldiers landed...and to this day, I've never forgotten them: Utah, Omaha, Gold, Juno, Sword. But, Dad, what you can't tell me is what it's like to walk those beaches and feel a Normandy breeze sweep across your face, to scoop the once-crimson sand and watch it flow between your fingers, or to gaze over the rows of white-marbled crosses that fill the cemeteries. I now have the chance if I take this job in Europe."

Before my parents could regain the momentum, I took a quick sip of juice to wet my parched throat and continued my speech.

"Mom, you couldn't tell us enough about your beloved Mozart, the master musician who began playing various keyboards at age 3, wrote his first symphony at 8 and his first opera at 12. Remarkable for someone as young as he, I know...but that's what the history books say. Mom, what you can't teach me is the impression the uneven cobblestones make as they weigh into the soles of my feet when walking the streets of his town, Salzburg. Or, the sensation of hearing Mozart's music in the very house he was born on Getreidegasse... I now have that chance."

Knowing that my words were resonating, I was gaining confidence.

"I've made up my mind. My things have been mailed home from school. I've withdrawn from my classes and signed out of the dorm. I'll pay you back for lost tuition and housing fees, I promise. In Germany I'll have a place to live and a steady job. My plane ticket will be waiting for me at the airport, and I've decided to go with or without your blessing. It's only for a year and then they'll fly me home. Maybe by then I'll know what it is I want to do."

Dad was trying hard not to look at me. He wasn't convinced.

"Come on, Dad. I want to make the next few months memorable with you, Mom, and Alex...please don't ignore me. On March 12th, I'll be on the plane and out of your hair."

He looked me squarely in the eyes. "I don't suppose we can stop you. You're old enough to make your own decisions, even if they are all wrong. You'd better be damned sure you know what you're doing and that this whole deal is kosher before you go. I'm not flying 5,000 miles to bail you out. GOT IT!?"

With a tremendous sigh of relief, I jumped from my seat and clutched Pops around his chest, giving him a big hug. "Got it! And if I have to...I'll bail myself out. I'll be fine, Dad. I will."

Bon voyage
PART X

The three months at home were spent catching up with family, working a part-time job, and preparing for my overseas move, which included getting a passport and completing a background check. When March 12th rolled around I found myself standing in line at the airport with a small carry-on bag and my backpack comfortably adjusted. My nerves became cumbersome foes as deep down the same thoughts kept echoing in my head: What if this whole thing is a big sham?

Behind the check-in counter stood a tall, thin man wearing a pilot's hat, blue suit, and the airline logo stitched to his breast pocket. "Hi! Your passport and ticket please."

"Here's my passport, but I was told my ticket would already be in the system. I'm on your 11:50 flight to Munich, Germany."

"Uh huh, I see... Miss Endicott, Munich, Germany," uttered the airline employee as he keenly stared into the computer while his fingers danced across the keyboard. "Endicott...Germany," he repeated, still gazing into the monitor. I stood in hopes of liberating the monkey off my back.

Finally, he looked up. "Miss Endicott...would you like a window or aisle seat?"

Whew. "Yes!"

I Need a Break 25

"Was that a 'Yes' to the aisle seat or...?"
"I'm sorry, that was a 'Yes' to the window seat."
"Here you go, Miss Endicott. Enjoy your flight."

My hand clenched the boarding pass as I pondered the forthcoming hours on a plane that would transport me countless miles from my family and home to a foreign land. Yet, despite last-minute jitters, everything seemed okay — that is until we reached the security line. Mom broke down, sobbing. She hugged me until my ribs creaked. Unleashing my own emotions, we dissolved into a pool of tears.

Dad cut in and handed me a small book. "Your mother and I wanted you to have this; it's a travel journal. Someday you'll be thankful you kept an account of your experiences."

He reached out for a simple embrace and bid farewell. "Please always remember and don't ever forget...we love you, Sydney."

Dad gave me a half smile, turned away and led Mom out of the terminal. They disappeared. For the first time in my life, I was really on my own.

Goodbye Mom, Dad, Alex.

Goodbye America. *'Bye home.* [1]

---

[1] Resort Europe, as portrayed in this book, is an Armed Forces Recreation Center (AFRC). In the year 2003, the U.S. Department of Defense shuttered AFRC Chiemsee by the town of Bernau am Chiemsee due to property consolidation and the downsizing of military forces in Europe. In 2008-2009, the former Lake Hotel and Chiemsee resort underwent a multi-million euro renovation (while maintaining the historic integrity of the property) and reopened under local German ownership as "Medical Park Chiemseeblick," facilities for modern medicine and therapy. There is, however, one AFRC property remaining in Europe, located 90 minutes west of Chiemsee. The 250-room Edelweiss Lodge and Resort is nestled in the Bavarian ski town of Garmisch-Partenkirchen, site of the 1936 Winter Olympics and starting point to reach Germany's highest peak: Zugspitze. This means that Sydney's job — along with a number of other employment opportunities — is real and you, too, may be eligible to live and work in the Alps and acquaint yourself with Europe like she did. (Go to www.edelweisslodgeandresort.com then 'about resort.')

A New Beginning
(Chiemsee, Germany)

Chapter 2: PART I

Sleep on the plane proved more difficult than I had expected. For some strange reason, I assumed airplanes rolled off the assembly line with bucket seats and generous legroom. The terrifying pockets of turbulence we encountered, tossing us frantic passengers around like salad, didn't permit forty winks. Nevertheless, several time zones later we landed at Munich airport, safe and sound.

Grainy-eyed and lifeless, I waited in a monster line at Customs. I thought they'd ask a zillion questions, rifle through my bags, and look at me suspiciously. When it was finally my turn to face the blitz, the officer in the booth asked for my passport and customs declaration.

"How long vill you schtay in Germany?" He questioned in a thick German accent while examining my documents.

"Thirteen months," I replied.

The officer looked baffled. "Zat lengz of time ist not auttorized in Germany."

"But, I'll be working here." I stated.

"Verrking?! Du you haff a verrk veesa?"

"Oh, no, I have a contract with the U.S. government, Department of Defense." I produced my work assignment printed on official DOD letterhead.

After verifying my paperwork, the officer stamped my passport and handed it back to me. "Auf Wiedersehen."

I smiled then exited through the sliding doors behind Customs that led to baggage claim, where I plucked my backpack from the carousel, and skipped into the arrivals hall. Instantly, I spotted my contact, a bright-eyed girl with strawberry blonde hair holding up a sign with my name on it.

"Hi! You must be Maddison from the Chiemsee resort?"

Her watchful eyes disengaged the exiting passengers and turned to me. "Yes," she replied, beaming, "and you must be Sydney Endicott?"

"That's me!" I extended my hand for a welcoming shake.

Maddison reciprocated and our hands linked. "Nice to meet you. Did everything go okay?"

"Wonderful!" I answered, before asking an essential question. "Is Chiemsee far?" I could feel my eyeballs rolling around in my head, and if I didn't find a horizontal surface to lie on soon, I'd start snoring standing up.

"It's about an hour and a half. Come on, the van's outside."

She escorted me to a white Volkswagen van, paid for parking, and sped away from the airport. Before I knew it, we were driving along a modern expressway with cars racing past us as if they were modified with jet engines.

"This must be the world-famous autobahn?" I surmised.

"Yep... sure is."

Glancing at the speedometer, I noticed she was driving 120 kilometers per hour and cars were squirting past us as if we were standing still. I wondered where all of these people were going in such a hurry. Maybe they were late to their college lectures? The last thing I remember before falling asleep was wondering why I'd never heard of Ausfahrt, Germany. It seemed to be an unbelievably large city, because every exit sign pointed to it.

Maddison woke me as we drove past a security gate entering the hotel grounds. It was an overcast, bleak day. March proved to be unlike any of the resplendent pictures I had seen on the resort's Web site. The lake appeared steel gray and quite delicate with its small whitecaps standing up to the brisk winds that made the flags in front of the hotel snap smartly.

In the foreground of a considerable two-tone building, which Maddison said was the Lake Hotel, were manicured lawns, well-tended shrubs, and leafless trees that stood like fragile skeletons. We turned left onto a short circular drive that brought us to the front entrance where I saw a U.S.-style newspaper stand and an ATM. Seeing a bit of familiarity made me feel a tad more at home. As we walked up the steps to the hotel, I stopped just shy of its front doors to read a bronze plaque mounted on the wall.

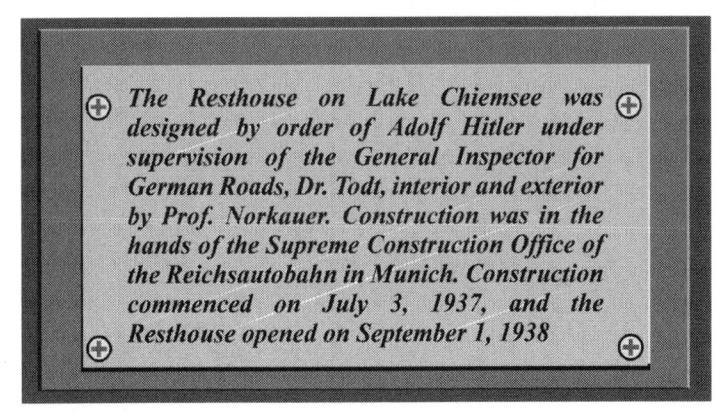

> *The Resthouse on Lake Chiemsee was designed by order of Adolf Hitler under supervision of the General Inspector for German Roads, Dr. Todt, interior and exterior by Prof. Norkauer. Construction was in the hands of the Supreme Construction Office of the Reichsautobahn in Munich. Construction commenced on July 3, 1937, and the Resthouse opened on September 1, 1938*

Unfreaking believable! I hadn't really considered Hitler's whereabouts before; it was like living in my tenth-grade history book. Then, a man emerged from the hotel in an outfit I had only seen on TV. He wore tall gray socks, knee-length brown leather pants with matching suspenders, and his handsome white shirt was embroidered down the front with small cream-colored spiky flowers; atop his head rested a green felt hat with a brush of animal hair pinned to its side.

Maddison pulled open the entrance door and smiled over her shoulder. "Oh, almost forgot. Welcome to Bavaria!"

The Waldheim
PART II

Maddison offered the general tour of the hotel, introducing me to my boss, his boss, and my co-workers. The orientation of the ground floor concluded in front of the combined gift shop and tours office, where Maddison informed me that I could sign up for any of the advertised tours for free. I watched the guy working at the tour desk, whom Maddison introduced as Jesse, enthusiastically recommending a local restaurant to a gentleman buying a souvenir beer stein. Jesse had wavy dark hair, deep brown eyes, zesty good looks, and an infectious smile with blazing white teeth. His hands waltzed around with dramatic flair while describing the meal he had eaten at the restaurant and its fine service. By the time the gentleman had left the shop, I was craving to eat there myself. I figured that employing Jesse was no accident; with his dynamic personality, one could probably sell air conditioning to Estonians.

The hotel might be almost a century in age, but surprisingly it had an operational elevator. Maddison's office was on the upper floor next to the executive suites and Internet café, the latter having a trio of computers for staff to use. The second round of introductions began with the hotel manager's assistant and the head honcho himself, Mike. He was much more sociable than I had expected and appeared to keep things pretty casual, since everyone from Maddison down to a lowly chambermaid was on a first-name basis with him.

Interrupting our tour, a phone call from the States concerning employment was transferred into Maddison's office. I could hear familiar questions pouring in from the other end. Maddison did her best not to sound like a broken record. "Yes, the ad is for real...."

This was my cue to jog next door and kick-start the Internet. I knew Mom and Dad would want to know I arrived safely. Plus, I had to check to see whether ShoSho12 had e-mailed anything regarding the crucifix.

Maddison ended the phone call and I promptly zipped back to her office. "Ah, there you are," she said. "I'm sorry about the disruption. I get about 20 of those calls a day." Maddison turned to her desk and invited me to the chair opposite. "Now, where were we...?"

I got my first taste of life working for the U.S. government as I filled out more paperwork, had an ID card made, and set up a new bank account. This was all choreographed a half-hour away at the resort's support center, otherwise known as Bad Aibling military base. In addition to the bank on base, there was a library, gas station, barbershop, post office, K-12 school, medical center, department of motor vehicles, bowling alley, bookstore, and a supermarket. It seemed a presentable place, a little America, where everyone spoke English and paid for their goods and services in U.S. dollars. Not exactly what I had come thousands of miles for, but handy just the same. If I absolutely had to have my Fruity Pebbles, I knew they would only be a yabba-dabba-doo away.

Back at the hotel, my eyes were weighing in like lead, but somehow I kept myself propped up. In consideration of my condition they gave me a day's reprieve to shake the jet lag before starting work. However, I had to hang my hat somewhere and rest, which meant there was still the matter of employee housing to wrap up. My new home was to be in a building called the Waldheim, a few hundred yards from the Lake Hotel.

Maddison and I walked outside to a small vehicle parked in the circular drive. She tossed my backpack into the trunk, we buckled up, drove around the flagpoles and out past the security gate. Maddison paralleled the autobahn for a short distance while explaining that Hitler had it built decades earlier. The autobahn looked great for a highway so old, but folks tended to build things better in those days. Now things only last until the warranty expires.

A New Beginning

We drove past the Park Hotel and Maddison said that it, too, was part of the Chiemsee resort. Our paved road turned to gravel and dead-ended at the edge of a wooded reserve. Nestled amongst the trees was the Waldheim, which fittingly translated to "Forest Home."

The Waldheim was a single-story, elongated building, and unless I was mistaken, it had a definite lean to the right. Maddison escorted me up the path and into the housing corridor. I was thankful my parents weren't here. In disagreement with the lean I'd noticed outside, the door frames inside skewed left. The yuck-green carpet in the hallway had untold stains, and the deep cracks in the walls had been creatively utilized as receptacles for cigarette butts and ash, which told me these coordinates did not exist on the housekeeping grid. Apparently, Hitler had these digs simultaneously built with the resort. Obviously, no one had bothered with any improvements since. The Lake Hotel's hallways and common areas were immaculate. I don't think that word had ever been used to describe a single area of the building I was about to call 'home.'

Maddison waved me into apartment 428, where I met my roommate and housekeeping colleague, Janie. "Hi. Welcome to Germany!" She said, grinning.

Meanwhile, Maddison motioned towards the door. "I'll go now and let you two girls get acquainted... and Sydney, if you need anything, just give me a call or stop by. You know where my office is."

"Thanks, Maddison. Thanks for everything." She left and I dropped my backpack to the floor.

"Where are you from?" Janie asked.

"I'm from..."

There was a short knock at the door and Maddison popped her head back in. "Sorry. Forget to mention... Sydney, I had an extra key to the room made. I'll drop it by tomorrow."

I thanked Maddison once again before returning to the conversation in progress. "So, where do you hail from, Janie?"

"Chicago! Born, bred, and schooled...the whole nine yards. I couldn't think of anywhere else I'd prefer to live," she paused, sweeping her pensive eyes over the various photos strategically placed near her bed.

There appeared to be more at stake in Illinois than just family. There was a young buck in her clutches.

Janie's pause became a recess, and I wasn't quite sure if she had simply lost her train of thought, or if she was in the middle of some sort of extrasensory psychic communication with someone. I didn't know what else to do but interrupt the supposed telepathy in progress.

"I like your photo collection." I pointed to one in particular. "Is this your boyfriend?"

"Yes! That's Johnny," she gushed. Judging by her tickled reaction, it was obvious I touched on her favorite subject. "We're engaged to be married when I return home in six months."

"Congratulations!"

Staring into the photos, Janie sighed aloud. "Having a boyfriend like him is like opening a present every day."

She had fallen ass-over-tea-kettle in love, all right. However, one can't deny the dreamy feeling.

"Hey listen," Janie said, shaking herself out of a romantic haze. "I'll get out of your hair for a few hours so you can get some rest."

"Thanks, but don't worry about me."

"It's no problem. Really. This is around the time I usually take a walk along the lake to think about home and my fiancé."

"Okay. I'll see ya later then."

She slid into a jacket and a pair of gloves before disappearing.

I glanced around my new home; it wasn't spacious, a tiny room with two single beds only a few feet apart. There was hardly a place for the sink, but thank goodness the builders maximized their millimeters and muscled one in. Somehow the previous occupants had managed to squeeze two cumbersome wardrobes through the door. One rested against the wall at the foot of Janie's bed and its twin occupied the same position on my half of the room. Outside our window, naked trees cluttered the view and the cold ground was littered with gopher holes.

Speaking of outside, the toilets and showers were down the hall. Unfortunately, there was no bathtub, which would've been lovely to soak in. But as tired as I was, I would have only fallen asleep and possibly drowned.

In any case, my roommate seemed compatible and rather tidy from the state of our room. She had a van Gogh print framed on the wall above her bed, a mini cube-like refrigerator neatly tucked in the corner, and a broad shelf systematically swollen with books, cereal boxes, pastas, coffee cups, a handful of dishes, silverware, and a saucepan. On the nightstand adjacent to her bed sat a small arrangement of dried flowers along with several more photos of home. Lastly, the clock radio rested somewhere in between. Since we worked together, chances were we'd never forget to set the alarm.

Preparing my side of things was going to be a mere formality. I was far too exhausted for anything ambitious. I hung my clothes in the wardrobe, stuffed my jeans and underwear in the two bottom drawers, parked my cosmetics bag above the sink, set a picture of Mom and Dad on the corner table, and made my bed with the sheets provided before passing out.

Good night, Waldheim. I look forward to the months ahead.

Chambermaid Extraordinaire
PART III

My first day of work began at 8 a.m. I reported to Sean, the executive housekeeper, who escorted me through a network of hallways to my workstation at the Lake Hotel, thus beginning my illustrious career as Sydney, international chambermaid extraordinaire.

He assigned me to train with Caitlin, a chirpy Irish girl from Dublin, who spoke with the most melodious accent. "Gudd job, Luv." I hung on her every word as I emptied wastepaper baskets, made beds, and scrubbed toilets.

By the end of my shift, I was tired beyond belief, which I attributed to unshakable jet lag and vacuuming more rooms in one day than I had in my entire life.

The e-mail,
Tuesday afternoon, eight days later
PART IV

The moment work finishes, my colleagues race to the time clock in hopes of punching out first to secure one of the three Internet computers in the café. Something kept telling me it was time to join the race and hasten the search for the crucifix. The fact that I hadn't heard anything from ShoSho bugged me, thus I commenced my own investigations.

Surfing the Web I located a fair amount of information on King Ludwig II, which I had expected since he is a notable figure in Bavarian history. However, a general search on relics revealed no such crucifix or any similar tale. It became apparent that long, tedious hours knee-deep in lake water were the key to finding the proverbial needle in a haystack.

Checking my Inbox one last time before logging off proved positive;

an e-mail from ShoSho12 had finally appeared. Anxious, I double-clicked "Open."

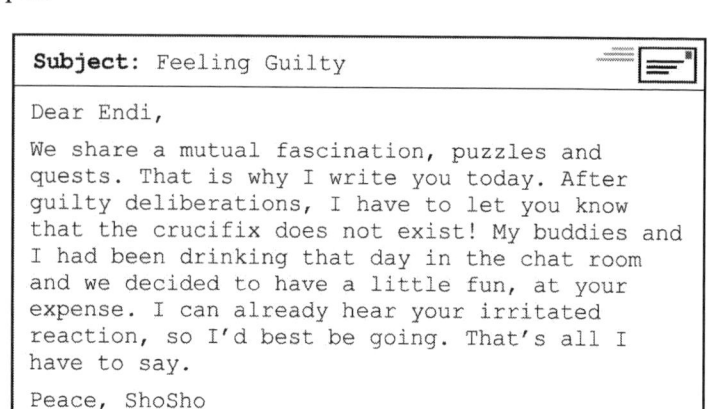

> **Subject:** Feeling Guilty
>
> Dear Endi,
>
> We share a mutual fascination, puzzles and quests. That is why I write you today. After guilty deliberations, I have to let you know that the crucifix does not exist! My buddies and I had been drinking that day in the chat room and we decided to have a little fun, at your expense. I can already hear your irritated reaction, so I'd best be going. That's all I have to say.
>
> Peace, ShoSho

That's all he has to say! Yeah, he'd best be going. I guarantee he just threw himself a bad-karma boomerang.

What a disappointment. I felt as though I'd been punched in the stomach. I guess that's what I get for giving an Internet stranger instant credibility. Was Dad right? Maybe I should have listened more carefully to his arguments.

What now? Wandering out of the hotel, I pondered the future: My college education hung in limbo, I live in a shoebox, and I'm in a country where I don't speak the language.

Best I fall into bed and throw the covers over my head. With any luck, I'll fall asleep and be abducted by aliens.

The hallway pick-up
PART V

Is it possible that ShoSho had lied? Maybe he had second thoughts about letting someone else in on the quest.

Nevertheless, I do know one thing for sure — which is exactly what Dad would say — consider your actions before acting on them.

After entering the Waldheim at a swift pace, I glanced back to make sure the access door closed behind me. That's when it happened. Wham!

Upon turning the corner, I walked directly into a scantily clad man heading to the showers, temporarily dislodging the towel from around his waist and briefly exposing his nether region. He hastily managed to wrestle it back in place, anchoring it with both hands.

His face looked familiar. Then it came to mind. It was Jesse, the tour-desk guy, standing all but naked in front of me with his delectable six-pack abs. My focus momentarily slipped away with his loincloth. I never once saw a naked man in the hallway of my dorm at college.

Tongue-tied, I looked for somewhere to hide. Perhaps I could turn green and blend in with the carpet.

"Hey, don't I know you?" He double blinked, smiling.

I was a little surprised. I expected him to accuse me of trying to disrobe him right there in the hallway, or at least tell me to watch where the hell I was going. But here he was, turning on the charm while readjusting his towel.

As I attempted unsuccessfully to hide my embarrassment, the part of my brain responsible for intelligent conversation crapped out. "Yeah, I, err... met you briefly in the tours office, 'bout a week ago. Maddison introduced us."

His eyes lit up. "Now I remember! You're Sydney, aren't you?"

He was infectious, all right.

"Correct, Sydney Endicott."

"How's housekeeping treating you?"

I managed to clear my throat. "Good."

Looking down, he administered the final tuck to secure his towel.

"Have you ever been to Europe before?" he asked.

"No...this is my first trip overseas. You?"

"I've been here a few times. I live to travel. Luckily, the hotel had a position available in their tours office and I jumped on it. That was nearly three years ago. I keep meaning to move on, but Chiemsee is captivating. I can't seem to leave."

"It certainly is beautiful. I'm eager to see as much as I can but I haven't yet had the time off. I'm free this Friday and Saturday, where do you suggest I go?"

"Salzburg, Austria! Why don't you tag along on our tour this Friday?"

I smiled and let out the breath I didn't realize I was holding. "I'd love to!"

The only tour I'd ever experienced was on our madcap family vacation when we walked around Washington, D.C., in 90-degree heat listening to some blasé woman in an ill-fitting purple blazer talk about the formal dining room at the White House. As a 10-year-old, I didn't care much about politics or distinguished guests sitting around the presidential table.

"Great, it's a plan then," Jesse insisted. "Bring an overnight bag... I can recommend a little Salzburg nightlife."

"Yeah, why not?" Reckless thoughts came from my evil twin; please tell me he's available. Reality revisited. "Well, I'd better start making some dinner and call it an early night. I've had a hectic day."

"I'm beat, too." He grinned. "I was out late last night with my girlfriend."

Jesse was sincere, intriguing, alluring, and *not* available. He gestured toward the shower while bidding adieu. "Nice talking with you, Miss Endicott. I'll see ya Friday morning."

CHAPTER 2

CHAPTER 2

Jesse's Tour
(Salzburg & The Sound of Music)

Chapter 3

I woke abruptly as Janie slammed her hand down onto the alarm clock, putting an end to "Bailando" by Enrique Iglesias — and my spicy dream.

It's been a long time since I voluntarily got out of bed before 8 a.m. on a day off. I recall as a young, annoying snot of 9 years old putting my hair in little pigtails with red-velvet ribbons in preparation for church. God could hardly expect me to show much enthusiasm for dressing when I wanted nothing more than to go back to bed, curl beneath the quilt that Grandmother made, and snuggle up with Tipsy, my stuffed rabbit. Although, the smell of Mom's pancakes wafting through the house always succeeded in gravitating my butt to the breakfast table.

Things are much different now as a young woman working for the U.S. government in Europe. I can honestly say that dragging my bones out of bed at zero dark-thirty for a tour to Salzburg wasn't so tough.

It was a pleasant morning, the kind I'm readily accepting in Bavaria. Outside our bedroom window, rousing rays of sun cut through the light morning mist suspended in the trees. A squirrel scampered across the cold ground and up the paper-white trunk of a birch tree, whacking its head on the first branch. *Ouch!* I felt that one ruffle through my pajamas. I don't think I've ever seen a blind squirrel before. As much as I'd like to find out where our fuzzy friend was going, a shower beckoned, towing me away from the nature channel.

Upon returning from the women's bathrooms, I glanced out the window to see Fuzzy nibbling on a golf ball. A blind squirrel that appreciates golf, huh? If this is an indication of the day's peculiarities to come, then it should be fascinating, to say the least.

Preparing for the next 36 hours might have been overkill. I packed everything but the furniture in the room. The last thing I grabbed when heading out the door was my umbrella in case the rain forecasted by the weather bureau came our way.

Over at the hotel, the conditions appeared disheartening. There was no hint of the sun and the mist thickened into one of those foggy mornings that just seemed to hang around. The bracing cold air was amplified with every breath. I had a few minutes to spare before the tour left, so I wandered into the cafeteria for a hot cup of cocoa. Once inside, I wish I could tell you the wafting smell of pancakes, bacon, and hash browns coming from the grill reminded me of home, but it just didn't equal Mom's.

Back outside, a group of about 20 hotel guests waited for someone to unlock the tour bus. A slightly built gentleman, sporting a brown mustache and a navy-blue jacket, walked up through the crowd, opened the bus and politely beckoned everyone aboard. I glanced back to see whether Jesse was coming, but there were only a couple of women in sweatpants, fleece jackets, and large shoulder bags making their way from the hotel.

Directly in front of me stood a silver-haired couple complaining about everything from the weather to how rude the younger people were for not offering to let them board first. The pair in front of them, equal in age and guilty of being within earshot, heard every whining word. They turned and eyed the irritating couple with a piercing glare. Hopefully the warmth of the bus would mellow the mood.

My turn came to board and I patiently proceeded up the few steps behind the irritating couple. For what seemed an eternity, I waited while they discussed who would sit where and in which overhead compartment their coats would be stored. The silver-haired man, as if he were a bus-safety inspector, swiftly backed up two paces and bent over to examine the available space under the two front seats. This shoved me in reverse motion, and like a human domino, I expected to fall lifelessly onto the women boarding behind me. Instead, I was propelled into a hard, angular object that dug into my left butt cheek and inflicted the kind of acute pain that makes you call out for Jesus. This in turn thrust me forward, knocking the silver-haired man into the seat face first.

Massaging my throbbing buttocks, I turned and stared accusingly at the angular object that dealt the pain. Meanwhile, the silver-haired man recovered from his plight and kicked off a series of scowling looks that provided invaluable training techniques for the aspiring thespians onboard. With a few stern expressions of my own, I squeezed by his outstretched frame and took refuge in a seat halfway back, making myself as comfortable as possible considering the swelling of an egg-like formation on my rear end.

Within a few minutes everyone had settled and Jesse stepped onto the bus grinning from ear to ear. He said a couple of words to the driver, an exchange that was obviously much funnier to them than to the emotionally constipated passengers up front who sat stone faced and unamused, resembling guests at a funeral. Jesse then grabbed hold of the angular object and pulled it outwards — which opened into the tour guide's jump seat — dropped his messenger bag to the floor and sat with his face all but plastered against the windshield.

A thirtyish brunette with big, pointy boobs like a porn star, sitting a couple of rows behind the driver, yelled out to Jesse with eager curiosity. "Are you our tour guide?!"

He cranked his head around and answered, charmingly: "Yes, indeed, Miss. I'm your escort for the day."

By her euphoric reaction, one could only presume that Cupid had materialized with a quiver of arrows and struck a bull's eye upon her heart.

Our escort blushed. He then signaled the driver with a snap of his fingers. Subsequently, the bus pulled away from the hotel like a train gathering steam. Jesse fiddled with the microphone and after a few seconds of tapping and thumping, his voice boomed through the bus: "GOOD MORNING EVERYBODY!"

Startled by the volume, Jesse inadvertently won everyone's undivided attention. Wearing a sheepish grin, he quickly reached down and adjusted some dials on the dashboard. "That better, everyone? Sorry, didn't mean to deafen you straight off."

Our driver lurched his bus past the guard gate and security pylons, taking the narrow, curvy road ahead in defiance of gravity.

Jesse glanced back to his audience and began the pre-tour formalities. "Allow me to introduce ourselves. Your chauffeur today is Bernie from Cologne; he's been driving with the resort for more than 25 years... so let me assure you, folks, you're in safe hands. As for me, my name is Jesse and I hail from California."

We entered onto Autobahn 8, southbound, in the direction of Salzburg. Bernie merged into traffic jockeying for position in between a Danish 12-wheeler carrying a load of fish and an old Fiat towing a rickety camper displaying "Roma" license plates. With its engine sputtering and tailpipe spewing exhaust, Italy seemed like a long shot. In contrast to our lumbering bus, lead-footed speedsters were blazing past us in their sports cars leaving a vapor trail in their wake.

Jesse diverted our attention by beginning his tour:

"Ladies and gentleman...you are traveling on the world's first freeway system. Adolf Hitler, in a speech given on May 1, 1933, announced his ambitious autobahn construction plan. He appointed Doctor of Engineering Fritz Todt to equip Germany with an efficient, multilane transportation system. Work officially began in September that same year under the authority of the Reichsautobahn bureau with ceremonies near Frankfurt. The initial crew assembled was that of a thousand men, and within a few years this increased to a workforce of 130,000 paving a vast network of concrete to link the developing cities of Hitler's infamous Third Reich. Without the knowledge of the German people, Hitler entertained secret plans for these super highways to hasten the mobilization of armies in case of war. Ironically, this logistical vision proved advantageous for the Allies as they raced across Germany to defeat Nazism in 1945." Jesse paused briefly, scanning the crowd with enthusiastic eyes before striking the finale. "And since the autobahns were constructed with a dual purpose, swift as well as scenic, your Chiemsee resort is idyllically situated on the sandy shores of an alpine lake. Today, the resort is registered as a national landmark in addition to the world's first hotel built along an expressway."

Jesse seemed genuinely interested in the topic and not simply spewing a scripted, monotone narration typical of other tour guides. His enthusiasm was sincere, even playful, and his guests wanted more. Jesse continued by gesturing out the window, naming the villages we passed and reciting their histories. His charisma was magnetic, and without pausing he pointed to the snow-white mountaintops and quoted the heights of their peaks.

The Alps were traveling along with us, regularly changing shape from soaring summits capped by a Latin cross to foothills stamped with ski runs. Every so often I could see a cable car lifting people over the fir trees to the mountain top. My eyes lowered to ground level. Tranquil beauty blanketed the farmers' fields. Patches of melting snow accented the rural mosaic. Charming villages dotted the valleys, each punctuated by a church spire jutting into the sky, looking heavenly against the fairy-tale landscape.

I gazed at the distinctive farmhouses; barns appeared to be built into the houses forming one cozy residence for the farmers and their livestock. Several hundred years of sun, wind, and snow seemed to have had no adverse effect on these practical structures. The facades were warmly decorated in swirling trim outlining the windows and doorways. Local histories were inscribed onto the walls by what appeared to be Gothic typeface. Colorful murals depicted dramatic scenes. Gables and support beams were exquisitely carved. Logs for the fireplace were evenly stacked waist high along three sides of the house, perfectly cut, a true testimonial to the cold winters. There was no doubt that Bavarians took extreme pride in their real estate.

Jesse interrupted these scenes of timeless tradition by pointing to the remnants of a concrete structure nestling at the side of the autobahn that he said was a former anti-aircraft position from World War II. It was certainly interesting to see possible evidence of a war long since past, which had been little more than passages in my history book and Grandpa's stories relayed via Dad. I pondered the brave soldiers Dad always talked about, who fought for the liberty that many of us take for granted. Perhaps witnesses of the war were sitting on this very bus. I wondered if the older gentleman behind me, or the irritating one up front, had been here before under less casual circumstances.

Moments later our tour guide was back in action. "How many fans of the movie 'The Sound of Music' do we have with us today?" The excitement was palpable; most everyone raised his or her hand enthusiastically. "I ask because Bernie and I think you've been a pretty good group so far, and as a thank you we'd like to make an extra-special stop to show you where one of the stars of the movie resides."

After that gracious offer, a number of elated tour-goers seemed they would require smelling salts to regain consciousness.

"Plus, at this sojourn, there are *free* toilets...which in itself is worth the stop. How many of you folks have already ran out of pocket change in Europe to relieve yourself?"

Jesse's followers were eating out of his hand. He kept the offerings plentiful and they lapped it up.

The bus began descending into Berchtesgadenerland, giving us a commanding view of the Salzburg valley.

"Gang, before us is the Austrian border." Jesse momentarily paused, lowering the mic to his chest to survey his guests before continuing. "Kids, that means keep your eyes open for kangaroos."

The middle-aged, married couple in front of me began whispering busily.

"Honey, did he say kangaroos?"
"Yes, Larry."
"Really...? That's great."
"No Stupid, it's a joke!"

"What makes you say that, Darling?"

"Because we're in Austria, not Australia."

There was a pregnant pause. Obviously, this gent did not possess the brains in the family.

"Austria?" Larry sniveled.

The wife eyeballed her man with disdain. "That's why he made the joke." Larry looked at her cockeyed. "Never mind!" she snarled.

I couldn't help but giggle to myself. I'd heard that some tourists forget to pack their common sense when traveling, but apparently this guy didn't have any to start with. My ponderings were again interrupted when Jesse manned the mic.

"Welcome, ladies and gentlemen, to the Republic of Austria, comprised of nine states and eight million people, with Vienna as its capital. Due to the Schengen Agreement, the borders in western Europe have been open since 1995, thus we'll scoot through this international boundary without stopping. The German autobahn has now ended, and the Austrian autobahn will soon split in two directions: The A1 heads east, accessing Vienna, Slovakia, Hungary and the Czech Republic. The alternative route, the A10, is the gateway to the south, leading to countries like Italy, Slovenia, Greece and Turkey."

After having recently seen the movie "Midnight Express," set in a barbaric Turkish prison, I didn't have a strong desire to visit Turkey — let alone drive there. It was nice, however, to know that should the mood strike me, I could take off to somewhere like Venice for little more than time and gas money. I figured at the very least I'd have a working knowledge of which direction to point lost tourists.

Bernie veered onto the A10, exiting at the first "Ausfahrt." We rolled lazily through the village of Anif and arrived at the gates of a buttercup-yellow palace called Schloss Hellbrunn. Jesse walked us beyond its golden walls and into the manicured gardens, where he stopped next to a seemingly out-of-place gazebo. An excited babble of voices erupted from the crowd: "Could it be...? The real one?!"

"This is the 'gazebo,'" Jesse announced, "featured in the movie 'The Sound of Music.' Anyone care to entertain us with a song, perhaps

'Sixteen Going on Seventeen'? And, folks, before I lose your attention, behind us are the toilets."

A race ensued to see who would be first to get his or her picture taken with the famous gazebo. The diehard 'Sound of Music' fans could hardly contain themselves, clutching at its panes and bursting into song. Two girls even brought along a life-sized picture cutout of their girlfriend because she couldn't make it on the trip. They insisted, "This is the next best thing to having her here with us." Accordingly, Jesse played host to a flood of photo requests.

Above and beyond the call of "The Sound of Music," my main goal here was self-relief 'number one.' *Desperately!* Several women were already pacing anxiously in line for the toilets. I guesstimated a 10-minute wait. Sometimes being a female isn't all it's cracked up to be, and this was one of those times. So I crafted a plan, waited until the coast was clear, and dashed into the men's bathroom, finding sanctuary within a stall.

Quickly I dropped my pants, squatting while being careful that no skin touched the seat, and let nature flow. A stealthy exit was essential before a male decided to reoccupy his headquarters.

I pulled up my jeans, buttoned them snuggly to my waist, unlocked the stall door, and began to exit with the finesse of a renowned Austrian: "Hasta la vista, baby!"

I then heard approaching footsteps. "Oh shit!" I mutely cursed. Frantically, I jumped back into the stall and kept still.

The footsteps became louder. Suddenly, they halted and the men's room became as quiet as a confessional. The male had found the urinal he came for. The tearing of a zipper pierced the silence. A steady flow of fluid began its course while the depositor exhaled a sigh of relief against the wall tiles. I psyched myself into tolerance, knowing he'd be zipped up in a jiffy and I'd be a free girl.

My bubble burst. I heard more footsteps enter the restroom. I couldn't believe the scene unzipping around me. The new male must have sensed a bowl movement and occupied the adjacent stall, pants to ankles. Back at the urinals, the man zipped up and headed out. With one leaving and the other engaged on the neighboring throne, this was my cue to escape purgatory.

Then the unthinkable happened: additional males felt the urge to use their headquarters. The urinal flow began anew as there were now two or three more customers relieving themselves. One broke wind, encouraging the others to indulge in a fusillade of flatulence.

Abruptly, the lock on my stall door jiggled aggressively. A male was trying to get in. I knelt down and saw his shoes in a holding pattern, waiting their turn to land.

In a moment of desperation, I threw back the stall door and bolted past the open-mouthed faces of stunned men in a blue flash.

Lightheaded, but ecstatic to be outside delighting in the fresh air, I rested momentarily on the nearest bench to recover from sensory overload and admire the budding tulips.

∞

Bernie and Jesse rounded up the gang to hit the road. Once underway, Jesse announced the time change. "Folks, we've just passed through the millennium warp. Please set your watches back 2,000 years."

We were soon swallowed up in old-world Salzburg as the smooth roads narrowed into cobbled lanes. The city encouraged tidiness and cleanliness. There was no trace of graffiti, anywhere. Nothing dirties a city more than buildings defaced with spray paint. Moreover, everything appeared so authentic, and quaint, compared with the sleek and modern world I had left behind.

I glanced around to see whether any of the other passengers were as taken as me when I heard a child excitedly yelp. "Mom, look, a real castle!"

Then I noticed everyone perk up to what Jesse began describing ahead. "Ladies and gentleman...in front of us is the medieval fortress of Salzburg, one of the largest fully preserved castle complexes in Europe!"

The history here is mind-boggling, to say the least. Lording over the city for more than 900 years, stark and imposing, Salzburg fortress is every bit the castle I had envisioned while listening to fairy tales as a child.

The castle's vast defense walls formed an impregnable curtain of stonework and turrets, which stood out from the forested bluff it sat upon. Its magnitude was impressive for sure, looking every bit like the fortress it epitomized. How could such a colossal structure be built way back then? Perhaps several he-men took a break from wrestling ferocious bears and hoisted gigantic blocks into place.

It seemed nothing could be so formidable, so impenetrable as the great hulk of stonework before us. Why hadn't I ever heard of it before? Something of such prominence must hold a place in history worth repeating to those outside the boundaries of its country.

Before long, the bus slowed and Jesse's commanding voice circulated through the overhead speakers. "All right, folks, let's hop off this beaten pony and go for a walk."

A handful poured out of the bus like prisoners being set free. As diligent as a wrangler, Jesse lassoed the ragtag bunch and herded them to a large info board featuring a map of Salzburg Old Town, officially listed as a UNESCO World Heritage Site. He explained our pedestrian route while instructing us to keep together and call out if he was going too fast.

"Okay, gang, let's go!" Like an army sergeant, Jesse waved everyone forward.

Judging by the elderly cluster of senior citizens following our guide, I was sure that if his gait were to exceed anything above slow, someone would certainly tug on the reins.

Jesse charged ahead, periodically glancing back to see whether his troops were hot on the trail. Contrary to my conjecture, the seniors gamely kept pace. At length we entered onto a broad expanse of asphalt, or as Jesse called it, Mozart Platz.

The thirtyish brunette with big boobs raised her hand and assertively inquired, "Is there a McDonald's in town?"

According to the clock on the church tower, the time was 10:30 a.m. She was officially late for breakfast if that was her purpose.

"Yes, there is..." Jesse said, as he turned to face Boobs. "I'll let you know when we're close."

"When do you think that'll be?" she insisted.

He gave her just enough attention as not to be rude. "'Bout an hour."

In the center of the square stood a statue of its namesake, Wolfgang Amadeus Mozart. Although it was prominent and considerably proportioned, I found the statue unremarkable, liberally splattered in bird ca-ca and more akin to a resident of the Planet of the Apes than that of the legendary composer. And the writing instrument clutched in his right hand looked like a ballpoint pen, which I'm certain did not exist in the 18th century. I bet Mozart wasn't impressed either, most likely turning in his grave at the thought of this eternal tribute. Etched into the base of the statue were Roman numerals equating to 1842, the year of its unveiling.

When we were kids, my mother used to tell Alex and me bits of trivia from Mozart's life. One of those referred to the death of his wife, Constanze Weber, in that same year of 1842.

Mom's Mozart narratives will remain with me for the rest of my life, and now that I'm here in his city, in his square, I couldn't think of a better time to reflect.

Wolfgang Amadeus Mozart, child prodigy born in 1756, began playing the keyboard at age 3, wrote his first symphony at 8 and his first opera at 12. Leopold Mozart, or Mozart senior, schlepped little Wolfgang around for months at a time during his youth to perform for the royal courts of Europe. During one of these tours, when Wolfgang was about 6, Leopold covered up the piano keys with a cloth to increase playing difficulty. Much to the astonishment of the crowd, Wolfgang tickled the ivories without missing a note. As an adult, Mozart favored the sophistication of Viennese culture over the intolerable holiness of small-town Salzburg. And so, in 1781, Mozart tired of composing "table music" on order of Salzburg's ruling archbishop and moved to Vienna, where he married Constanze Weber. Tragically, four of six children born to them died at birth or shortly thereafter. If things weren't depressing enough for the young couple, Mozart's lavish routine as a spendthrift brought heartache and hardship. In 1791, the prolific composer became ill and died on December 5, at the age of 35. Except for the gravedigger and the priest, no one showed up for his funeral, not even his wife. A crestfallen rock star of his time, Wolfgang Amadeus Mozart was unceremoniously tossed into an unmarked commoner's grave for a large amount of people.

©Salzburg Tourism

It was incredible to think that the musical maestro was born only a few hundred meters from Mozart Platz, where I now stood. Perhaps he played in this very square as a child, that is if he had the time.

While Mozart held me mesmerized, our group had strayed from the asphalt expanse. I felt dreadfully alone. They were marching ahead into a graveled plaza. Stuffing my hands into my jeans pockets, I hustled to catch up.

Jesse distanced himself a few feet from his guests, and like a circus ringmaster, he spread his arms out wide. Needing only to throw on a top hat and coat to complete the image, he announced: "We are now in Residence Platz, the largest square in town."

The prominent building at the far end of the square was the Residence, the former stately home of the archbishop. Its four-story facade was stacked with windows, one on top of the other, and the princely archway was just that. I pondered the thought of calling this place home, end of thought. I'd never make it past the first month's heating bill. I was thrilled at college just to have a room to myself in the dorms outfitted with a worn desk and dresser, and a sagging couch.

"The jewel of the square is the Residence Fountain, built in 1658. It's one of the most impressive Baroque fountains north of the Alps, featuring four horses spouting water from their noses and mouths. The horse facing the 'Hypo' bank was made famous in the movie 'The Sound of Music' when Julie Andrews pranced through the square while singing 'I Have Confidence' and splashed water in its face."

As fascinating as this was, our tour marched on — but now the humming of "The Sound of Music" soundtrack could clearly be heard coming from members of our group, which I swore was on auto-replay.

Lined up in front of the Residence stood a dozen horse-drawn carriages and their drivers waiting to clip-clop tourists through Old Town.

A carriage ride began to look extremely attractive as I puffed to keep up with Jesse, who was all but sprinting ahead toward six tall archways opening into yet another square. I glanced over to the older folks; they were keeping pace with gusto. Although, chances were they hadn't just postponed college, moved a world away, endured a depressing case of electronic deception, or been kept up late every night by a roommate keen to chat about her amazingly wonderful fiancé, so they had somewhat of an advantage over me.

In the next square — which was similar to the previous two, sparse but featuring a themed attraction — I followed the group past a statue of the Virgin Mary. The Cathedral of Salzburg stood magnificently before us as we craned our necks backward to get the holy perspective.

"We are now standing in Dom Platz, or Cathedral Square. In front of us is the largest Baroque building north of the Alps, Salzburg Cathedral, having the capacity to hold more than 10,000 people. It was originally built in the year 774, and gutted by fire in 1598, to be rebuilt and reconsecrated in 1628. Some 300 years later it was heavily damaged in 1944 during a World War II bombing raid; pictures inside the cathedral depict this awful day. The structure was again rebuilt and reconsecrated in 1959."

Jesse led us across Dom Platz and inside the sacred confines of the cathedral. Along the main aisle, I noted the pews and kneeling benches, both of which looked uncomfortably hard. I reached the high altar where streams of light poured in from the massive octagonal dome above, charging my body with newfound strength. Time seemed of no concern. I stood motionless, absorbing the entire spectrum. The cool, white interior was elaborate and awe-inspiring. Heavenly ceiling frescos depicted scenes from the life and suffering of Christ. I felt humbled by the presence of such beauty, antiquity, and workmanship devoted to an undying faith. My eyes closed as I breathed the divine air and sensed a feeling of unconditional love seep up through the floor and into my body. If it had been possible, I would've embraced the entire room.

The seniors, meanwhile, had been silently milling around in a similar manner, simply staring in wonderment. Most dipped their fingers in the basin of holy water before kneeling in front of the pews. Foreigners in a foreign land they may be, but home in any church.

By the main portal were pictures of conflict displaying the cathedral's tragic past. They revealed a dome that was no more; the bombing raid had all but destroyed it. The entire sanctuary was filled with piles of wood and stone, the rubble of war. It seemed an abomination that evil hostilities would have touched this place dedicated to faith, love and hope. I was deeply moved by a power greater than any on Earth.

On the way out, I dropped a few coins into a contribution box manned by a clergyman distributing little remembrance cards to all who donated.

Outside, Jesse approached me. He wore a huge smile that seemed brighter than the sun, which shone curiously upon us. I'm sure I felt God tapping my shoulder with one of those vibrant rays, double-checking that I wasn't hitting on our shepherd right there on his front porch. Without breaking his smile, Jesse managed to juice out a greeting.

"Hi! How's it goin'?"

"Wunderbar! And what a church, huh?"

"Yeah, fantastic," he double blinked. "You enjoying yourself so far?"

"Overwhelmed! I still find it hard to believe that I'm actually here."

"I know what ya mean. I feel the same way myself, and I've been here nearly three years. Hopefully the magic will never fade."

I nodded. "It would be tragic to tire of such a fascinating place. Frankly, I'm surprised not to see any stone gargoyles out on grocery runs."

"Wouldn't that be an exciting addition to the tour?!" Jesse then pulled a loose hair off my sweater before changing the subject. "As for tonight, you staying?"

"Yep, I have everything I need in this daypack." I swiveled my upper body to remind Jesse of what rested upon my back. "You said...you've got a place in mind?"

"Sure do. It's a youth hostel that's cheap, clean, and fun."

This was good news. I had hoped my budget of 80 euros would cover sleeping arrangements, dinner, and return train fare. I'd been assured that I had enough, but I was still grappling with a little overseas insecurity.

"I want to show the guests a few more things before we break," Jesse said, "then we'll have some free time and I can get you situated. Maybe I'll even head back down tonight and join you in town. I'll likely find you in my favorite bar, Hüftgold. Everyone ends up there at some time or another."

His words required no reply. A simple smile was sufficient.

The gang was again set in motion and a stringent hike ensued. This time we headed out the opposite set of arches and into the next square, where a titanic view of Salzburg's landmark fortress presented itself. Jesse charged across the square, leading us towards a narrow cobbled lane. On the way we passed souvenir stands filled with Mozart mementos, useless knickknacks, colorful postcards, and T-shirts printed with catchy phrases like "No kangaroos in Austria," "I met Mozart," and "Salzburgers do it with salt."

On the plaza I also saw what must have been Europe's biggest chessboard painted onto the asphalt. The accompanying pieces were the size of children.

Jesse stopped in front of the Festungsbahn, or cable railway, that climbed to the fortress. He told us tales about Salzburg's medieval archbishops, who ruled the city-state from the citadel before moving down to the luxury of the Residence. It didn't seem very Christian-like of the archbishops to keep a cruel dungeon or a royal toilet that "flushed" onto the peasants below. Jesse concluded his narration then led us through a wrought-iron gate and into a cemetery.

Larry, the kangaroo comic, who happened to be walking next to me as we entered, wisecracked: "Who said you can't quit smoking? All these people did."

His wife scowled at him as if he were a life-sized turd. "Larry, you really are a nitwit! Stop bothering the poor girl and mind your own business. I don't wanna hear another word out of you!"

"But, Honey, I..."

"Not another word," she exclaimed, jamming her finger into his brow. "Is that clear?!"

"Yes, dear," he answered, obediently.

Even if I didn't want to believe it, the pair left no doubt that marriage can be a challenging commitment.

During the marital spat, rhythmic sighs from the group assured me something was up. Of course, I should have known, we were in the cemetery where Hollywood hid the von Trapps during the escape scene in "The Sound of Music."

The cemetery proper was a mix of old and new graves linked via slender footpaths and encompassed by a succession of vaulted burial chambers belonging to titled families. In the center of the graveyard sat a petite, frail church — the date above its portal read 1491. It's amazing to think that Europeans were already building cathedrals, fighting wars, and brewing beer long before my country was even a twinkle in our forefathers' eyes.

I noticed a few of the older headstones were leaning, awkwardly sunken into the rich, coffee-brown soil. The monument adjacent to me had a black-and-white picture of its occupant set in crookedly. Otherwise, the plot was immaculately cared for and dressed in a breadth of multi-colored flowers like red begonias and burnt-orange marigolds. On each grave a candle burned, perhaps to break the black stillness of the night when ghostly spirits come out to play.

Jesse broke the peculiar silence by beginning his spiel on the Who's Who of gravesites. "As we stand here in the center of the burial ground, we see the plot of Harry J. Collins, an American World War II general attached to the 42nd 'Rainbow' Division. After the war General Collins remained here in command of the occupying forces until 1955, when Austria became a republic and our boys were deployed elsewhere. By that time it was too late for the general to leave; he had fallen madly in love with Salzburg and a local Fräulein. The general died in the early '60s and is buried here with Frau Collins. His headstone reads, 'Honorary citizen of the cities of Salzburg and Linz.' Ironically, behind the general is a memorial dedicated to the Axis soldiers who fell in defense of the city during the war."

Interrupting our narrator, Boobs verbalized a reminder that she was on the verge of starvation. "Is McDonald's near?"

Most of the group thought she was being rude, including Jesse. "I'll let you know," he firmly replied, grimacing.

"Okay..." she said over her rumbling stomach, "but don't forget."

Jesse continued the tour. "Going back a few years, before the general and World War II, are Salzburg's so-called catacombs, Christian dugouts secreted in the rock face from the Romans in the third century A.D. At its entrance to our left you'll find the grave of Mozart's sister, Maria Anna, affectionately known as 'Nannerl.'"

We exited the cemetery through an archway continuing our platz hop into St. Peter's Square.

"Ladies and gentleman, in the year 696, the Catholic Church sent Bishop Rupert from the German city of Worms to form St. Peter's Monastery, where we now stand, to bring peace and prosperity to the region. From these roots, more than 13 centuries ago, came the first archbishop and the settlement's new name, Salzburg, meaning 'salt castle.'"

Jesse further explained that Bishop Rupert was entombed in the church to our right, and to our left was St. Peter's Stiftskeller, the oldest restaurant in Europe, dating from the year 803!

At that juncture a voice rang out from the group. "Have the prices gone up since then?" That, I hate to say, came from Larry. He snorted with laughter at his own jest.

There was only one thing to do, shield my eyes from the punishment Wifey was about to administer. Regrettably, I forgot that other sense called hearing.

"Ooooooouuch...let go of my ear, Honey!"

I removed my hands to see Larry being dragged off into the restaurant by his wife, probably to get personally acquainted with the prices.

The group appeared to be aghast by the couple's actions. No one could believe his or her eyes, but what could we do. Maybe that's how Larry and Wifey get their kicks. Jesse had seen and heard it all before. He simply continued.

"I assume you're familiar with Hitler and his planned 'thousand-year' Third Reich. Well, the court scribe Alcuin first recorded St. Peter's Stiftskeller into the history books during a visit in the year 803 by Emperor Charlemagne, founder of the First Reich, which actually did last a thousand years under the so-called Holy Roman Empire."

Before Jesse could continue, an elderly woman wearing a hot-pink pantsuit, as if to impress us on her ability to count to three, yelled out: "Was there a Second Reich between the first and the third?"

In a pleasant pitch, our knowledgeable guide responded, "Why, yes, there was. The Second Reich was the brainchild of Germany's 'Iron Chancellor,' Otto von Bismarck, who helped to unify the German states into one empire in 1871, lasting some 48 years until its collapse in 1918 after the Kaiser's defeat in World War I."

We bid adieu to St. Peter's Stiftskeller then marched across the monastery grounds, paralleled the sheer cliffs that bolstered the fortress, through yet another set of archways and into a secluded courtyard called the Toscanini Hof. Facing us were two huge iron doors bordered by six stone blocks chiseled into masks and muses symbolic of drama. Seemingly suspended above, protruding from the wall, sat an enormous, acidic-green organ. Using this offbeat locale as a backdrop, Jesse waited for everyone to catch up.

"This, gang, is the south end of Salzburg's festival halls. From here they appear to be rather insignificant, but once around the corner you'll see the building extends the entire length of the block. Within this massive 17th-century complex are three theaters. The middle theater is distinctively one of a kind due to its 96 arches hewn into the cliff face, which can be seen during the movie 'The Sound of Music' when the von Trapps perform their farewell songs before fleeing to the cemetery."

The group let out an expected gasp.

Jesse relocated us to Old Market Square. Everything in this town seemed astonishingly old. Case in point: To our left was Café Tomaselli, Austria's oldest coffeehouse, established in 1703, where Mozart played cards and drank his preferred almond milk.

The far end of the square connected to Getreidegasse, a narrow shopping lane and birthplace of the legendary composer. Nearby sat another glorious church. To our joy, Salzburg's many churches continuously rang their bells, seemingly competing for parishioners.

On our way through the old square, Jesse challenged us. "Okay, folks, let's see if anyone can pick out the smallest house in Salzburg." Immediately the group embarked on their quest. I lagged behind, again.

A succession of beautifully Baroque facades bound our location. They reached six stories tall and were painted in soft pastels, perhaps suggesting the warmth of the square. To the right stood a fountain crowned by Saint Florian, patron of fire protection, pouring a bucket of water over a burning castle. Behind it sat a sweets shop having pounds of chocolate in its front window. Boxes upon boxes, in all shapes and sizes, filled with little chocolate balls wrapped in shiny foil featuring the likeness of Mozart. I gladly plucked a sample from the lady standing outside offering passersby the toothsome treat. Yum.

Abruptly, my attention was diverted to a chorus of sighs and people pointing. What, or who, could it be this time?

Of course, the smallest house in Salzburg. Not much of a house, more like a stuccoed matchbox betwixt buildings. Add a door, a window, throw on a few tiles for a roof, nail in a gargoyle and call it the smallest house in town. Marvelous advertising for the converted jewelry store.

At this pit stop I pulled ahead of our group and milled around a cluster of market stalls while Jesse waited for the last of his guests to finish taking pictures. One stall in particular stood out. It was brimming with spiritual trinkets and a wealth of crosses: gold, silver, hand carved. My interest roused. I walked over for a closer look. The stall owner must have sensed I was a tourist and offered her thoughts in textbook English. "I see you are interested in my crosses. Can I help you make a choice?"

"Well, actually, I'm interested in a 19th-century gold crucifix covered with jewels that may have come from King Ludwig II."

The stall owner's face curiously tilted. "Sorry, there's nothing like that here. But a short time ago I did read a magazine article that described a cross similar to the one you speak of."

Intrigued, I pressed the stall owner for details. She said the article stated that a jeweled crucifix was dug up in the mid-1930s at a construction site along Hitler's new autobahn between Munich and Salzburg, but that's where the story ended. However, that was enough information to sway me to believe that ShoSho had second thoughts about letting someone else in on the quest — especially someone living in Germany so close to the action.

Meanwhile, Jesse had his hands full. The assertive hot-pink pantsuit lady had managed to bog down the gang who had otherwise adopted the motto 'Keep on truckin'.' Her modus operandi effectively puppeteered the seniors into photo shock. "Chuck, put your arm around Martha. Okay, smile, and...perfect!" *Click!*

Pantsuit Lady searched for new recruits. "Ethel, I want you and Thelma in this next one, just in front of the smallest house. Great, now a bit more to your left, a bit more.... Stop! Okay, say, 'Peanut butter balls.'" *Snap!*

"Good grief. I'm out of film! Hold your positions everybody, this'll just take a second."

Ethel and Thelma stood impatiently while Pantsuit Lady clumsily opened the foil packaging of a film cartridge and loaded it into her dated camera.

'Good grief' is right; that Kodak would serve a better purpose in the Smithsonian.

Pantsuit Lady, unfortunately, was back in business. "Okay, people, let's take a group photo. Jesse, I want you standing up front with me!"

"Yes, Ma'am," Jesse replied, as if she were his grandmother and he the young, obedient grandson.

Afterward, she rudely grabbed a passerby and asked him in English if he would take their photo. She forced the recording device on him and walked away before he could answer.

The man stared confusingly down at the contraption that rested in his hands. He searched for the correct button to push, found it, then politely took the picture. Embarrassed, Jesse graciously thanked the man in German, "Ich danke Ihnen ganz herzlich."

That consequently wrapped things up on the photo front and the gang began marching onwards, ignoring Pantsuit Lady's requests for more group pictures.

Our next move led us onto Getreidegasse, where throngs of shoppers shuffled past. Bang on the corner stood a pair of manufactured models in the window of a provocative lingerie shop flaunting its scant merchandise.

If mannequins could speak, I wonder what they would say? Probably something like: It's freakin' cold!

These life-sized dolls were quite exposed with their thin shapes and erect nipples, making a trio of passing monks blush. Over here, nudity seemed to be accepted. Much more than back home, anyway. I can honestly say that few people have seen me as naked as these ladies, but that's a conversation for another time.

If it were mandated to select one's best assets, I would choose my feet. They're not sexy or beautiful or anything like that, I simply mean they get me around town with no problem. I often hear people complaining about their feet, like having a corn, blister, bunion, something. Fortunately, I've had no difficulties — knock on wood — and my feet are perfect just the way they are.

Yet, to a number of men, a woman's breasts or backside seem to be the focus. Maybe there's nothing wrong with that, but there's something lacking in the way they go about it. 'Hey, Honey...nice tits, nice ass!'

Come on guys, show some class. Treat a lady with respect, give her flowers, spring for dinner once in awhile. There's more to a woman than her butt and breasts. You've got to take your time. Give her long, slow caresses, define her curves with gentle strokes, hold her tight and feel how she radiates warmth. Look deep into her eyes — you'll see there's nothing sexier. And most importantly, listen to what she has to say. Gentlemen, do this, I guarantee you will get what you want.

I'd better conclude there, because as arresting as this was, it became evident that no one else had noticed the willowy window models.

The gang had already arrived at the next attraction and was patiently waiting for me. So, I hightailed it out of eroticville. Jesse had just begun counting heads outside Mozart's birthplace and museum. I was last, but punctual.

"Good. Everyone's here!" Jesse faced us like a conductor to his orchestra. "Gang, this is where I say goodbye. I'm sure you're all ready to do your own thing and I do hope you've enjoyed our walk together. The museum is in English and there are toilets inside. If you have any questions, stay behind, otherwise I'll see you again at 3 p.m. on Mozart Platz. Enjoy Salzburg, and I bid you *auf Wiederseh'n*."

The guests were all smiles, telling Jesse he had done a great job as they filed past him into the museum. Well, that is, except for one.

"Where's McDonald's?" By this time Boobs' stomach was a shock wave of malnutrition; abdominal rumblings rocked the Mozart house to its Baroque foundations.

Without delay, Jesse pointed the way. Boobs turned and shot out of Mozart's place like a pair of melons launched from a catapult.

Fast food and fleshy fruit aside, thoughts of Mom flooded in. How she would love to be here to witness the history. Yet, I would have to visit this museum on behalf of my mother another day. Jesse was heading in my direction and there was the issue of lodging to address.

"The guests are all settled. We're free to explore," Jesse said with a smile while shoving a stick of gum in his mouth and recycling the wrapper into his jeans pocket.

"How 'bout we grab a quick bite to eat," I asked, "before finding me somewhere to sleep?"

"Deal. I know the perfect place."

Not far from Mozart's, secreted midway along a cobbled passage, Jesse led me to the Bosna Grill, a literal whole in the wall, serving Salzburg's favorite sausages of Bulgarian origin since 1950. The man working behind the window had little more than elbow room to serve a queue of customers. Apparently this elfin eatery was so hush-hush that the local regulatory agencies responsible for health and safety inspections hadn't yet discovered its sausage success.

The Bosna menu was short, simple and spicy, having five options to choose from, each consisting of two sausages slotted into a hot-dog-like bun loaded with condiments. By the time it was our turn to order I had decided on No. 3, the Bosna with mustard and curry spice. Jesse opted for the works, No. 4, with onions.

We ushered our savory sausages to the riverbank and sat next to the Mozart Steg, dating from 1903, the footbridge used in the filming of the Do-Re-Mi curtain-wearing sequence in "The Sound of Music."

Good thing our group wasn't picnicking with us, otherwise arms would have been flinging up everywhere at the movie reference and possibly knocking the Bosna out of my mouth.

We sat alongside the river, delighting in the stunning beauty of this age-old city. The pleasant weather conditions, the chirping birds playing by the water, the castle on the hill. I felt so fortunate to be here, in Austria, at this moment. Hopefully Jesse didn't notice the mustard that dripped off the Bosna bun nto my lap.

Our conversation turned to travel, and we discussed the pros and cons of a backpack versus a suitcase. The backpack had no cons.

"So, what brings Sydney Endicott to Europe?"

"Ha! Where should I begin? How 'bout a break from college, a sense of self-achievement, the quest for a golden crucifix, and the opportunity to travel and meet new people."

"Huh...? The quest, for what?"

"A golden crucifix studded with precious gemstones that is supposedly buried around Chiemsee and came from the fairy-tale king, Ludwig II. Sound familiar?"

"Uh," he looked at me, scratching his head in perplexity, "no."

I didn't think so, but it was worth asking. Although, I'd better change the subject before he thinks I'm some kind of nut. "So, what brings you to Europe, Mister Tour Guide?"

"I guess you could say that I'm on a global mission for knowledge. It's the fuel that drives my engine. As a tour guide, I especially love to watch the expressions of people when I show them something they've never seen before. One guest, for example, was so overwhelmed by a cache of sacred relics that she actually fainted on tour."

"Nuh-uh. Serious?"

"Really! We were in the heart of old Vienna admiring St. Stephen's Cathedral, the city's most sacred monument. Our hands shielded us from the sun as we gazed upwards beyond the stained-glass windows and gargoyles to the Heathen Towers. In the year 1683, I told them, some 150,000 Ottoman Turks rode from the east to capture Vienna and its glorious cathedral. Locked in mortal combat, the Muslims were beat back from the city gates when a Christian relief army struck a counterblow. In their retreat, the Turks left behind sacks of coffee beans on the battlefield, beginning a stimulating odyssey of Viennese coffee trade and culture that continues to thrive to this day."

"And the fainted one," I inquired. "What about her?"

"Oh, right, yeah... I summoned the guests into the cathedral, along the left aisle and down the steps into the catacombs to witness piles of decayed bones and skulls from plagues past. That's when I lost her. She dropped like a sack of potatoes right there in the heart of Vienna."

"Yikes! What did ya do?"

"Well, I happened to have a slice of Sacher chocolate cake in my bag. I wagged it past her nose and said if she didn't get up, the medieval trolls were gonna come and whisk her away. And you should have seen her jump. She snapped to attention like a soldier in Patton's Third Army!"

Jesse had whetted my appetite for travel. There's so much to see and do in Europe. Vienna had been just another grand city from the history books, but now — I'm here! Could a year possibly be enough time? I do know one thing for sure, out of the 1,440 minutes I get to spend every day, not one will be wasted.

After lunch, Jesse insisted on walking me through the Mirabell Gardens on the way to the hostel.

I was excited all right, as this was my first of many adventures in Europe. Not to mention, my first night ever in a youth hostel.

The Mirabell Gardens were immensely beautiful, like a painting with tourists. At the entrance appeared to be two Greek-inspired statues of nude discus throwers in the after-release position, and beyond them were another two. We walked past the statues, as if being careful not to be struck, and were drawn to a symphony of flowers breaking through the earth, reaching for the sun. Jesse walked to the back center of the gardens and planted himself opposite a bed of budding roses.

From this spot, the splendor of the gardens, skyline of Old Town, and the majesty of the Alps were all at our photographic disposal. Truly a postcard-perfect picture!

CHAPTER 3

My First Youth Hostel
(Salzburg, Austria)

Chapter 4

We exited the Mirabell Gardens via the Do-Re-Mi steps portrayed in the movie "The Sound of Music," walked up a few streets and through the hostel's front door. A welcoming sign read *Yoho, International Youth Hotel, Easy to Find — Hard to Leave.*

Standing behind the reception desk, a twenty-something woman cordially greeted us in excellent English. "Hi! Can I help you?"

Unknown to me, Jesse had called ahead and made a reservation.

"Yeah, hi, I talked yesterday with Stephanie and booked a dorm bed for my friend here, Sydney." Jesse eyed the receptionist hoping she could verify his call.

"Sure, I remember." Jesse looked instantly relieved. "I'm Stephanie. You seemed a little concerned, so I took the opportunity and roomed her with some free-spirited travelers in a four-bed dorm." She then scrolled her finger down the guest book in front of her. "Was that for one or two nights, Miss Endercut?"

"Just one night," I answered, not worrying about the name difference.

Jesse, however, insisted on clearing up the discrepancy. "In case there's a problem of any sort..." he turned to me with a cheeky grin, "the name is Endicott."

"I'm sorry!" Stephanie apologized. "That does have a nicer ring to it."

"Oh, thank you." I accepted Stephanie's compliment, turning to Jesse with a cheeky grin of my own.

She offered me the room key and a suggestion. "Happy hour in our bar is from 6 to 7 p.m. Enjoy your stay!"

Mister Tour Guide escorted me upstairs to my room. I turned the key in the lock, pivoted to face Jesse, and pushed the door open. "My first room in Europe. What do ya think?"

By the look on his face, I knew something was wrong. Were the curtains a horrible color? Was there a dead body on the floor?

Turning to see for myself, I saw two bunk beds, a sink, heating radiator, and my very first hostel roommates: two girls sitting on a bed and braiding their snow-white hair, each wearing a sheer lace bra and panty set. Unabashed, they stood up in a relaxed, welcoming manner. Both had lean, athletic bodies like that of a dancer.

"Hello. You must be our roommates," one of them said.

"Hi," I responded, awkwardly. "It's just me who is staying tonight." We entered the room and closed the door behind us. "My friend here will be leaving, soon. Right, Jesse?" I gave him a double nudge to the ribs. "Jesse?"

He appeared flushed and somewhat googly eyed. "Right, yeah...I have ahh, err...some people, a tour to catch up with." Jesse stammered, glancing at his watch.

The two girls, lacking a shy bone, remained stationary with their enviable figures and suntanned skin on full display. It was as if the window models from the lingerie shop on Getreidegasse had checked into the same hostel as me.

The room abruptly lit when the sun penetrated the afternoon clouds, emphasizing every detail of their toned bodies as the rays beamed through the curtainless window. Jesse offered his hand to divert from the obvious distractions. "Hiii I'mm... Jesse."

He struggled to maintain eye contact, the up-and-down motion of the handshake was too much to bear. His intense concentration disintegrated into a hot mess as he introduced himself directly to their breasts. Jesse recognized his *faux pas* and searched for an out. I dove in for the rescue, alerting him that the time was 2:30 and he needed to meet his group. Without hesitation, Jesse agreed and waved goodbye, walking straight into the door as he exited.

Embarrassed, I apologized on Jesse's behalf. "I'm sorry for my friend; he's not usually so...shy."

"No need to apologize," said one of the girls. They looked at each other and giggled. "He seemed very friendly," said the other.

"Ahh...yeah," I agreed, "friendly."

"Are you traveling around Europe?" questioned one of the girls as they continued getting dressed for the evening.

"In a way, yeah. I'm working at a hotel just north of here for a year, and in that time I'd like to see as much as I can while searching for a golden cross. How about you two?" I abruptly cut the sentence short and winced. "I'm sorry, I seem to have forgotten your names."

On that note they both thrust their hands at me. "Hi, I'm Liselott," said one.

"And I'm Britte," said the other. "We're university students from Sweden."

Stephanie had clearly made a clairvoyant decision to room me with these girls. Not only did I sense their sincerity, but maybe we had college frustrations in common.

"How long are you traveling for?" I asked.

"Well..." Liselott shrugged, "we wanted to take the semester off and tour Europe, but our parents didn't go for it and we were lucky to steal two weeks around the Easter holidays."

Our ping-pong chatter lasted nearly two hours before we realized the time. During the conversation, the girls invited me to join them for dinner and drinks. I accepted, but first I decided to take a shower, which was down the hall.

I jumped in, soaked under the rain shower head, and quickly realized I had no towel. There were no towels. How could there be no towels?!

Upon returning to the dorm, I walked in on the Swedes talking to our new roommate, an attractive girl with honey-colored, shoulder-length hair that complemented her striking green eyes. As the Swedes eyeballed my conspicuously wet clothes with amusement, she introduced herself as Onoma from Prague, Czech Republic.

"You have an interesting name," I stated. "Is that Czech for something?"

"That's a familiar question. My mother originally comes from Greece and she wanted to hand down something traditional. Onomastics is the study of names and their origins and Onoma is the Greek word for 'name.'"

"Now I really like your name," I said.

"Děkuji." Onoma stopped immediately when she understood her slip. "Sorry, that's Czech for what I wanted to say in English, Thank you."

"You're welcome. But, it's also interesting to hear your language."

"Britte and Liselott told me your name is Sydney. Is that after the Australian city?"

"That's also a familiar question. Actually, it comes from my grandfather and father. Because of how hard I was kicking in my mother's stomach, my parents assumed I was a boy and automatically had all the paperwork filled out as Sidney Lee Endicott III. So, of course, it was a shock for them when a girl popped out. Nevertheless, they left things as planned except for changing the 'i' to a 'y.'"

"Now I especially like your name," Onoma said, returning the compliment.

"Děkuji," I countered, hoping my memory served me correctly.

Onama's face lit up. "I'm impressed! I think you, Sydney, have a gift for languages."

While the four of us were getting acquainted, I concluded that hostel life boasted many similarities to dorm life at college. The only differences were bunk beds, international camaraderie, and sharing your room with adventurers. I felt extremely blessed to be here.

We all agreed that since none of us knew the city, 'happy hour' should be our first stop and we would take the night from there. It was getting close to 6 p.m. and valuable time was slipping away.

The first drinks were poured and unsurprisingly the popular choice was the local beer, Stiegl. Our opening gesture of camaraderie was a toast to new friendships and the night ahead. I began.

"Here's a little drinking ditty I learned in Bavaria. Okay, girls, you ready? Raise your glasses and repeat after me...

> Into each other's eyes we stare.
> Our glasses clink with flair.
> Down to the table for a tap.
> We raise 'em up and throw 'em back.
> Stomach and liver, have no fear,
> This is how we drink our beer!"

Our sips became healthy gulps. We couldn't help but laugh at each other's foamy moustaches and the teeny burps that followed. Conversation flowed, especially when the girls found out that I had showered without a towel, having to dry off with my shirt and jeans. Joking aside, the girls graciously informed me that sometimes when staying at a hostel one needs to either rent a towel from reception or, better, bring your own. I guess I should have known, but it was my first youth hostel.

What a great experience. I was having so much fun talking to the

My First Youth Hostel 67

people we met: Canadians, Australians, New Zealanders, British, Japanese, Koreans, fellow Americans, and other passionate travelers from faraway lands. It was much easier than I had anticipated — sharing a drink, discussing common interests, and exchanging travel tips to new adventures. Everybody had a story to tell, a dream to grasp. Though, I must admit, no one was searching for a lost crucifix.

Happy hour wound down, but the night was young. The word going around shifted the partygoers to Hüftgold. I chuckled at the mention of the place. It reminded me of Jesse, which in turn reminded me of his earlier facial expressions when he awkwardly attempted to introduce himself to Britte and Liselott. He would've had better luck tackling a plate of spaghetti with chopsticks.

Although a liquid dinner was alluring, my new acquaintances and I elected to grab something to eat. A friend at Chiemsee had given me directions to a historic riverside restaurant just outside Old Town known for its pocket-friendly prices and authentic Austrian fare. The girls approved and we found our way by public transportation.

We exited the bus and into the Bärenwirt on Bärengässchen in the district of Mülln. According to legend, in the year 1562, a black bear swam up from the river and rested here on the bank, thus today's storied Bear Inn on Bear Lane. We arrived with ravaging hunger.

Inside, a gentleman came to our service. "Grüss Gott, Sie schauen aus, als hätten Sie einen Bärenhunger."

We girls looked at each other wondering who was going to answer.

The host swiftly acknowledged a language barrier and switched to something familiar. "Allow me to introduce myself, my name is Herr Boss. You girls look hungry!"

Boy, were we ever. He sat us at a table with a view and promptly handed us menus. After a quick flip through, I saw what my stomach craved. The others hardly took as much time.

Herr Boss and a co-worker arrived a minute later with our drinks and an order of goulash soup with four spoons. We began the dinner toast the same as our happy-hour *Prost*, but this time it went like clockwork. It had become our theme.

> "Into each other's eyes we stare.
> Our glasses clink with flair.
> Down to the table for a tap.
> We raise 'em up and throw 'em back.
> Stomach and liver, have no fear,
> This is how we drink our beer!"

Out the window, a natural wonder set before our eyes. The sun went down like a ball of fire, filling the horizon with a glowing medley of color. The fiery sphere continued its descent behind the mountains, painting the twilight sky deep red before disappearing into the arms of Mother Earth.

The dazzling sunset electrified the mood in the restaurant. All were jovial as they ordered additional drinks and appetizers, keeping Herr Boss and his staff moving at a brisk pace. The couple at the next table commented on the stunning colors of twilight and introduced themselves as Karel and Silke. They said they got a kick out of our energy, as did other patrons. Karel told us they were from Vienna and visiting Salzburg for a few days.

"Karel, are you originally Viennese?" Onoma asked. "Your name sounds more Slavic than Austrian."

"Actually, my grandparents are from the former Sudetenland, so you could say I'm a little bit Czech, German and Austrian," he said.

"Can you talk the talk?" Onoma inquired, entertaining the notion of conversing with him in her native tongue.

We all stared and waited for an answer. It wasn't as if she was trying to hit on Karel — his girlfriend was sitting right next to him.

"I can get by," he modestly replied. This triggered a fluid conversation in Czech. At least that's how it sounded to us.

Britte and Liselott began chattering in Swedish, which left Silke and me linguistically handcuffed. I felt like a weed in a flower box when it came to speaking German, and Silke wasn't much better in English.

Salvation came when Herr Boss arrived with our meals, interrupting the language debacle. *Mmm...that smells delicious* is how I interpreted everyone's expression.

My wild boar sausage, served in a skillet with potatoes and cabbage, looked scrumptious. The girls ordered the house specialty, fried chicken, said to be Austria's best!

"Bring another round of beers for myself and the traveling girls," Karel requested. "Oh, and Herr Boss..." he gestured as if he'd forgotten something, "could you also pour a soda for my friend here? Danke."

Uh oh, it was his girlfriend he had forgotten. We gave a hearty thank you to our admirer, much to the chagrin of Silke.

We washed our meals down with freshly tapped Augustiner, beer brewed by the monks since 1621 in the neighboring monastery, now called Müllner Bräu. The trick at Bärenwirt, with all its scrumptiousness, is to leave room for dessert.

To complement our heaping portion of Black Forest Cherry Dream ice cream, we indulged in a round of short stories from our lives back home. Liselott began.

"Britte and I grew up in Jönköping, a historic trading city in southern Sweden. We've known each other since we were 3 years old when our parents started an ABBA cover band, The Dancing Queens. The band was a local success, playing weekends. That is...until a very cold Saturday in November when they played to a sell-out crowd at Fernando's, the biggest club downtown. The first two songs that night went smoothly. By the third song, their groove intensified and they belted out 'Mamma Mia,' bringing the crowd to its feet. That's when it happened. My father tripped over a power cord, fell off the stage and into the arms of a beautiful blonde woman dancing in the front row. My father had the sympathy of everyone until it became apparent he was in no hurry to leave the woman's comforting embrace. My mother burst into tears. Backstage, our parents decided that life in a rock band was too demanding and from then on they would spend their weekends raising sheep at their country homes. Even though we miss the old ABBA days, we enjoy being with our parents and playing with the animals on the large farms they've built."

With the delighted look of a child being tucked into bed anticipating a story, Britte rotated to Onoma. "What do you miss about home?"

"My grandparents!" Onoma gushed, taking a sip of beer and positioning herself better to face us. "They're getting older now, so I worry about them. They live in a two-story farmhouse in the Bohemian countryside with their rat-catching cat, Hanka. The farm dates from the 1700s and it needs regular assistance to keep the rodents at a minimum, the perfect job for Hanka. She's a bubbly creature that wanders the property licking the faces of the baby lambs and torments the cows by jumping on their backs and playing cowgirl cat. About twice a week, during the early hours of the morning, Hanka will come to the bedroom window and scratch her paws against the glass, waking Grandpa and Grandma. Grandpa usually rolls over and insists, 'It's your turn to comfort the cat, Dear.' Grandma then gets out of bed, walks over to the window and affectionately says, 'Ahh, good cat...you caught a rat. Now go run off and play, my darling.' Hanka leaves to play with her new toy and dear Grandma and Grandpa go back to sleep."

"Cute story," Liselott tweeted. Then the girls focused their attention on me. "It's your turn, Sydney."

"Well... I grew up in America with my brother, Alex, and two loving parents, Dolores and Sid. One summer about 10 years ago we took a family trip to the southern states in our minivan. We spent the day touring Mobile, Alabama, and the nearby alligator wildlife park. It was getting late so we started to look for a place to stay the night, but the hotels were full.

"We continued our route east. Soon, we heard a repetitive clunking sound. 'What's that?' my fretful brother asked.

"'Oh no...' said our panic-stricken mother, 'I think we are on a bridge.'

"At that moment, we learned our mother was deathly afraid of long bridges over water, especially at night. Dad told Mom not to worry. A few uneasy minutes later, we reached the other side...Florida.

"The time was approaching midnight and we agreed that anywhere on the side of the road to sleep would be wonderful. We eventually found a rest area and parked for the night. We got as comfortable as humanly possible, using towels for blankets and sweaters for pillows. Dad and Alex were a little warm, so they cracked the windows for air. Morning came and we woke to uncontrollable itching.

"We pulled into the first gas station to fill up. The attendant noticed our scratching. 'Looks like you've been bitten by the noseeum.'

"'The what?' we asked.

"'In Florida, we call them tiny bugs 'no-see-ums'...because ya can't see 'um. But don't worry, we sell a powder here that'll fix y'all up in a jiffy!'

"The end."

The girls applauded. Onoma then suggested we finish our drinks and head into town.

"As we say in Sweden," Britte said, "Skål!"

"Our drinking theme girls: Eins, zwei, drei...."

With frothy smiles we waved Herr Boss over to pay compliments to the chef and settle the bill.

Karel made a proposal while Silke kept a watchful eye. "We're driving into Old Town, if you girls would like a ride."

"Sure. If it's no problem," we innocently responded while trying not to look at Silke, knowing the intensity of her glare could probably burn holes through us.

She seemed a pleasant girl, and there's absolutely no need for her to be jealous — unless she has reasons from the past. If that were the case, maybe she should feed Karel to Hanka, the rat-catching cat. Nonetheless, that's their issue and we weren't going to turn down a free ride into town.

In a few short minutes we turned onto Salzburg's bumpy cobbled streets and were soon at the bar's front door. The girls and I bid farewell

My First Youth Hostel

to Silke and Karel and entered Hüftgold arm in arm. I felt as though we had been friends for years.

Once inside, it had the feel of a cantina from Mexico's past. The walls were a painted hodgepodge of Aztec symbols, brightly colored parrots, and little sombrero dudes resting against cacti.

"Arriba, arriba ... andelé, andelé," I crooned.

Liselott eyed me strangely.

When four girls walk into a bar unescorted, eyes will follow.

Inspired by the décor, I suggested a round of margaritas. With drinks in hand, we browsed the scene. A pair of musicians stood on a modest stage, one playing guitar and the other a saxophone. They were performing the "Tequila" song, whipping everyone into a whirlwind as we danced our way through the crowd.

Farther back amidst the heady atmosphere, we saw a table available. Upon sitting down, four guys who were also staying at our hostel came over to say hello.

The waiter interrupted our salutations by delivering eight shots of flaming sambuca to the table.

The guys, two Australians and two Canadians, clearly had premeditated our meeting, and although I'm sure it was a ploy to get into our pants, free drinks on my already stretched euro budget were welcome. Besides, sometimes it's entertaining to take advantage of male weaknesses.

The guys raised their sambuca up high and made a toast to new acquaintances.

The idea of flaming sambuca is to kill the flame and drink the liqueur. You do this by lowering the palm of your hand over the shot glass to choke the oxygen and extinguish the flame. As a result, the glass will affix to your palm, like a leech to skin. Remove the glass and consume your warmed beverage. Sounds simple, right? Sure, until it was my turn to give it a try.

As soon as I released my flambéed hand from the top of the shot glass, the sambuca spilled — spreading the flame with it. Panicked, I knocked the glass to the floor, where it smashed and created a mini firestorm. Luckily, the bar crew scurried over to help stomp out my little mishap.

Embarrassed, I began to apologize to our group. "I'm sorry, but.... Hey, where did everyone go?"

At some point while the barkeeps mopped the floor and I picked glass bits out of my shoe, our group had shifted to the dance floor. I joined in the fun. With modest room to rumba, we all jumped and bumped into each other with little care.

During the next song, "Do You Love Me," the girls and I danced amongst ourselves. Not overly dirty, but apparently provocative enough to arouse the guys, who were gawking at us like they were good to go.

Our dance was interrupted when we saw Karel enter the bar — without Silke! Britte, Liselott, and I swiftly turned to Onoma.

"I had nothing to do with this!" she protested, flinging up her arms.

Onoma was offended that we had even considered such a thought. Feelings aside, she walked over to him to see what's up.

The rest of us resumed dancing, but our harmonious octet dwindled into an offbeat party of five. Liselott had interlocked with Dazza, one of the Australians. His hands glided up and down her body as their tongues did the tango. Without delay, Dazza's friends felt this was their cue to move in and mimic the action. Britte and I weren't keen on the hormone overload. We pried their hands from our backsides and retreated to our table for a deserved break. Besides, it was still possible that Jesse might show.

Britte signaled the waiter. At the same moment two guys sat down and made themselves comfortable. "Ciao, yu girls a free?"

Luckily, the waiter arrived. "Vhat kann I get you?"

"Two white wines, please," I answered.

"We a paya for yu girls," one of the guys said. "It's a no problema."

"Where do you come from?" Britte asked.

"Yu girls bella, beutiful." They each lit a cigarette. "Yua want smoke, I can giva yu?"

"No thank you." This time I asked the question. "Where do you come from?"

"We cuma from Italia, yua like my country?"

"Yes, of course..." Britte said, "I went last year to Rimini with my 'ex' for a beach holiday."

"Oh si, si, yua meet lots Italian man."

"No man," Britte explained, "I went with my ex-*girl*friend!"

"Oh capito, si... yu and other girl make it weth Italian boy."

"Hier ladiez, two vhite vines." The thick-accented waiter, thank goodness, had returned. "Zat vill be sieben euro fünfzig, pleaz."

One of the guys reached for his wallet. "Rememba, we paya for yu beutiful girls." He handed the waiter money. "Here, keepa the changa."

"Schönen Dank," replied the appreciative waiter in his native tongue.

My First Youth Hostel   73

Meanwhile, Britte reached over and began stroking my hair. "This sensual woman is now my monogamous partner."

Despite Britte's anti-male strokes, they persisted like starved animals. Homoeroticism had only encouraged their arousal. It was like watching two male dogs drooling over prime rump roasts.

"Yu girls cuma weth us, we showa yu how real man maka luv... *Italian-style*."

If these guys would stop staring down our tops and listen, they might get the hint that we're not interested. They act like the type of slime balls who come on to every girl they meet. It was time to give these degenerates a verbal vasectomy.

"Listen up!" I said. "We're not interested in having relations with you now, later, or ever...so put it back in your pants and save it for someone who's desperate enough to fall for your charade." On that final note, we snatched our wine and waved *arrivederci*. I hated being so mean, but they deserved it.

A prudent woman is a wise woman.

Still trying, the guys expressed their *amore*. "No ragazze, stai, stai. We luva yu!"

Before losing ourselves in the crowd, we turned to see the guys standing awkwardly. It was more than obvious that our company had made them rise to the occasion and their swollen spermatozoon heads were primed to erupt like volcanoes!

On the other side of the dance floor, we mocked our wannabe lovers. "Oh baby, I giva yu spaghetti and vino, now we maka luv."

"Si, si, I showa you my pasta, you showa me yours."

It was time for another toast, this round to European travels.

> "Here's to meeting different peoples;
>
> Castles, cobblestones and church steeples.
>
> Let's drink our white wine,
>
> To escaping the swine!"

One drink and a few dances later landed us at 2 a.m. Time to call it a night. Britte went to retrieve Liselott, and I strayed in the direction of the front door to see how Onoma was doing. Sliding through the crowd, I arrived in time to observe her reaching back with an open hand and slapping it forward. *Whack!* It was a sure bet that someone was ready to leave. She must have seen me approaching, because she immediately rushed over.

"Is everything okay?" I asked, grabbing both her jittery arms and looking her straight in the eyes.

"I'm fine!" Onoma insisted. However, she appeared rattled and her face glowed cherry red.

She quickly told me about the incident: Karel was giving her the sad story about how he and his girlfriend got into a fight, which brought him back to the bar for a cheer-up. Onoma, being polite, tried to console him, but I could see in her eyes that she was suspicious of his spiel. He tried to pull a fast one by putting his lips on hers and that's when she gave him a complimentary outline of her hand across his face.

"Are the girls ready to go?" Onoma questioned.

Britte then walked up, followed by Liselott and Dazza.

I asked Liselott the question I'm sure we were all thinking. "Are you coming with us, or staying?"

"A foursome," she briskly responded, "is better than a threesome!"

"But..." Dazza reasoned, "I thought we made a pretty good twosome."

That was the smartest thing he could have said in his plea to win her heart.

"Maybe tomorrow night you'll get lucky?" Liselott proposed.

"What does that mean?" Dazza asked as he casually leaned against the doorway portraying the bad-boy image with his knotty hair, sweat-drenched T-shirt, and lipstick-smeared face while cocking his head and lighting a cigarette.

"Be here and find out," Liselott replied.

Arm in arm, like our entrance hours earlier, we exited Hüftgold.

Onoma was bothered by her previous actions and began to apologize.

Britte cut her off. "You need not explain a thing. We've all had bad experiences with the opposite sex."

Back at the hostel, we stripped from our smoke-rich clothing and snuggled deep into our beds. Our chatter soon petered to a soft snore as we drifted off to sleep.

Good night, Salzburg

My First Youth Hostel

CHAPTER 4

Look, But Don't Touch
(Baden-Baden, Germany)

Chapter 5

Five weeks later, beginning of May

Jesse had been conducting some investigations of his own, as I found out when he excitedly burst into my room and explained that it's possible the crucifix was dug up right here beneath the Chiemsee resort. He said he'd been speaking with a local elder who had worked on the original construction of the Lake Hotel as a kid in the mid-1930s and recalled unearthing a golden crucifix. He wasn't sure what happened to it after that since the on-site foreman, a high-ranking Nazi official, immediately spirited the cross away. What's more, the individual Jesse interviewed hinted that the hotel's cellar might hold a clue.

Upon hearing this, I grabbed my coat and we dashed out of the Waldheim for the Lake Hotel. At the reception desk, Jesse signed for a special key and grabbed two flashlights.

The spirit of the adventure had me wrapped tightly within its grasp.

After a few hours of successful sleuthing, we were cotton-mouthed from the cellar's musty air. Lucky for us, it was karaoke night in the resort's bar! We rushed back to our rooms to change out of our cellar clothes and then joined our colleagues, who were already in the bar hoisting brews and murdering popular tunes.

Karaoke night always attracts a full house. Locals pour in from the neighboring villages to practice their English while sharing a friendly drink with hotel guests and staff. Shyness is checked at the door and everybody sings a song. Some try to impersonate Bon Jovi, others Elvis. The Bavarians especially love getting up on stage and singing Jimmy

Buffett's "Margaritaville" with margarita in hand. By night's end there is always one superstar who is half a drink from passing out and dabbles in the metal of Iron Maiden's "Run to the Hills."

Last drinks are called at 11:30 and the bar shuts at midnight, when sensible employees head back to their quarters. The unsensible migrate to a designated party room and continue the assault on their livers. On this particular evening in early May, I joined the glut. The designated party room belonged to Steve, 504 in the Annex, where about 15 of us boozehounds partied until dawn.

At 8:30 a.m., feeling awful, I rolled out of bed and gingerly made my way to the Lake Hotel for work, almost certainly resembling a red-eyed zombie from a horror movie. I was supposed to have the day off but elected to fill in for a friend who between parties decided on a spontaneous trip to Berlin. I couldn't reject her serendipitous spirit.

After clocking in, I reported to Sean, the head housekeeper. He handed me my work assignment, which consisted of four checkouts and nine stayovers on the ground floor of the Lake Hotel.

At my workstation I was met by a cheery, "Gooood morning!" It was my roommate, Janie. She got an early night's sleep.

I tried to equal her enthusiasm as best I could, "Mornin'."

"Have you seen Greg or Gabby around?" Janie asked of our housekeeping colleagues.

"No, sorry, I haven't. But I did see them last night partaking in karaoke festivities." They were in full swing impersonating John Travolta and Olivia Newton-John in a wowing rendition of "Summer Nights." On stage they looked so cute together dancing, singing, staring into each other's eyes. Maybe they finally got together like we'd all been hoping for, which would explain their absence.

Janie and I pulled our cleaning carts from the utility closet, arranged a time to meet for lunch, and went our separate ways down the hall.

The first room I had to clean was a stay-over, which meant the emptying of trash, replacement of towels, and a general clean where necessary, usually taking 15 minutes.

Operation Sanitize, as I call it, was put into action. *Knock. Knock.* "Housekeeping," I announced at the door.

There was no answer, so I said it again louder. "HOUSEKEEPING!" Still, no answer. Using my master key, I proceeded into the room. Inside, I saw a half-naked guy passed out on the bed. In my professional work voice, I asked: "Do you need any cleaning done in your room today, sir?"

With sleep packed around his eyes and a string of drool connecting the corner of his mouth to the pillow, he raised his head with great

Look, But Don't Touch 79

difficulty and articulated: "No, I'm fi...." His head crashed back onto the pillow before he could finish. I recognized him from karaoke; Iron Maiden wasn't his best selection.

This first-rate example of employee-to-guest dedication gave me an extra 13 minutes for lunch. With the next room, a checkout, I should have parked my senses at the door. Upon entering, the smell of sex was so strong it virtually reached out and slapped me in the face. The former occupants undeniably got their money's worth. Strewn everywhere were bath towels and bed sheets and used condoms. Instantly, I ran to the window for fresh air and calming thoughts.

Relax. I'm in Germany. I can readily travel on days off, tour medieval castles, shop European fashion, indulge in authentic schnitzel and strudel and chocolate-covered sweets.

Progressively, my plan worked. I began picking up the used latex items with a towel and I didn't vomit.

Tucked in the corner of the room, adjacent to the bed and partially hidden by an overhanging blanket, sat a black overnight bag. Curious, I lifted the blanket off the bag and pulled its zipper open.

"Yowza!" I exhaled as my eyes nearly popped out. Staring me in the face were the trade tools of a porn star: vibrator, whip, handcuffs, assorted creams. I zipped up the bag and let it be. It was destined for Lost and Found.

In an attempt to take my mind off of cleaning, I flipped on the television.

Knock. Knock. Someone lightly tapped at the door, making me jump. I turned off the TV and pretended to dust.

"Come in," I said, pivoting to see who it was.

A brunette in her mid-forties with schoolteacher looks entered. "Hello, I'm sorry to bother you..." she said in a soft, pleasant voice, "but I believe I left my overnight bag behind. By any chance, have you seen it?"

Boy, had I ever!

"I did notice a bag in the corner," I answered politely, pointing in the direction of her treasure trove.

"Oh, thank you. I'd be lost without it." She pulled out a $5 bill from her purse and handed it to me. "Thanks again...and I'm sorry for any inconvenience." Offering an innocent smile, she turned and exited the room.

Well, I guess stranger things have happened — just not to me.

By the time I completed the remainder of my checkouts, it was time to take a break and visit Janie to see how she was doing.

I found her sitting on a couch bawling her eyes out. "What's wrong?" I asked, rushing over to comfort her with a hug.

"My fiancé, Johnny, called. He said he'd been with another woman, and that our relationship...was over!" Tears cascaded down her face. She broke from my clutch and wept hysterically. "How could he do this to me? We've been together for three years and were planning on getting married and having children. This has got to be a mistake! I have to go back home and sort things out. I have to go immediately!"

"I am so sorry, Janie." I handed her a tissue before pulling her back into my arms. There wasn't much I could say to make her feel better; she was just too distraught. The only cure for a broken heart is time. However, to tell her that wouldn't have made any sense. I'm sure her mind was clouded by thoughts of desperation and anxiety. Most importantly, she needed a consoling shoulder to lean on.

One thing was certain: I had to get that crazy idea of going home out of her head. Maybe it's easy for me to say, but if that ignoramus loved her as much as she said he did, she wouldn't have this problem. This sounds like another job for Hanka, the rat-catching cat! There are plenty of good men out there who would love to treat my amazing friend with respect.

"How about if we take our lunch break early and go outside for some fresh air?" I asked.

"Ookaay," she replied, sadly.

We walked outside and took a seat on one of the benches facing the lake. I brought my sack lunch containing two quickly thrown-together peanut-butter-and-jelly sandwiches. Knowing she had to eat, I offered her one.

"No thanks. I'm not hungry." She seemed to be recovering.

"You've got to eat something," I insisted with my hand extended as though it were a silver platter, "even if it's a nibble."

She reluctantly accepted the PB and J.

"I've got an idea that will help get your mind off things. In a few days I'll be hooking up with a couple girlfriends I met two months ago in Salzburg. They invited me to join them in Baden-Baden, a health-spa town in the Black Forest that is famous for its hot springs. Why don't you come along?"

"Oh, I don't know. It sounds all right..."

I interrupted her, realizing this was going to take some persuading. "Just imagine Roman baths and saunas. Live the life of an empress for a day. Spoil yourself, Janie, you're allowed to once in a while, you know. Furthermore, it's near the Rhine River, which is the border between

Germany and France." I just about had her swayed. She needed only a dash more convincing. "Come on, Janie, you deserve better than that jerk! You can't just mope around and watch the world go by, at least not in my presence you won't."

"Maybe you're right, but..."

"But nothing!" I was starting to sound like my father. "We only live once, and you're coming along. I'll tell the girls our schedule and have them meet us at the train station."

I know I was being tough on her, but no doubt she needed it.

"You make me laugh, Sydney. I didn't know you could be so bossy. How could I turn you down." She shrugged, regaining her senses. "I'll talk to Sean or somebody and make sure I get the time off. They can't say no if I tell them I'm suffering from a mid-life crisis."

"Hi girls! Beautiful day, isn't it?" Jesse appeared, hands tucked into his jeans pockets, wearing an uplifting smile.

"Hi!" I countered, pleasantly surprised. "Sure is, it'd be an injustice to stay indoors. No tour today, Mister Guide?"

"It was cancelled, so I'm in the gift shop assisting guests with this and that. So...anything new goin' on, any gossip, trips planned?"

"Matter of fact, yes!" He had no idea how perfect a question that was. "Janie and I are taking the train to Baden-Baden on Saturday for a girls' weekend away."

"Oh...you ladies will love it!" Jesse's face lit up. "It'll be a time to relax and forget about the world for awhile, a real liberating experience."

"We're so looking forward to it," I replied. "How about you; anything new?"

"Funny you ask. I've just started the biggest undertaking in my life... and you're partly my inspiration."

"What?!" I exclaimed, genuinely surprised.

"It was your enthusiasm for traveling Europe that flipped the pages in my mind to the many unforgettable stories I hear from our guests and their journeys, and that's when it clicked! I decided to write a novel, an adventure novel."

"Sounds exciting! I wish you mountains of success."

"Thanks. But the downside of this grand plan is my social life will be nonexistent since I'll be chained to the computer. And for my girlfriend, she will be bored out of her mind sitting around and watching me type all the time instead of going here or there together like we used to."

"She'll get over it," I painlessly tendered. "Do you think I'll get a mention in the book?"

"It would be my pleasure, Ms. Endicott. And it wouldn't be complete without a mention of your attractive and witty roommate." Mister-Tour-Guide-Turned-Author pivoted to face the blushful girl at my side. "What do ya think, Janie, do I have your blessing?"

"Why of course, Jesse," she replied, adoringly. I couldn't have paid him enough for that compliment. She definitely needed some outside help in the cheering-up department.

Jesse saucered his head back to me. "I wanted to tell you...my best friend, Reuben McJiggy, from California is flying in next month for a week and I'm taking him to Berchtesgaden for a visit. Would you like to come along?"

"I'd love to!" No doubt I wanted to see Berchtesgaden, an alpine village on the Austrian border, but this would also be an opportunity to get to know Jesse better as well as to track down the crucifix.

"I was hoping you'd join us. Besides, I think you'll find Reuben on the cute side with his tanned skin and surfer good-looks."

"We'll see about that."

"Gotta get back to the grindstone. See ya girls later. *Ciao.*"

"See you later, Jesse. Don't work too hard," Janie playfully teased, as her new favorite man sped off. "You know, Sydney..." Janie wore a slight grin, "he seems like a really nice guy."

"I know."

It was time we got back to work. One thing for sure, my head was no longer hurting from last night — only eager for the days ahead.

While cleaning the last of the stayovers, it occurred to me that I never did tell Janie about my encounter with the loose brunette and her bag of tricks in the porno room. Oh well, I'll save that story for another day.

After work, I searched for Janie everywhere around the hotel with no luck. Eventually, I found her sitting in the hallway of the Waldheim trying to work things out on the phone with her ladies' man.

Their conversation was about as mind-numbing as any one of the lectures given by my blathering psychology professor. 'Yeah, yeah, yeah... blah, blah, blah.'

I'm sure Casanova gave her the usual lame excuses: *Baby, it's not you, it's me ...* or more pathetic, *It's just that I'm here alone without you and it's making me do crazy things.*

Oh, PUH-LEASE! That crap's been around since the Bronze Age. It's only a ploy to keep a girl baited on the hook while the male casts his rod elsewhere. There's no good excuse, but every double-dealing male will try.

Janie's hallway banter was becoming quite the spectacle as she

Look, But Don't Touch

broadcasted her love mush with several Waldheimers in attendance. "I wuv you too, Shnooky Bear, and I'll wait for as long as you want me to. 'Bye, love you.... 'Bye."

It wasn't until she finished the call that she noticed me. "Oh. Hi! Guess you just heard: My fiancé and I are back together. Isn't that great?!"

"I'm happy if you're happy," I replied with a pathetically fake smile. How could I tell her that she was making a big mistake. I decided to keep quiet, recognizing her love was blind. If I were to intervene, she would only end up resenting me.

"I knew it wasn't him speaking earlier," Janie glowingly gushed, as we traipsed over the grubby green carpet to our room. "Now it's the real Johnny talking, and he wants me back! I'm sorry, but it's probably not a good idea that I go with you girls to Baden-Baden this weekend. I mean, what if he tries to call me and I can't be reached?"

What is she saying? I think anyone would agree that Janie should let Shnooky Bear stew in his own juice for a while. I knew I had to act fast, before I lost her.

"You can't back out now, I've already contacted the girls and made the arrangements."

"Well..."

"Come on, Janie. How could you pass up a girls' trip to the Black Forest? What harm could come from a couple of fun-filled days away?" I said with a devilish grin, having less innocent plans for her.

"Maybe you're right; what's it gonna hurt. I'll call Johnny back and tell him that I'm going away for two days. Do you have the name of the hotel we'll be staying in case he needs it for whatever reason?"

"Sorry, I don't. The girls are making all the arrangements. I only notified them of our arrival time on Saturday so they could meet us at the train station."

Janie was hesitant to respond. "I guess I'll just have to call him after we check into our room."

"Okay, it's settled then, you're going! Trust me, you won't regret a thing." I motioned towards the door. "I'm heading out for some fresh air. I'll see ya later on."

I was really off to the Lake Hotel to e-mail Britte and Liselott because I hadn't actually contacted them about any of this. Real sly of me, I know, but I wanted to make 100-percent sure Janie was coming. Everything else was genuine. The girls were coming back to Germany to celebrate the end of the school semester, and they did ask me to join them in Baden-Baden. Besides, this was the perfect excuse to hit the road again. It was time to summon the girls.

```
Subject: Meet this weekend...

Hello Swedish scholars,

How's finals' week going - hopefully not too
stressful. I'm so looking forward to our trip to
Baden-Baden this weekend. I hope you don't mind
if I bring my friend Janie along; she's been
having boyfriend problems and I told her that a
good soak in the Roman baths would help to clear
her senses. Don't ya think? We're arriving Sat-
urday on the 16:37 train coming in from Munich.

Looking forward to new adventures ☺

C U, Sydney & Janie
```

Work dragged by the rest of the week because I could only think about the weekend ahead. When Friday night finally came, Janie and I packed our bags and went to bed early. Saturday morning our neighbor, Kevin, was nice enough to give us a ride to the train station.

The first stretch from Bernau am Chiemsee to Munich took an hour. Our next connection was scheduled to depart some 40 minutes later. We spent our time on the upper level of Munich's main station sharing a döner kebab and spying the guys below who were en route to their respective trains.

We got a few receptive looks, but most men were too focused on keeping to a schedule to notice us. One guy, however, was nothing but smiles and walked straight into a pole. Another guy caught our attention by wildly waving his arms as if he were stranded on an island and we were his rescuers. He jumped onto the escalator and began making his way up to us, but at that very moment Janie noticed the time. "Oh my gawd...our train leaves in one minute!"

Over to the escalator and down we raced, unintentionally bumping those around us with our backpacks as we wove in and out of the crowd. "Excuse us. Pardon me. Sorry!!!"

Like two hysterical mental patients on the loose, we darted through the station to our train that had just begun to pull away. The conductor must have noticed our desperation because he held the doors open giving us a fighting chance to make an Olympic hurdle on board. I motioned for Janie to attempt the first door while I dashed on to the second. With a running leap, Janie landed for a perfect 10.

I, on the other hand, was not as graceful. Upon landing, my legs collapsed like a house of cards; momentum sent me tumbling into the door opposite. I got up and immediately brushed myself off to act as if nothing had happened, precisely when the conductor waltzed over. "Ticket pleaz." He was trying hard to keep a straight face.

Janie and I regained our composure and settled into second-class seating. Several stops, a change of trains, and four hours later we approached Baden-Baden. Janie had made the right decision to come along. Child-like enthusiasm was written all over her face as she gazed out the window. To our left, quaint towns were pressed into valleys, trees were bursting with the colors of spring, and the green undulating hills rolled into one another like the perfect, rhythmic heartbeat recorded on an electrocardiogram. To our right were the flatlands that lay before the Rhine River, and according to my map, the opposite bank was the Alsace region of France.

"France, Sydney...France!" Janie exclaimed in delight. She grabbed me with both hands and gave me a spirited shake. That was enough. The weekend had already been worth it.

The train crawled into the leafy town of Baden-Baden and came to a stop. I shouted from the window as my Swedish friends were the first people I saw. "Liselott, Britte... HELLO!"

They came running to the train door, faces beaming. I gave them both a hug and a Euro kiss, pecking each cheek lightly. Another round of greetings followed when I introduced my traveling companion.

The Swedes suggested we head over to the hotel, drop our gear, and clean up. Slinging the backpacks over our shoulders, we boarded the 201 bus into town.

The ride took about 10 minutes. We exited and the girls led us through the pedestrian shopping zone and straight up 43 steps, passing a giant stone statue of a sword-clenching warrior named Bismarck, to the top of town and our flower-boxed accommodations: Hotel am Markt.

Britte and Liselott only needed to change their clothes before being ready to hit the town. Janie and I tried our best to match the Swedes stitch for stitch in tasteful evening attire.

Europeans have their own sense of dress style: muted colors, trendy shoes, excess denim, little makeup, flowing scarves. That's not to say Janie and I weren't fashionable, just more likely to throw on a pair of jeans and a shirt. Either way is fine. The most significant thing I've learned since arriving in Europe does not concern clothes but more importantly to be respectful, that we are ambassadors of our country wherever we go, and the locals will judge our nation by our actions.

∞

After a fantastically delicious dinner and dessert — smoked trout complemented by a large slice of Black Forest cake layered with cherries and chocolate, locally Schwarzwälder Kirschtorte — we decided to walk it off with a stroll around town.

It was a balmy spring evening, the perfect weather for a long-sleeved blouse and a skirt just short enough to show off a bit of leg. Confidence makes a person, and no doubt we looked confident.

Baden-Baden had all the telltale signs of an early summer. Restaurants and cafés spilled onto the sidewalks, encouraging the townsfolk out of hibernation. On every other corner a vendor sold ice cream. Yet, it was a cheery bar just off the pedestrian shopping zone that pulled us in like a magnet. Feeling the moment, we ordered a bottle of white wine, specifically a German Riesling.

"So, Sydney, do you have a little rhyme for wine?" Liselott requested.
"Hmm...let's see.

> We raise our glasses of this wine,
> Handpicked from vineyards of the Rhine.
> To an adventure bold and new,
> For this my friends I say, Thank you.
> So drink this drink with words of pleasure,
> One who finds a friend, finds a treasure."

The wine emptied promptly, compensating us with jovial feelings and a desire to wander. Arms interlocked, we skipped along our moonlit path like four friends heading home after the last day of school.

We came upon what appeared to be a large mansion built in Neoclassical style, perhaps Baden-Baden's version of the White House — spotlights illuminated eight lofty pillars supporting the landmark facade. Its sweeping front garden flourished with flowers, and dewdrops dampened the neatly trimmed lawn that glistened beneath the full moon.

So far we only knew Baden-Baden externally; now it was time to peek inside for a closer look. We strolled through the mansion's grand entrance and into a — casino?

The hostess told us the building was called the Kurhaus, and indeed it was a casino. But nothing comparable to those in Las Vegas; this one was quite different. It happened to be the oldest casino in Europe and, owing to its sumptuous décor, was dubbed by the legendary film actress Marlene Dietrich as the most beautiful in the world.

Look, But Don't Touch

I asked whether we could look around. We produced our ID cards and without delay the hostess waved us through to the gaming floor. Simultaneously, she stopped a middle-aged man from entering through the same door. Men, so we learned, had a fairly strict dress code. It's compulsory for them to wear a jacket and tie before entering. The hostess referred him to reception where he could rent the combo for a few euros.

Opulent chandeliers hung from muraled ceilings. Statues of nudes stood unabashedly near moneyed gaming tables. Walls were draped in red velvet and dripping in gold trim. Exquisite oil paintings of wealthy subjects and dreamy landscapes embellished every corner of every room. It reminded me of a French château I'd seen on TV.

"How about a quick spin on the roulette wheel?" I asked, trying to coax the girls into a little adventure. "We are ladies and they do call it luck." I don't think they were thoroughly convinced, but they were game enough to play the odds.

I inspired them to throw in 10 euros each and place it on black. A gentleman wearing a penguin suit sent the ball whizzing around the wheel. Round and round the ball rolled, mesmerizing us into a trance. I stood paralyzed with fear.

Even though it wasn't much money, I quickly realized that if we were to lose it was due to my persuasion. What if it spiraled into further losses, forcing us to hitchhike home and beg for scraps at a schnitzel stand all because I suggested gambling? Would I have to call home and ask Mom and Dad to bail me out? What was I saying? That would be the ultimate victory for them, especially for Dad. I could hear him now: 'I told you so! If you'd listened to me, you wouldn't be in this mess...now would you?!'

And what about the girls? They would be my immediate threat. Would they throw me into the Rhine with cement shoes?

The ball fell from the rim, causing it to bounce several times between slots — CLICK, *clink*, CLICK, *clink*, CLICK, *clink* — until it found its place. I closed my eyes and waited to hear the reaction from the others.

"Oh, no... I can't believe it!" Liselott trumpeted.

A shiver snaked down my spine. I opened my eyes. The numbered slot the ball sat in was a blur, but I recognized the color: Black.

"Yes! Yes! Yes!" Janie cried as though an orgasm had struck. "Eighty euros, that's enough to pay for our Roman baths tomorrow."

Janie gazed at the dealer with possessed eyes. "Let it ride."

"Janie, no!" I shrieked. "Are you crazy?! What's gotten into you?" I understood her enthusiasm, but we were lucky to escape with extra cash in our pockets. "Let's not get greedy," I begged her. Britte and Liselott echoed my pleas.

However, it was too late. The ball had already been set in motion. I could have knelt down right then and there and ripped a chunk out of the table with my teeth. After the first few revolutions I had convinced myself that this time it was not my doing, and Janie could possibly have three less friends if we lost.

What happened to that sweet, innocent girl I brought with me to Baden-Baden? Had I released the addict within? This was supposed to be a weekend of relaxation and deliverance. Instead, the evil of gambling had reared its ugly head and threatened to steal her soul. I silently promised God that if we escaped this moment, I would never, ever, gamble again.

CLICK, *clink*, CLICK, *clink*, CLICK, *clink*. This time it was Britte and Liselott who held their hands over their faces. Janie's eyeballs resembled giant dollar signs. The palpitations of my heart bordered on cardiac arrest as I pondered the abyss of bankruptcy.

"Black! Black!" Janie roared. "We won!"

"What a relief," Liselott exhaled.

Janie eyed the dealer with the same devilish intensity as before. I gestured to the Swedes, urging a kidnapping. Britte and I grabbed Janie, while Liselott stifled her arguments until she was safely outside the building with our little fortune. We marched her back to the hotel, giggling about our "gift" from the Kurhaus. In our room we counted the money like sheep, until we became very sleepy.

©Carasana Bäderbetriebe

Look, But Don't Touch

The next morning after breakfast we rolled down the cobbled lane to the bathhouse. The whole idea of our time in Baden-Baden was relaxation and, of course, my own personal mission of getting Janie's mind off her so-called 'true love.'

Of the two main bathhouses in town, we decided on the Roman-Irish baths at the Friedrichsbad. I had no idea what Roman-Irish baths were, but it sounded like an interesting combination. Perhaps they were bubbling hot pools, surrounded by tall green columns made of marble. Maybe even some leprechauns to sooth the aches and pains.

Britte told us that Baden-Baden, meaning Bath-Bath, was settled some 2,000 years ago by the Romans and named after its native hot springs. Romans discovered the special healing benefits of the thermal waters and, during the reign of Emperor Caracalla, spa culture thrived in the Black Forest.

We seemed to be in the right place. The brochure on Baden-Baden we picked up at our hotel touted the visit of the famous American novelist Mark Twain, who said of the baths: *"Here at the Friedrichsbad you lose track of time within 10 minutes and track of the world within 20."*

Dating from 1877 and bang in the center of town, the Friedrichsbad was instantly recognizable by its immense size and palatial facade featuring neo-Renaissance architecture. Above the main entrance, four flags flapped in the light morning breeze. We stepped inside and over to the reception desk. Although they offered several package-types, we opted for the works.

"We'll take your pamper package designed to spoil," I said.

"That will be our 17-step, Roman-Irish treatment with soap-and-brush massage..." replied the grinning receptionist, "which will cost 37 euro per person and last three and a half hours."

By her air of confidence, I got the impression her customers were never disappointed.

"That's what the doctor ordered," Britte proclaimed.

"Yeah...and the doctor's three-hour order came courtesy of the casino," Janie responded, giggling.

After receiving our entrance cards, we climbed a grand staircase that led to the women's changing rooms. Anticipation grew, as Janie and I had no idea what to expect. At least we had our swimsuits with us.

Inside the changing room, I eyed Janie with apprehension. She triple blinked. "Uh, oh!"

Women were entering the baths stripped of all their worldly possessions. We undressed hastily so as not to be nervous. I hopped in place with a foot stuck inside my jeans while Janie struggled with unbuttoning her shirt.

"Is everything okay, girls?" Liselott questioned.

"I've never been to a nudie bathhouse before," I confessed.

"Don't stress. Everyone is naked. You'll forget about it in no time. Besides, with a body like yours, you should show it off."

I realize nudeness is natural, but to parade around in the buff with others isn't something the typical North American is accustomed to. However, I don't know anyone here, so what reason do I have to feel self-conscious? I have little problem with social nudity, as long as I'm not involved.

Station 1: Virgin Mile to the Rinsing Showers

Gracefully, I strolled to my premiere in the world of informal bathing. Within a few paces we were met by Monika, the head spa attendant, and given towels.

"Maybe it's optional nudism," Janie said in a hopeful tone as we snuggly wrapped the towels around our bodies.

"We shouldn't worry anyway," I replied, trying to make light of a bare situation. "It's only women here."

Britte and Liselott held the towels in their hands and entered the bathing world like all the rest, naked as babies.

Stations 2, 3 & 4: Walt Disney's Inspiration

I followed the girls into the next area: the dry-heat rooms.

Station 2 suggested 15 minutes of unadulterated relaxation in the warm-air room. We each grabbed a lounge chair, stretched out and suspended all conversation. Colorful tiles accentuated the walls and ceiling.

Station 3 featured a similar room, only much hotter. Five minutes were suggested, talking recommended — and the towel was still intact.

"Where else have you traveled in Germany and Austria?" Janie asked, directing her thoughts to the Swedes.

"Other than Salzburg and the Black Forest," Liselott replied, "we've been to Innsbruck and Hohenschwangau."

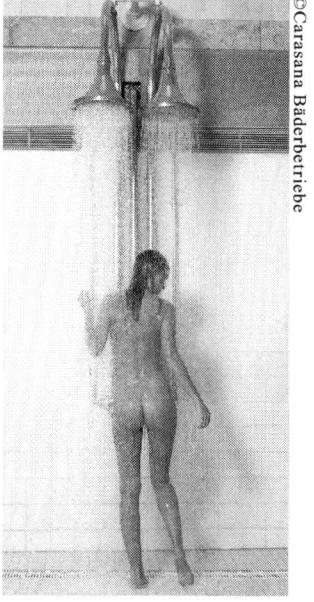

Look, But Don't Touch 91

"Hohenwhat?" I responded, curiously.

"It's an alpine community home to King Ludwig's fairy-tale castle, Schloss Neuschwanstein."

"Authentic medieval romanticism in modern times," Janie recounted. "I can see the storybook castle now with its high walls and pointy turrets perched upon the forested hillside. If Prince Charming is included in the package, I'm there."

Our five minutes were up and we exited the hot-air room for the rinsing shower at station 4.

Stations 5 & 6: No More Aching Muscles

The fifth stage of our journey was a real spoiler, the complete soap-and-brush body massage. My masseuse was a thick and stocky gal, characteristics that proved advantageous. The strength of her huge hands allowed me to envision any Herculean male from Muscle Beach I desired. Perhaps I could have a member of the Chippendales materialize to rescue my tender back, or my very own Hollywood hunk.

Instead, within our classical setting I imagined myself as Cleopatra on a visit to Julius Caesar. His troop of Roman menservants were assigned to fulfill my every desire. The cornucopia of males wearing white robes slipped succulent grapes into my mouth. Gladiators fanned me with enormous ostrich feathers as I lay on a golden lounge. If anyone were to fail my requests, they would be ordered to their knees to plead for

©Carasana Bäderbetriebe

leniency. "You've been a bad boy!" Concluding my thought and massage, the masseuse soundly slapped my butt.

"Who's been a bad boy?" Janie chirped, standing mere feet away.

Whoops! I had drifted into Fantasyland, out loud. "Ah, err... I said 'bath toy,' you know, like rubber duckies and things." I quickly changed the subject. "So...are ya glad you came this weekend?"

"I'll let you know when I'm wearing clothes again," she insisted. "Right now I really miss my swimsuit, and Johnny!"

I couldn't understand why she would miss a guy who cheated on her only days before and was probably on a repeat performance. Love sure seems to have a short memory.

The massage — mostly an exfoliating brush scrub — and subsequent rinsing shower were blissful, and over too soon. At this point, Monika pried our security towels away from Janie and me, leaving us with nothing more than our bare expressions.

"Don't worry, girls," Britte said, offering her contingency plan. "What you don't have, you don't need."

It appeared to be pure nakedness from here on in.

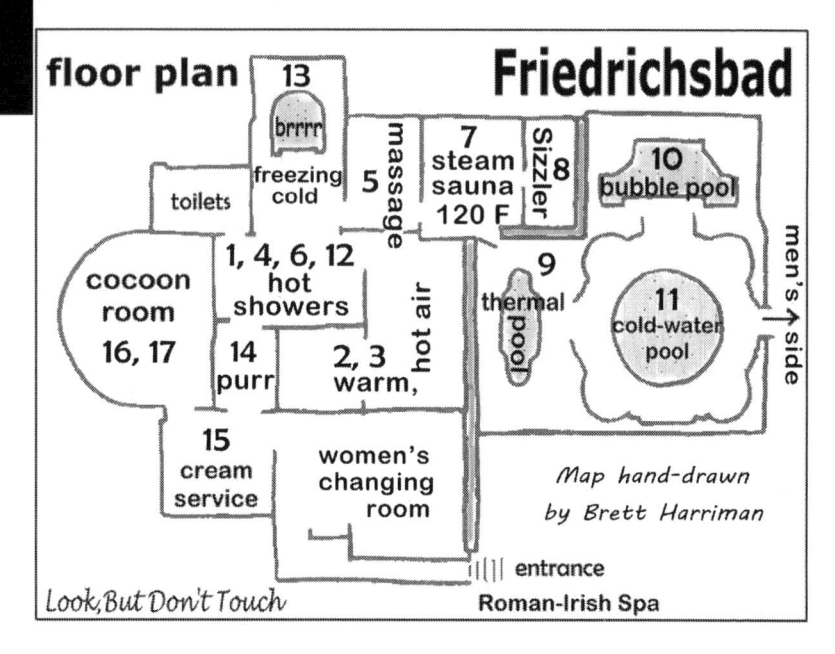

floor plan — **Friedrichsbad**

- 13 brrrr freezing cold
- toilets
- 5 massage
- 7 steam sauna 120 F
- 8 Sizzler
- 10 bubble pool
- 1, 4, 6, 12 hot showers
- cocoon room 16, 17
- 14 purr
- 2, 3 warm, hot air
- 9 thermal pool
- 11 cold-water pool
- men's side →
- 15 cream service
- women's changing room
- Map hand-drawn by Brett Harriman
- entrance

Look, But Don't Touch — **Roman-Irish Spa**

<u>Station 7</u>: *My First Nude Pow Wow*

...began with a 10-minute steam sauna at 120 degrees Fahrenheit. It wasn't a large room per se, having a brown-tiled resting block in the middle that offered body-length, stepped tiers for varying levels of relaxation. There were already a few women basking when we arrived. One was sprawled out like a lounging lizard on the middle tier while chatting to her friend who stood adjacent in a model-like posture as if she were the queen of saunas. On the top level, two French-speaking girls were marinating in the upper heat zone. They looked as if they could take but a minute more of the pitiless steam. We mapped out a few brown tiles on the lowest tier and sat our cheeks down.

©Carasana Bäderbetriebe

Look, But Don't Touch

"Sydney, what kind of guy are you looking for?" Britte asked.

"Well, someone who is intelligent, witty, has an adventurous spirit, and makes my heart thump."

"Sounds like someone I know," Janie claimed.

"I've had perhaps one unladylike dream about him."

"Who's this...anyone we know?" begged Britte and Liselott.

"No, just a guy we work with at Chiemsee. Wait! Actually, you have met him. Jesse, the guy who came with me to the hostel in Salzburg."

"Oh, yeah," said Liselott. The girls turned to each other and giggled. "The guy who introduced himself to our boobs."

"That's him. Anyway, he has a girlfriend and I probably shouldn't even consider him a possibility. It's just that he's so... edible."

Janie gave me a loopy grin. She then rose to her feet and ordered us off our behinds with a few sharp claps of the hands. "Time to change to the hottest sauna of 'em all...five minutes at 126 degrees Fahrenheit. Come on girls. Get moving. Chop! Chop!"

Each sauna was hotter than the last, from sweltering to unbearable.

Station 8: The Sizzler...126°F!

We saw the same four women lounging in similar fashion as in the last sauna. But this time upon sitting down we felt obliged to say something, even if it was trivial. "Hot, isn't it?" Janie said, in broken German.

The French girls knew we spoke English so their reply was easy to understand. "Yes, very! Our five minutes are over. We'll see you in the mineral pools." They stood up and proceeded out the door, followed by Lounge Lizard and Sauna Queen.

The condensed steam ran off our bodies in meandering rivulets. Janie held her right leg rigidly outwards, wiping collective beads of sweat off herself in long sweeping motions. The intense heat was stifling; with every deep breath I felt as though I were going to suffocate. But I couldn't die here in the buff. I mean, what would my parents think? And the crucifix, what about that? I have to find it. If it's the last thing I do!

"Hey, Sydney," Britte inquired, "...how's the search going for that golden cross you mentioned in Salzburg?"

She must've been reading my mind. "Well, the other day Jesse and I went into our hotel's cellar. With flashlights in hand, we illuminated numerous wall murals that were painted during the Second World War when frightened nurses, doctors, and patients gathered there to wait out the air-raid sirens. See, during the war our hotel was converted into a hospital to treat wounded German soldiers, so the basement became a shelter and makeshift infirmary." I paused briefly to change positions and wring more sweat from my limbs. The girls stared at me, patiently waiting.

"During our explorations, Jesse and I came across some fascinating history. In particular we found one very revealing wall mural, which showed carpenters, laborers, and stonemasons building the hotel in the 1930s. Cleverly painted into the scene, we discovered a symbolic cross with the name *das Bayernkreuz*."

"What does that mean?" Liselott questioned.

"The Bavarian Cross."

I glanced at Janie for a reaction, but it was obvious that she had left the conversation. No doubt she was still deeply troubled by her relationship with The Cheater. At times Janie seemed just plain out of it, more or less on a different wavelength. This was one of those times. Out of the blue, she began telling a story.

"I have this friend, Sarah, who had been dating her boyfriend for almost two years. During that time she and a girlfriend went to Europe for a month. Sarah missed her boyfriend tremendously, phoning and e-mailing him regularly. Even though the two girls were having the time of their lives, Sarah came home as planned at the end of the month while her friend decided to stay longer. When Sarah arrived home, her boyfriend wasn't there to greet her. Naturally, she didn't understand why. The next day she heard rumors he was seeing another girl. When Sarah asked him if it were true, he replied: 'Sorry...it's over between us.' Unsurprisingly, Sarah freaked out! Partly because he didn't tell her while she was away. Two days later, Sarah bought a plane ticket back to Europe to meet her friend." Janie, seemingly drained, halted the tale and rested her head against the tiles.

Britte, Liselott, and I turned curiously to one another, hoping there was more to the story. "Is that it?" Britte asked.

Liselott and I had questions of our own. "Did Sarah get revenge? Did she return to Europe?"

"Both!" Janie exclaimed, her face flushed from the heat. "On the way to the airport she took a baseball bat to his Corvette and did at least a plane ticket's worth in damage. The last I heard of Sarah she was training to be a winemaker in Bordeaux, France."

Janie did a fabulous job of keeping our minds off the thermostat, which we were half expecting to melt off the wall at any time. This was our cue to move on to the next station.

Outside the Sizzler, Britte pulled open the door leading to the mineral pools.

Station 9: Look, But Don't Touch

"OH SHIT...!" I gasped. Terror struck me. There were men, lots of them — and all butt-ass naked! I stood frozen in the doorway, mouth open.

My first instinct was to grab my towel. I had zilch to grab. My every detail was exposed with nothing left to the imagination. Dexterously, I crossed one arm over my breasts and used my other hand like a fig leaf to cover my privates below. I felt like Eve in a room full of ogling Adams.

Meanwhile, the Swedes had proceeded straight to the thermal pool. "Will both you girls come through this door right now," Britte demanded with mock sternness.

We had no choice but to run the gauntlet. Naked as a maple tree in December, I closed my eyes and held onto Janie's shoulders as she led me out to the display pools.

"Sydney, you can open your eyes now," Britte insisted, tapping me on the shoulder.

Even Janie demanded my full attention. "Sydney...!"

I turned to my roommate in astonishment before muttering like a whacked-out prude, "Aren't you worried about all these strange men seeing you in your birthday suit?"

Undaunted, Janie replied, "It's just a human body...get over it!"

My jaw hit the floor. I couldn't believe what I was hearing. The Swedes stood next to me wearing nothing but white-teethed smiles. I had no alternative but to throw in the towel, so to speak. Plus, Janie was correct. Strength comes from facing reality, and now was the time to be fearless.

Chest out, shoulders back, head upright, legs firm: I boldly went where no other Endicott had gone before. Wading leisurely into a pool of poised men, I displayed my goods like a vendor at the market.

"Hallelujah..." I bellowed under my breath, "I did it!" Glancing behind me, I saw the girls just standing there. "What are you waiting for? The water's wunderbar!" They stepped into the pool and dog paddled over to me.

"It's good to see you've gotten over your shyness," Liselott said.

The experience seemed like a type of baptism. I was purified, initiated, and ready for the neighboring pools.

A gutsy grouping of nude people in all manner of shapes and sizes and ages united in the mixed bathing area. Noticeably spying the female populace, two twenty-something guys of Italian appearance coasted between pools delighting in the fabric-free setting.

On the periphery, an adorable middle-aged couple debated their courage, which I could wholeheartedly identify with. He stepped cautiously as if signs for a minefield had been posted while his better half tiptoed faithfully in his wake. This I would have to say reminded me of my parents, but Lord knows they'd never leave home destined for a nudie spa. Or would they?

This was an excellent opportunity to spy the male gender and their mannerisms. They were certainly not a bashful bunch, displaying their doodads as if judges were handing out awards. Cheryl, my neighbor at college, would no doubt have a season pass if the baths were within 100 miles of her bed.

Standing mere meters from the edge of our pool was an older, weight-challenged man with his hands resting upon his hips, legs apart and shrunken penis scarcely visible beneath his rolls of belly fat. Not a pretty sight.

"Psst. Hey," I whispered to the girls, "...what's with this guy?"

"What...which guy?!" Janie countered in a booming voice.

"Never mind." He presumably felt a draft because at that moment he retreated from his post, repositioning himself next to the center pool.

Since being generously exposed to the variety of male organs, I was curious about my latest observation. "Have you girls noticed that many of these men are uncircumcised?"

"I have," Janie said. "It's a good thing the saunas are segregated. I'd hate to see their steamed noodles."

"They resemble a snake hiding in a blanket," Britte contributed, giggling.

"Is it a fashion over here?" I asked the Swedes.

Britte and Liselott looked at each other, shrugging their shoulders.

"They look so...petite," Janie remarked.

"Looks can be deceiving," Liselott claimed. "My ex-boyfriend, Sven, had a little noodle that when aroused grew into a large serving of beef chow fun."

Britte raised a skeptical eyebrow; water cascaded off her fit body and onto the tiled floor as she exited the pool.

Station 10: Fifteen Minutes of Bubbles

"Ahh..." Liselott exhaled, "this is heaven." Her eyes lay closed as she floated on her back in our new location, a pool of bubbles generated by a network of air jets. "How about we stretch our time here to 20 minutes, girls?"

Immersed up to our necks in a vortex of hydrating minerals, we were too busy floating in our own little dreamworld to respond. That is, except for Janie. "I've always thought of European women as having hairy armpits and mild body odor. But in my few months here, I've changed my opinion."

Britte took the ball for Team Euro. "That's in the past. Modern times call for regular bathing and shaving. I think I'm a good example of both."

"No doubt about that," I asserted, referring to Britte's preference for full Brazilian waxing.

Meanwhile, I noticed one of the French girls rubbing shoulders with presumably her boyfriend in the center pool. According to the list of stations, this was the cold-water bath.

©Carasana Bäderbetriebe

Resembling an enormous rotunda with an ornate dome, the central pool area was the traffic circle of the complex, a temple dedicated to the art of bathing. The focal point was the cold-water bath, surrounded by rose-marbled columns that bolstered arched recesses — two having been outfitted into communal showers. Above stood curvy statuettes of mermaids that appeared to supervise every titillating move.

The affectionate French duo rose from the pool while each teasingly pursued the other's private parts, or in this case: public parts. Her short dark hair and beautifully brown, toned body complemented her lover's ripped muscles and Nordic blonde hair.

They frolicked into an arched recess for a shower. It provided no refuge, yet the French couple persisted with their promiscuous program as if a curtain sheltered them from the growing audience. Sliding tongues hit all the bases; loving hands telegraphed their carnal desires.

All men were already in, or scampering towards, the cold-water pool for safekeeping. The mermaids above were blushing.

Watching the passionate pair ignited distant memories: soft touches, cozy cuddles, sweet kisses, and long, caressing strokes that aroused my body. The bubbles floated me weightless like an astronaut in space. The sensations from the jets below were tremendous. I wondered if my head was still attached to my body.

Station 11: Cold-Water Pool, 300 Seconds Suggested

It was frigid, but refreshing. This I know we all needed. The overall scene was more than hot and spicy. For the moment, the French couple had wrapped up their affair and progressed elsewhere. Voyeurs weren't far behind. We passed the five minutes required here the best we could.

"How was your trip to Innsbruck?" Janie asked the Swedes.

"Excellent," Liselott trumpeted.

"The city is amazingly beautiful, framed by the Austrian Alps," Britte added. "Majestic mountains rose up all around us in every direction."

The suggestion of soaring summits and dramatic scenery seemed to be an apt segue to the hunky guy strutting past. He stopped an arm's length from our location, allowing us to study every erectile inch of his anatomy. It was obvious that when God was handing out organs to men, this guy received the freakishly large penis package. Suddenly the water didn't feel so frigid.

"It's funny how nipples go hard when it's cold," Britte commented, interrupting my theological thoughts.

Look, But Don't Touch

Liselott glanced down at her nipples and began playfully stroking them with her thumb and index finger.

"Brr. It's freezing!" Janie affirmed. "Let's get outta here."

The concluding portions of the therapy cycle, stations 12 through 17, directed us back inside the women-only area.

Stations 12 & 13: Fire and Ice

Station 12 offered a handful of showerheads budding from a tiled wall, expelling tremendously hot water. Opposite was station 13, a much-smaller and much-colder pool than station 11. Multiple jumps back and forth between the two extremes generated unusual feelings and tingling sensations. We did this for the 10 minutes suggested.

Station 14: The Towel Was Back

Monika appeared and handed us each a warm towel to dry off with. The snug warmth had us purring like kittens. Although four heavenly minutes weren't nearly long enough, we had to move on. Like the white tufts of a dandelion that wishful children blow into the wind, our towels vanished. Monika giveth, and Monika taketh away.

Station 15: Cream Service

Here the idea was simple: pamper yourself by putting velvety-soft lotion on your body.

The room was small and outfitted with floor-to-ceiling mirrors. As we entered, a couple of ladies were generously applying cream from the dispensers that sat in holders affixed to the wall. The perfumed fragrance of the moisturizers filled the air.

I claimed the nearest spot in front of the mirror, took a few pumps of lotion, warmed it between my hands, and massaged my arms, breasts and stomach. It was so invigorating that several more pumps were essential to cover the rest of my body.

Thoroughly hydrated and silky, our group continued on to the last venue.

Stations 16 & 17: Half Hour in the Cocoon Room

The final stations were set in a considerably sized room furnished with raised table-like beds that resembled those used by a therapist to give a massage. Monika reappeared and guided us to separate beds, neatly spread out a large white sheet on each and instructed us to lie comfortably on our backs. One by one, she wrapped us in the warm sheet until we were completely cocooned. My thoughts drifted.

The room is silent. My body is bound. My eyes closed. My mind clear. I am drowsy. I am tranquil. I am floating. An indescribable sensation.

Forty-five minutes had passed. I must have fallen asleep. The girls were also dead to the world. Others had since been cocooned.

"Liselott, Britte, Janie," I whispered, giving each a nudge. "We have 20 minutes before our spa time expires. Let's head back to the sauna for a wake-up." Groggy, they unwrapped their naked bodies and followed.

At station 7 the steaming sauna was conveniently empty, which meant freedom to stretch out where we pleased on the brown-tiled block.

Now seemed a good time to ask Britte the same question she had put to me earlier. "What kind of guy are you looking for?"

"A generous lover! One who's all about me."

"I have a confession," Liselott admitted. "My ex-boyfriend, Sven, is the best lover I've ever had but I quit our relationship after I caught him cheating on me. Once a cheater, always a cheater, right? One thing I miss about him, though, is after he'd orgasm his nipples would shrink rock-hard, which turned me on for more."

Janie piped up. "I've made love to only one person in my life and I've never noticed if his nipples were hard or not."

With the candidness of our conversation, I felt comfortable to share some otherwise private thoughts. "I think the most electrifying part of sex is the 'after-max,' the last sensual moment of lovemaking. When bodies glisten with sweat after a simultaneous orgasm, it's magic to gaze into your partner's eyes while nestling in his firm embrace."

Janie sat up from her lounging position. Doubt clouded her face. "I'd say I'm making myself sound naïve, but I honestly didn't know."

Janie then turned reflective. She had a realization. "When Johnny and I made love, he usually jumped in my pants for a quickie. Since our intimate experiences were virtually over before they began, I wanted Johnny in me as much as possible. I thought we were truly in love, but now I believe he was just using me. After what happened this past week and considering the three years of what I thought was the perfect relationship, I realize he cheated in more than one way. He never once told me I looked nice, gave me flowers or a back massage. And he probably wouldn't even be at the airport to pick me up on account of the other woman.

"That's it, my next phone call to Johnny will be my last. One day he'll come to his senses and realize what he's lost."

Janie had released her pent-up tensions. It was a catharsis, a rebirth, a fresh start.

The Swedes and I congratulated her. Janie had a new air of self-confidence and concluded with gratitude. "I really want to thank you for sharing this weekend with me. It's liberating to let go of the past and move forward. My future looks brighter than ever, and that...I owe to you girls."

One by one, we got up and gave our reborn friend a hug. We were in our own little world, four young women absorbing the thermal magic.

Back in the changing room, where insecurities were shed and virtues gained, Janie admitted: "I've never felt more relieved in my life. Kind of like an orgasm. I guess?"

"What could be better than a naked romp through a bath house?" Britte asked no one in particular.

As we dressed, I posed a thought to Janie. "Now that you're a single woman again, what's on your to-do list?"

"Well, it'll be awhile before I start dating again, that's for sure, but I'm thinking of traveling to Bordeaux, France. I owe a friend a visit."

Fully clothed and heading out the door, Liselott turned to me and commented: "That wasn't so bad, was it?"

Funny she should say that, because until now I had forgotten I'd even been naked. In fact, it feels a tad strange wearing clothes. It makes me wonder what the girls back home would say. They'd never believe this one!

∞

Baden-Baden really impressed me. A wonder unsurprisingly named twice. The streets were clean, the gardens flourishing and fragrant, the restaurants appetizing, the hotels welcoming, the shops upscale, and the Victorian homes quaint. The community was rich in culture, from music and theater companies to Europe's oldest casino. Above all, it was an enriching thermal paradise, recharging us with its therapeutic gifts.

Our time in Friedrichsbad was worthwhile, overwhelming in fact, because today we all learned something new about ourselves — and maybe we were a little more independent because of it.

Good night, Black Forest

An Alpine Village
(Berchtesgaden, Germany)

Chapter 6

The wind blew through my hair as Jesse's car zipped down the autobahn at speeds that were highly illegal back home. He spent almost the entire time in the fast lane passing columns of motor homes with Dutch license plates. Jesse compared this annual journey to bird migration in which the Dutch flock southward, from the dikes of Holland to the docks of Palermo, offloading their euros in exchange for fresh pasta and guaranteed sun.

Schooled on the relocation of the Netherlands, I sat back and digested the names of the towns we passed: Marquartstein, Ruhpolding, Neukirchen, Teisendorf, Bad Reichenhall. I wondered if learning to spell took longer for German children, since each word has so many letters. Perhaps they feel the same way about Americans naming a state Mississippi.

It was a gorgeous blue-sky day in the middle of June. Geraniums in vibrant reds and pinks lit the balconies of rustic farmhouses. Bedspreads aired over windowsills. Cattle roamed freely in their pastures. Bales of hay sat five and six to a field, wrapped in white plastic, resembling giant marshmallows. One farmer mowed his pasture with a modern tractor, while his older, traditional neighbors clipped theirs by rocking a scythe back and forth in a motion similar to a pendulum on a clock. Beyond the farmers' fields, bulbous church towers shimmered in the morning sun. It was the perfect inauguration to summer, which couldn't have been better timing for Reuben's visit and our trip to Berchtesgaden.

The back seat was small but comfortable. Van Morrison's "Bright

Side of the Road" boomed through the rear speakers while Jesse and his buddy from California reminisced up front.

Interrupting their chat, Jesse eyeballed me through the rear-view mirror. "I have a feeling we're gonna find another clue regarding the crucifix today, since Berchtesgaden was formerly the base of operations for Nazi Southern Command."

"I hope you're right."

"Err... crucifixes, and Nazis! What are you guys talkin' about?" Reuben asked, looking slightly unnerved.

"Right now," I explained, "we're chasing legends concerning a very old cross that could be worth a fortune."

"Fortune?" Reuben's face lit up. "Count me in!"

"It's too bad you're only here for a week..." Jesse clarified, "or else we might."

Reuben's smile collapsed.

"Have you ever been to Berchtesgaden?" Reuben asked, apparently trying to learn a little more about the girl riding along in his best friend's car.

"Nope. Never." Moving forward between the seats, I positioned my upper body into the front portion of the car. "I've ridden a bike around Chiemsee, toured Salzburg with Jesse, and about a month ago I was in Baden-Baden with my roommate and two friends. Other than that, I'm pretty new at the art of traveling. How 'bout you...first time in Europe?"

"Sure is! And it's everything Jesse said it would be, and more... including you."

"Hmm. How shall I take that?" I replied, blushing.

"Take it as a compliment."

I rested my elbows upon either passenger seat, getting comfy. "You seem like a nice guy yourself."

Jesse cut in. "I have an idea for you both...a tour of Munich, the capital of Bavaria. Unfortunately, my hectic work schedule won't allow me to take Reuben as planned, and he certainly could use a companion." He glanced at me again through the mirror. "If you could arrange some free time in the next few days, I'll do all the rest. How does that sound?"

"Sounds good to me," I answered, surprised but delighted.

"Reuben?"

"Couldn't think of a better traveling companion!"

"Fine, it's settled then," Jesse said, concluding his matchmaking endeavor. "In the meantime, kick back and admire the edelweiss on the Alps."

"Edelweiss?" Reuben wondered aloud.

"It's a snow-white flower unique to these parts that typically blooms at 6,000 feet and above from July to September. If you're hiking, edelweiss is easy to spot since it grows in mini clusters and has an unusual woolly texture and star-shaped symmetry."

"Have you ever seen one?" I asked.

"Several times, and on each occasion edelweiss epitomized its German translation: 'noble white.'"

"That would explain why it's Austria's national flower."

"Not totally true," Jesse stated. "It's the country's unofficial flower, but its representation is used for the official logos of the Austrian and German mountaineering clubs. And if you ever do hike the Alps and cross paths with a cluster of edelweiss, know that it is a nationally protected flower and illegal to pick."

Switching gears, Reuben began a list of praise for his best friend. "Lucky for me, Jesse's a world traveler and considerate host. I simply base my vacation every few years around his new whereabouts. Sometimes, though, he can be tough to keep track of. His parents miss him a great deal, which gets me invited over for dinner once a month to fill them in on what's new with our crowd. I'm the next best thing to their walkabout son." Jesse took his eyes off the road momentarily and aimed a smirk at Reuben.

"Sounds like you've known each other for a long time," I said.

"Since we were two years old!" Reuben affirmed. "We grew up across the street from each other in Dana Point, California. We've been through a lot together: kindergarten, catechism, Little League, Boy Scouts, high school. Occasionally, we even liked the same girls...which usually ended in a fight, but we're as good as brothers because of it. I remember our parents sending us out the door, with lunch boxes in hand, to school for the very first time. We strolled to the bus stop, pausing every few feet to wave to our misty-eyed mothers. A couple of years later, our teacher tried separating us into different classrooms because our regular chatter was, supposedly, upsetting the other students."

"What do you mean, 'tried'?"

"Well...the classrooms we were moved into only got noisier, until the teachers decided to return things to the way they were. We weren't really all that bad, it's just...kids will be kids, and we were loud."

"So I'm sitting with a pair of troublemakers, eh?" I announced from my perch between the driver and his best buddy.

After a few childhood stories and about 40 minutes of pedal-to-the-metal German-style driving, we exited the autobahn.

Jesse switched on his touring voice. "We are now entering the town of Bischofswiesen, meaning 'Bishop's Meadow.'" He pointed to our right. "There are the bishops now."

Two statues stood in front of the most beautiful jade-green stream. We paralleled the watercourse for about half a mile before making a left turn in the direction of Berchtesgaden.

Our meandering route led us past lethargic cows basking in the sun and gnawing dried grass while farmers took advantage of the good weather and stacked hay on tall wooden stakes. The balconies of charming farmhouses were flush with flowers resplendent in color. Clean washing puffed with the breeze as it hung on a line to dry. In the rural hamlet of Stanggass, the quintessential Bavaria I've come to know and expect is perfectly presented.

Our tour guide then pulled the car over before the Reitoffen bus stop so we could stretch our legs.

"This narrow road to the right," Jesse informed us, "formerly led to the official headquarters of Nazi Southern Command and the residences of Wilhelm Keitel and Alfred Jodl, Adolf Hitler's chiefs of staff."

"It's incredible to be here..." I declared, "at the end of the line for the Allies, their strategic goal." Again, I was delving back to my history books and Grandpa's stories relayed via Dad.

"You haven't seen anything yet!" Jesse trumpeted, shifting his body 90 degrees. "From this vantage point we can see two local landmarks. In front of us, perched upon the summit of Mount Kehlstein at 6,000 feet, is Hitler's former 'Eagle's Nest,' and to our right is the pride of Berchtesgaden, the Watzmann massif, Germany's second-highest mountain, rising to 8,900 feet.

"The Watzmann is comprised of seven peaks. Legend refers to the largest of these as the 'king' and 'queen' and the smaller crests huddled in between as their children. As the story goes, the real king and queen were pitiless to the people, taxing them into poverty while ruling with an iron fist. The royal children weren't much friendlier, running through the farmers' fields and trampling their crops. The townsfolk prayed for an improvement of any kind. Then, one morning after a wicked storm, the people awoke to see the royal family on the mountain, having been transformed into stone. The people lived happily ever after."

"You made that up, right?" Reuben said, unconvinced.

"What kind of question is that?!" Jesse snorted, annoyed. Then a wrestle broke out. They riveted together like two rams locking horns.

"Guys, break it up! Heeello!" I jumped in to stop the tussle, but it was too late. They were already laughing at my sincerity.

"Let's say we get a move on," Jesse proposed, as he brushed off his shirt. "I can tell you more on the road."

A minute later we arrived in Berchtesgaden, passing the town-limits sign. Beyond the sign were two abandoned hotels that Jesse said once belonged to our Chiemsee resort. The first one was formerly the General McNair, which was still in reasonable shape. The adjacent hotel, separated from the McNair by an empty swimming pool, was the Berchtesgadener Hof. It appeared in dire need of a makeover. Large sections of plaster had fallen off the walls and elsewhere the paint was peeling. A far cry from how I imagined the building to look after viewing its 1945 recreation in the final episode of the miniseries "Band of Brothers" when the boys of Easy Company entered and began lifting Hitler souvenirs.

Further down the road the majesty of Berchtesgaden opened like a picture book. Authentic Bavaria was on full display in this quaint village nestling at the toes of the Alps. Cute wooden houses resembled chalets with their pitched roofs, decorative window shutters and overhanging eaves. People milled around at a leisurely pace as if time ticked slower here. Hikers carried ornamented sticks, men wore traditional lederhosen, and women were resplendent in busty dirndls. If Jesse were to tell me that Berchtesgaden and its abundant pine-fresh air doubled as a doctor's prescription for stress associated with inner-city living, I'd believe him.

On the other side of town Jesse took us into the Berchtesgaden National Park for a spectacular boat ride on der Königssee, the only lake in Central Europe most similar to a Scandinavian fjord, surrounded by the dramatic scenery of vertical rock walls belonging to gigantic mountains that rose from its azure waters.

From the national park Jesse drove Reuben and me to the salt mines where we donned miner's uniforms, rode a narrow-gauge railway half a mile into the mountain face, and slid down wooden chutes from one salty cavern to another. By the time we resurfaced from our subterranean adventure, it was nearly 1:30 and our starving stomachs were in competition for the loudest growl.

This brought us to the Berchtesgadener Inn, a handsome three-story gasthaus in the center of town. Although we found the traditional décor inside the restaurant inviting, we elected to sit outside and enjoy the pleasant weather on the scenic patio. Our view of the Alps, including the Eagle's Nest, was prettier than a painting.

A personable waitress took our order. It didn't take long. Jesse did it for us.

"So...what's on the grill?" Reuben asked, dying to know what his buddy had in mind.

"I'm not going to spoil the surprise. Just think Bavarian. I suggest you kick back, relax, and bask in the scenery."

Shortly after ordering, our first course arrived: liver-dumpling soup for Jesse, cheese-onion for Reuben, and asparagus-cream for me. Judging by the guys' expressions, they were enjoying their fare as much as I was.

Next came the main course. Our server placed the dishes randomly on the table, commencing the festivities.

"Amen," I thanked the Almighty before digging into the Jägerschnitzel, two sautéed veal cutlets smothered in a creamy mushroom sauce, served in a skillet with homemade egg noodles known as Spätzle.

Jesse ordered his favorite, Schweinshaxe, an entire pork knuckle doused in beer sauce, paired with a baseball-sized bread dumpling and a side of braised red cabbage, locally Blaukraut.

Reuben received Sauerbraten, three medallions of beef marinated in red wine, accompanied by butter noodles and a house salad.

Jesse took a few bites of his meal then abruptly disappeared. Reuben and I were too engrossed in the scenery and clearing our plates to take much notice.

When Jesse returned he anxiously told us: "I think I just found our next clue. Follow me!"

Jesse had spotted his friend Heinrich, a local retiree and former tour guide, walking past. He asked him whether he'd heard anything about the crucifix. Amazingly, Heinrich had, which led us behind the Berchtesgadener Inn to the entrance of a bunker that remained from the days of Hitler's Third Reich.

From the lane running alongside the restaurant, Heinrich escorted us to an inconspicuous, wooden portal that fronted a labyrinth of concrete tunnels cutting through the cavernous depths of Berchtesgaden. He opened the large door with an old stylish key that was seemingly a family heirloom from the Middle Ages, walked us a short way in, and explained that the crucifix had been brought from the Chiemsee construction site and held in a tunnel system similar to this one at Obersalzberg, Hitler's neighborhood. Upon Hitler's next trip to Berlin, he personally took the crucifix with him and secured it in the vaults of the Reich's Chancellery.

In April 1945, during the waning days of World War II, the Soviet Red Army entered the outskirts of Berlin and the vaults were hastily cleared with its contents transported to western Germany by truck convoys constantly under fire from Allied aircraft. Heinrich admitted things were unimaginably chaotic then and nobody knows for sure where the crucifix ended up, or if it even survived.

Although Heinrich's story didn't provide us with a solid lead, it did give us a reason to believe the crucifix existed.

"Come on you two," Jesse announced to Reuben and me. "I want to show you something else before we leave."

We nodded in agreement, then waved goodbye to Heinrich.

Jesse piloted us across the street into the leafy church cemetery filled with a myriad of tall, dignified tombstones. The first grave on our right was that of Anton Adner.

"Check out the dates, 1705 to 1822," Jesse said, pointing to the monument.

After some quick number crunching, I calculated Adner was 117 years old when he died.

"He's Bavaria's oldest man," Jesse stated, "whose secret was walking. Adner's hobby was to knit warm garments and craft wooden toys for kids. In those days, goods were taxed when crossing borders, unless they could be transported on your person. Thus Adner strapped a large wooden box to his back to carry his handiwork to distant markets to sell. During these journeys, Adner would knit socks and carve figurines as he went. Not surprisingly, the Bavarian king heard of Adner's remarkable story and at the mature age of 113 he was honored as one of the 12 worthiest men in the kingdom. According to tradition, this warranted a trip to the palace in Munich for the annual 'washing of the feet' by the king on Maundy Thursday, the Thursday before Easter, which is symbolic of Jesus washing the feet of his disciples. For the next four years, Adner was invited to Munich for a royal scrub until his death in 1822."

"Whoa, totally cool!" rolled Reuben's California tongue.

Opposite Adner's grave and running the length of the cemetery, memorial markers were embedded in the wall remembering Berchtesgaden's beloved sons. Their names and living dates spanned two world wars, inscribed for all to see: where they fell in combat, what year, their age. Some had a poem; most featured a black-and-white photo of a proud soldier in uniform. Many families lost two young men, some lost three. One marker remembered a father and his son, Josef Ponn senior and junior.

I felt a twinge of homesickness at the tremendous loss of family represented here and wished my dad could share this moment with me. I wondered if Grandpa encountered any of these men on the battlefield.

"Their faces look so young...so innocent," Reuben noticed.

"Yes, you're right," Jesse agreed. "Endless names affixed to an endless wall. These proud men, like those of any nation, fought and died for their country. Many Wehrmacht, or German army, soldiers were regular guys drawn reluctantly into war. Today, we barely understand their times and troubles. Things were different then."

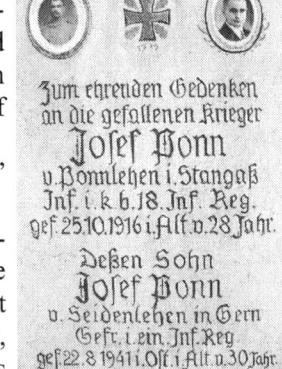

"Like how different?" I inquired.

"Well...let's go back about 150 years and outline a simple German history lesson. Up to the year 1945 there are four main dates one needs to know: 1871, 1914, 1919, and 1933. Once you understand the latter periods, you'll have a better idea of what motivated these young men to march off to war."

"This should be good; yesteryear in a cemetery," mused Reuben while folding his arms into his chest and leaning against a healthy pine tree in preparation for something longer than just a historical outline. The only things missing were a movie seat and popcorn. I did, however, have a fresh bag of gummi bears. Yum.

"In the year 1870," Jesse began, "a Prussian statesman named Otto von Bismarck championed the idea of bringing together a related group of territories to forge an empire. By design, Bismarck orchestrated a confrontation that became known as the Franco-Prussian War. You see, at this time there was no Germany, only the southern states and the northern confederation, or Prussians. Between the territories there were underlying tensions, kind of like the North and the South before the American Civil War. But in this case there were other countries that could be exploited as a common enemy to prevent a possible interrelated bloodbath. Bismarck provoked a united German response against its unpopular neighbor, France, by publicly misrepresenting French documents, which induced heated dialogue and ultimately the Franco-Prussian War. The Prussian and southern-Germanic armies formed a military alliance

A Quiet Village 111

and the so-called aggressor was swiftly defeated. In the Hall of Mirrors at Versailles, France, on January 18, **1871**, the King of Prussia, William I, was proclaimed the first German emperor of a unified Germany, thus began the so-called Second Reich."

"What does Reich mean?" Reuben asked, chewing on a blade of grass. It was a valid question, but one I'd already learned from the Salzburg tour.

"In this case it means, 'Empire.'" Jesse paused, brushing back the fringe of hair that kept dropping onto his brow.

"During the Second Reich, Germany became a mighty industrialized nation, and the factory worker embodied the state's robust economy. Within two decades of the unification, William I died and was succeeded by his grandson, William II, infamously known as 'Kaiser Wilhelm.'

"In **1914**, Germany jumped into the First World War, which crippled an entire landmass for four years and stole the lives of millions of Europe's beloved sons. Germany lost this ghastly war, devastating its economy, people and their will. The Kaiser fled to Holland and the Second Reich was kaput!"

"Remind me; who were the bad guys in World War I?" Reuben wanted to know.

"And why did it take the U.S. so long to enter the war?" I added.

"Excellent questions. But keep in mind, the war was a European conflict, and the Atlantic Ocean was especially challenging to navigate in those days. Moreover, the U.S. didn't quite know who the bad guys were. See, World War I began as a local conflict between Austria and Serbia after the assassination of Archduke Francis Ferdinand, heir to the Austrian throne, in Sarajevo on June 28, 1914, by a Serb nationalist. Within weeks the various European countries took sides and by August the world was at war. Germany and Austria were neighbors and natural partners, and with millions of immigrants from both sides of the conflict living in America, U.S. neutrality was understandable. It wasn't until early 1917 that Germany became America's sworn enemy when it brought about a change to war policy with the commencement of unrestricted submarine warfare upon all vessels heading Britain's way. This meant the sinking of ships belonging to still-neutral countries, like the U.S. The Germans figured that by cutting off Britain's supply route once and for all, victory would be theirs within a year, or even months. This turned out to be a gross miscalculation because Germany was then seen as the aggressor and the U.S. declared war on April 6, 1917. The land battles raged on but under a new light, the doughboys, or American soldiers, were on the field, and advancing. The deadly gunfire finally came to an end on the eleventh hour...of the eleventh day...of the eleventh month in the year 1918."

"What about World War II?" Reuben asked.

"We're getting there, Ruby. Be patient," Jesse said with a grin, knowing his audience was devouring the lesson.

"Remember the Hall of Mirrors at Versailles where William I was proclaimed the first German emperor of the new, unified Germany? Well, to add to the wounds of Germany's defeat in World War I, the victorious nations gathered near Paris to draft a peace treaty and decide the fate of the losers. The victors concluded that Germany must pay war retributions, but these greatly exceeded the capabilities of a shattered nation and on June 28, **1919**, the Treaty of Versailles was signed in that very same Hall of Mirrors."

"History coming full circle," I commented as I scanned more names on the remembrance wall.

"Yeah, it really did. And, Reuben...here begins the buildup to your previous question." At this point, Jesse walked us deeper into the cemetery.

"It later became evident that the Treaty of Versailles had a disastrous impact on Germany and was heavily to blame for the evils that brought forth the second European war of the century."

Reuben and I knew no more questions were required, as the finale was at hand. Our measured pace was halted in front of a large, featureless tombstone with the lone inscription: Dietrich Eckart. Jesse said he was Hitler's mentor.

"Post-war Germany had to produce a new government. And since the nation's capital, Berlin, was considered unsafe from revolution, politicians convened some 200 kilometers southwest in the historic town of Weimar, where a constitutional democracy was adopted. To honor the location of the document's signing, Germany's new era in politics was called the Weimar Republic; but it was essentially doomed from the beginning. Within the first few years the German people were beset with mass unemployment, political instability, and hyperinflation that spiraled the currency into a black hole. During these challenging times it literally took a briefcase full of money to buy a single loaf of bread. Millions, eventually billions, of German marks were necessary to equal just one U.S. dollar.

Consequently, the victors seized Germany's industrial region, the Ruhr, for collateral on defaulted war payments. The streets were frequently in chaos, which generated the ideal climate to breed a broad range of political parties with each having a leader speaking of, yet again, a new and unified Germany. Their forum was the town square, the local beer hall, even the circus. People came to these staged events to hear a way out of the mess their government had failed to alleviate. They congregated to hear solutions to the crisis. Germany's most impassioned speaker and political rising star was Adolf Hitler, a decorated World War I veteran who promised order and blamed the crisis on the Communists and the Jews.

"Economically, in the mid to late 1920s, things somewhat stabilized thanks to the resumption of foreign support. Until, that is, those nations revoked their assistance when the Great Depression struck in 1929, leaving Germany in a state of peril, once again. The Weimar Republic was on the verge of ruin, about to be ripped from the ground by its democratic roots.

"The following year, parliament held an election and the National Socialists, with Adolf Hitler as their leader, won second-most powerful party in the nation. As the world depression deepened, the stronger Hitler's party, the N.S.D.A.P., became."

Reuben interjected, "The N.S...what?"

"The Nationalsozialistische Deutsche Arbeiterpartei, meaning the National Socialist German Workers' Party, or more commonly...the Nazis."

"Whoa! Dude," said the open-mouthed Californian.

Jesse rolled up his sleeves and continued. "Amid bitter political wrangling between the Social Democrats and the Communist parties, Hitler snatched control of the government and abolished all other political groups. The year **1933** marked the beginning of Hitler's so-called thousand-year empire, the Third Reich. During the thirties, many Germans regained their sense of pride under Nazi rule. Jobs were created, the currency recovered, the Olympics came to Berlin, airports were built, and mass-transit highways paved.

"Once Germany got back onto its feet, Hitler avenged the Treaty of Versailles by reunifying territories lost to the Great War victors while building up the country's armed forces well beyond what was necessary for a continent at peace. First, the Nazis retook the Rhineland in 1936, followed by Austria and Czechoslovakia in 1938. Hitler achieved all this without so much as a reprimand from its passive neighbors. The German people had regained some of their lost dignity since their Führer, or supreme leader, Adolf Hitler, revived a deceased nation and produced a superpower within a mere seven years. A feat unmatched in history. He led the country into war and, of course, the people followed. That war, the Second World War, shattered the continent, bringing about 40 million dead, the Holocaust, untold homeless plagued by famine and illness, and the Stalinization of Eastern Europe. The Third Reich was undeniably an evil scheme cooked in the cauldron of hell!"

Jesse wrapped up our German history lesson then pointed to the Alps. "Look to that mountain and you'll see a structure at its summit. A road leads there, and midway up that road lies Obersalzberg, the former seat of Hitler's empire, where the dictator once lived, walked his dog, bullied generals, intimidated statesmen, and shuffled massive armies from the English Channel to the borders of Asia. Come on. Let's explore Obersalzberg."

Craving more, Reuben posed one last question. Jesse and I were already exiting the churchyard.

"That was a groovy lesson and all, but..." Reuben then raised his arms outward, practically touching the snow-capped mountains themselves, "can you teach me to yodel?"

This should be interesting. Jesse even had a laugh. Reuben stood eager, and so did I.

"Okay. I guess we have a minute. You ready?" Jesse began clearing his throat. "Now repeat after me: *Any ol' lady'll do*."

He insisted Reuben sing this three times rapidly with a Texas twang.

Reuben did, and he yodeled all the way from the cemetery gates to the guardhouses leading to Hitler's former command center.

∞

Upon turning right at a set of lights, Jesse pointed left. "This structure was the first of several security checkpoints leading up to Obersalzberg, Hitler's former hood. Above the door once hung a wooden version of the Reich's iconic eagle, clasping the swastika with its talons."

Berchtesgaden sat 1,700 feet above sea level; where we were headed was twice that elevation. The narrow road climbed at a seriously steep grade. On either side of us were lush maple trees, beech, and evergreens. We even passed a petite, multi-tiered waterfall. The beauty of God's work was overwhelming.

A Quiet Village 115

Jesse negotiated every bend in the serpentine road with caution. After about two miles in low gear, we reached a green sign marked 'Obersalzberg.'

Obersalzberg 1933-45

Map hand-drawn by Brett Harriman

Locations shown: coal bunker, Göring's adjutant, Göring, Eagle's Nest 6.5 km, air-raid warning center, Bormann, greenhouse, SS, Kindergarten, Archives & Admin., Hotel Türken, Mooslahnerkopf, Adolf-Hitler-Str., Hitler, Volkshotel Platterhof, post office, view to Salzburg, VIP guest haus, Haus Eckart, # = guard post, Kampfhäusl, path, pig stables, 2,000-seat theater, grazing meadows, Gutshof, Studio Speer, Haus Speer, Berchtesgaden 4km

MAP NOT TO SCALE
To walk from Haus Hitler to the greenhouse would have been less than 5 min.

= guard post

Our guide was faithfully on cue, imparting his tour as he was so used to doing. "Obersalzberg translates to Upper Salt Mountain. We were in this mountain earlier when the narrow-gauge railway delivered us deep within the salt mines. Now look to your right." He pointed. "The driveway you see formerly led to Albert Speer's home and studio."

"Who was Albert Speer?" I asked, before popping a pair of gummi bears.

"He was an architect. Such a good one that Hitler took Speer under his wing and made him one of the Reich's primary designers. As a teenager, Hitler aspired to be an artist and architect himself, but the Academy of Fine Arts in Vienna twice rejected him, saying he lacked talent. Speer was the architect Hitler dreamed of being: gifted, intelligent, charismatic.

"In 1942, Hitler appointed Speer as Minister of Armaments and War Production, succeeding Fritz Todt, who died in a plane crash. Unfortunately for the Allies, Speer did his job too well, doubling, tripling, and sometimes quadrupling output. Later in the war, when the Allies were bombing the smithereens out of the manufacturing plants, Speer had them reassembled underground where they sustained 80 percent output until the end of 1944. During the opening months of '45, Hitler's Reich was on the verge of collapse and Speer did his best to stop the annihilation of the Germans themselves. Since Hitler believed his people had failed their mission to conquer Europe, he issued orders to 'scorch' Germany, leaving nothing for future generations. Defying the madness, Speer drove around the nation persuading local leaders to disobey Hitler's orders."

"How come Hitler didn't have him executed?" Reuben asked from the back seat.

"For two reasons: First, Hitler was suffering from Parkinson's disease, thus his doctor prescribed a regular cocktail of drugs that more often than not left Hitler in Fantasyland. The second reason, and I'd say the main one, was that Hitler really admired Speer. He was among the rare few in the Reich who gained Hitler's unwavering trust.

"Speer's fanaticism to salvage whatever he could persisted to the very end. In the final days of the war, during the Battle for Berlin, Russian artillery pounded Hitler's command bunker knocking out all means of communication, except for one. Contact with the outside world fell to Hitler's personal pilot, Hans Baur, who flew daring missions in and out of the capital using a makeshift runway in the nearby Tiergarten park. To prepare the runway, Baur ordered his men to fell the few remaining trees. This drove Speer mad. He chased down Baur's men yelling at them to stop the slaughter while grabbing the axes from their hands. An architect's purpose is to create, and at this point he'd seen so much destruction that every miniscule thing had a meaning of colossal importance. After the war, for his role in the Nazi regime, Speer was sentenced to 20 years in Spandau prison, Berlin."

"It's amazing," I commented, "how someone so intelligent could blindly follow the lead of a maniac like Adolf Hitler."

"My thoughts exactly...and Speer had two decades behind bars to reflect on that very question. His answer was as coherent as his character: 'One seldom recognizes the devil when he puts his hand on your shoulder.'"

"Whoa...deep, man," Reuben astutely contributed.

"What happened with the trees in Tiergarten park?" I inquired. "Did Speer save them?"

"Not a chance! Between Baur's men and Russian artillery, nearly all living matter in the park was obliterated. After the war, new vegetation had to be planted, and today many trees in Berlin's Tiergarten can be dated back to the years immediately following the war."

Ahead, we came to a junction. The main route curved right. Jesse continued straight onto a narrow road.

"We are now entering what used to be 'Adolf Hitler Strasse.' From this point we cross the former boundary into the spiritual heartland of Nazi Germany, or as Sydney said earlier: *the Allied goal, the end of the line.* On the hillside to the right is where Hitler lived in his three-story mansion called the Berghof."

Reuben leaned forward into the front part of the car. "What Berghof? There's nothing there."

"That's because on April 25, 1945, more than 300 British bombers flew overhead and royally pummeled this community into a mountain of craters. In 1952, local authorities, fearing Obersalzberg would become a pilgrimage site for neo-Nazis, had all remaining structures razed...blown up!"

Jesse continued our tour as we motored up the hill. "Only two properties were allowed to be rebuilt after the 1952 demolitions. In front of us is one of those, the Hotel Türken. Because of the Türken's handy location next to the Berghof, the hotel in the 1930s was appropriated by the Reich's Security Service to safeguard Hitler. As the war progressed, a bunker system was excavated beneath the Türken that ran directly under the Berghof. Loaded with specially trained SS guards and laced with deadly machine-gun nests, Hitler could have retreated here for a last stand. Today, the tunnel system at the Türken is open to the public and we'll return later for a closer inspection."

"Woo hoo!" hooted Reuben.

"Would this be the tunnel network that Heinrich referred to earlier..." I asked, "where the crucifix was stashed after its discovery at Chiemsee?"

"That's right, Sydney."

Continuing farther up the hill, the road leveled off. Nestling on the crest of a grassy knoll we saw the 5-star Kempinski Hotel, where Jesse said Field Marshal Herman Göring's house once stood. He commanded Hitler's terrifying Luftwaffe, or air force.

All around us were vacant lots wrapped in alpine flora that once prospered with structures devoted to a dictator's pursuit of world domination: administration buildings; archives and planning rooms; military barracks for Hitler's elite SS protection guard; an air-defense command bunker that signaled the approach of enemy planes and alerted local antiaircraft units; a kindergarten for the children of Obersalzberg personnel; and even a greenhouse.

"A greenhouse?" Reuben repeated with an inflection of curiosity.

"Hitler was a strict vegetarian who desired his produce fresh. Additionally, Eva Braun used the greenhouse to hold Easter-egg hunts for the officers' children."

"Who's Eva Braun?" Reuben questioned, refusing to miss a trick.

"She was Hitler's longtime mistress, whom he married in Berlin on April 29, 1945, only days before the end of the war, in the bunker system below the Reich's Chancellery. Hitler believed the German people had failed him, thus he divorced Germany to marry Eva. Some 40 hours after tying the knot, the wedding couple consummated their union by committing suicide in the bunker. Honoring Hitler's wishes, both bodies were carried outside to the chancellery garden by staff, doused in petrol, and torched. Lovely honeymoon, huh."

"How did they do themselves in?" I asked.

"Sitting on a velvet sofa, Hitler opted for the foolproof poison-and-pistol method, biting down on a cyanide capsule then shooting himself in the head. Sitting next to Hitler and wearing an elegant black dress, Eva bit into her poison capsule at the sound of Hitler's gun...ending her life with a simple but lethal pill."

"Killer!" Reuben roared.

Our raconteur flipped the car around and retraced our route, descending past the Hotel Türken and Hitler's former estate to the junction, where we turned left and climbed another twisting road.

At the last curve, Jesse pointed to the hillside on the right where he said the stone foundation still remains of the Kampfhäusl, the cabin Hitler resided in the mid-1920s while he finished revising his political manifesto, "Mein Kampf."

On the left side of the road Martin Bormann had his guest house built for visiting VIPs. Today, the structure accommodates the Documentation Center, a museum focusing on none other than the rise and fall of the Third Reich.

Farther ahead, Jesse hooked a left into a freshly paved parking lot and cut the engine, which concluded the automobile portion of our tour. From here we would explore Hitler's bygone neighborhood the old-fashioned way, on foot.

As we set off, Jesse explained that the parking area used to be the location of the Platterhof, a grand Nazi hotel. We learned the hotel was bombed by the British, rebuilt by the Americans, and recently razed by the Germans to become a revenue-making parking lot charging tourists 3€ per car for the privilege.

"What's that dwelling on the mountaintop?" Reuben inquired, rocking back on his heels looking skyward.

"That's the Eagle's Nest, where we're headed."

"Way up there?!"

Jesse dismissed his comment as sarcasm. We bought our tickets and waited for the bus that would deliver us to the summit.

In the distance three buses returning from the Eagle's Nest motored in our direction. They made a wide, sweeping turn, each stopping momentarily to unload its cargo before pulling forward into their predetermined loading bays.

"Which side has the best views?" Reuben queried with trepidation while I waited with enthusiasm.

"Merely pick a seat," Jesse responded. "Anywhere is fine with me." He was too occupied with talking to his friend, the bus driver, to notice Reuben's tense demeanor.

Again, he questioned the seating arrangements. "No, really... which side has the best views?" Reuben looked about as nervous as a long-tailed cat in a room full of rocking chairs. Possibly he was disguising the real reason for his continuing curiosity: fear of heights.

We boarded the bus and Reuben aimed straight for the back. He stopped just shy of the last row, twisted sideways and politely motioned for Jesse and me to pass. "You guys go ahead and take the two window seats." The acrophobia theory was proving correct.

Jesse squeezed by and slid over to the window. I stayed where I was to tease a reaction out of Reuben. "Thanks...but you go ahead and take the other window seat and I can sit between you two. I'll have plenty of opportunities to revisit."

Reuben's face contorted. He appeared to be swallowing his tongue.

"What's going on; is someone coming over to join me?" trumpeted Jesse.

Reuben was visibly distraught, thus I decided to cut him some slack and praise his mock politeness as I stepped past him to the other window seat. "Thanks," I extended my hand and waved Reuben over, "I hope you don't mind the middle seat."

"I don't mind," Reuben confidently replied, his manhood still intact.

All three buses fired up their engines, and one by one respectively rambled out of their bays, forming a motorcade that traveled through a raised boom gate opening onto a road so narrow that it could only be one way.

We began heading up, straight up, and fast! Everyone was forced into a recline as our driver challenged the steep gradient. We must have looked like primed passengers in a rocket ship readying to launch into orbit.

In a manner suggestive of a Broadway thespian, Jesse dramatically explained our ascent. "We are about to embark on a four-mile stretch of road at a 22-percent grade to an elevation of 5,500 feet, more than one mile in the sky. From there we'll walk through a 400-foot tunnel blasted into the mountain face, where Hitler's former elevator will lift us another 400 feet within 45 seconds directly into the heart of the Eagle's Nest." I felt deep within the pages of a Stephen Ambrose novel. Reuben sat motionless and pale.

Our bus wrestled through the trees, traversing its alpine path. Eventually the dense tree line broke and superlative views developed in abundance. Reuben clutched the seat in front of him with both hands. There was no let up, his grip intensified as the driver played a game of cat and mouse with the guardrails. Higher and higher the bus climbed its narrow lane. Reuben's knuckles compressed to knots of ivory-bone as the objects on the earth's floor became minuscule. We passed through a few tunnels and suddenly Reuben's eyes bugged out as he braced the seat in front of him with all his might. What had been, for some, a long and nauseating road — abruptly disappeared.

"0oO...o0oo0...o0o0o0...h*hhh*h*hh*h*hh*!" roared our fellow passengers as the driver whipped around the 180-degree hairpin turn, no doubt scaring some into a change of underwear. The worry-free travelers on the left side of the bus now found themselves frightfully on the cliff's edge.

The driver raced even higher towards another tunnel. We were deeply camouflaged in the mountain face, becoming absorbed by the magnitude. A few scattered trees still held their roots, living life unabated in the dense mountain rock.

Jesse broke from his gaze out the window to express caution. "All right you two, hold on to your pretzels."

The bus whipped around another provocative curve that appeared to be a one-way ticket over the mountain's edge, exhausting the last of Reuben's bravado. He lowered his head into his lap. I thought he was going to be sick, or was he praying to the patron saint of bus catastrophes? This caught his best friend's eye. "Hey McJiggy...you okay?"

"Fine," he answered, in a less than fine voice.

While we studied the movements of our ill friend, the bus crept up to level ground and our destination of several thousand feet.

Jesse led us off the bus and over to the mouth of the 400-foot tunnel. Reuben was slow to react, but he made it. Small pockets of snow kept the clean air cool. I threw on a sweater, as did the others.

A Baroque-style medallion crowned the tunnel entrance displaying its birth year: 1938. Jesse pointed to a name etched into one of the mammoth bronze security doors: "*Stellan Anderson. Rockford, Illinois. 1945. 100th Division.* The boys were here!" he exclaimed, before shepherding us into the subterranean passageway.

"Sweet!" Reuben was impressed and, apparently, on the mend.

The tunnel's interior, built out of roughly finished rose-marble blocks, was damp and cold. Our three bodies kept pace with the throng in front of us while Jesse imparted more inside info.

"Hitler's chauffeur, SS Colonel Erich Kempka, would drive down this confined passage to the elevator and drop off his boss. Kempka then carefully reversed Hitler's supercharged Mercedes out of the tunnel, turned it around, and slowly reversed back to the elevator."

"Imagine if Kempka dented the fender in the process," I quipped.

Reuben was quick to complete my thought. "Hitler would probably say: 'Schultz...hand me the Luger!'"

Jesse laughed.

"Wasn't this tunnel a smidgen cold for the goofy-mustached tyrant?" I asked through chattering teeth.

"Cold! Not at all...the tyrant had heating. Check out the vents near the floor." Jesse pointed to the right, where we counted 11 along the way.

At the end of the tunnel people were cramming into the original brass elevator like it were a New York subway during rush hour. We were next to load but I stopped us in front of the doors.

"Kommen Sie doch bitte herein," said the elevator operator.

Jesse responded by squeezing forward into Hitler's brass box. Now all the squashed people were staring at Reuben and me, including Jesse.

"What's going on?" Reuben questioned.

"He told us to get in. So, get in!" Jesse insisted.

Reuben and I looked at each other. We then elbowed our way in, and for the first time in my life I truly understood the idiom 'packed in like sardines.' We were face to face, shoulder to shoulder, butts against cheeks as the elevator doors closed and our cabin shot upward like a missile. The predicament of 50 mashed individuals in a snug environment wasn't a picture of harmony. If I were to move any part of my body, my neighbor would more than likely sue for sexual harassment. Forty-five ear-popping seconds later, the elevator doors opened and we landed in the Nest.

Jesse escorted us through the door on the right and into an oak-paneled banquet room. We followed him past tables and chairs and down a few steps into a circular hall featuring a red-marble fireplace and five significant windows providing an abundance of light. He then proceeded to lead us through a portal on the left and down a few more steps into an intimate tea room, a said favorite of Hitler's mistress, Eva Braun. The walls were finished with knotted panels of pinewood that emitted a refreshing fragrance suggestive of an evergreen forest.

The room had a large picture-frame window opening to remarkable views of the national park below. Chief among the park's wonders were its sweeping forests of conifers that jacketed snow-peaked mountains, rising above the azure waters of Königssee lake, bright blue in color like a cloudless sky. I felt as if I were in a capsule hovering above God's greatest creations.

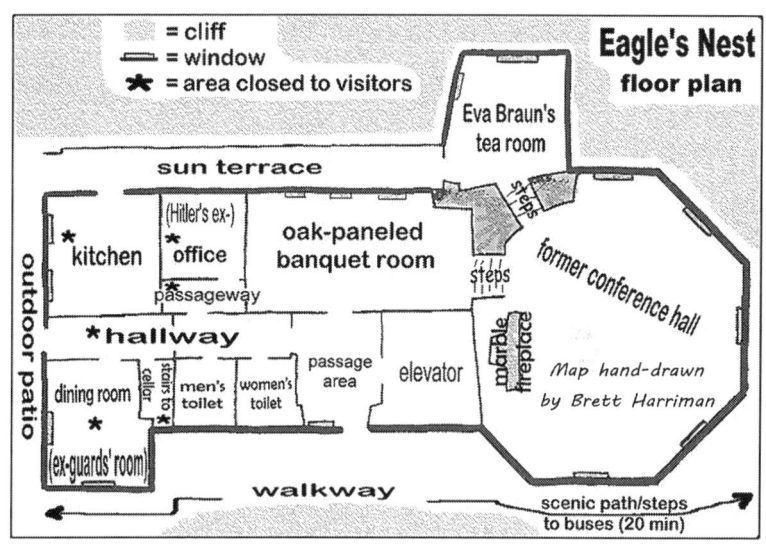

Eagle's Nest floor plan

- = cliff
- = window
- ★ = area closed to visitors

Areas shown: Eva Braun's tea room, sun terrace, *kitchen, (Hitler's ex-) *office, oak-paneled banquet room, passageway, steps, former conference hall, outdoor patio, *hallway, dining room, cellar stairs to *, men's toilet, women's toilet, passage area, elevator, marble fireplace, (ex-guards' room), walkway, scenic path/steps to buses (20 min)

Map hand-drawn by Brett Harriman

"So, what did you think of the Eagle's Nest?" Jesse said.

Reuben and I looked at Jesse curiously. "What do you mean?" I asked.

"You've nearly walked through the entire structure. The only parts you haven't seen are the bathrooms, kitchen, and former guards' room."

"Where did Hitler sleep?" Reuben queried.

"He slept at his house, the Berghof. Remember, we saw where it once stood...by the Hotel Türken?"

Reuben rubbed his thumb and index finger against his chin trying to mentally retrace our tour.

"This place must be tiny," I said.

"Not only is this place tiny...Hitler had a fear of heights and experienced claustrophobia in the elevator on the way up, thus he wasn't a huge fan of the property. Hitler officially visited the Nest 14 times between September 1938 and October 1940. The biggest function held here was a wedding reception in June 1944. The guests of honor were Eva Braun's sister, Gretl, and SS general Herman Fegelein. Hitler did not attend. A year later, Hitler had Fegelein killed in Berlin...but that's another story."

"Whoa. Nice guy!" Reuben exclaimed, rocking back on his heels again.

Jesse steered us out of the tea room, back into the former conference hall, and over to the red-marble fireplace. "Allegedly, this was a 50th-birthday present from the Italian dictator Benito Mussolini to Hitler on April 20, 1939."

"Not a bad rig," Reuben expressed. "I imagine it could warm the hall in a heartbeat."

"The edges and corners are drastically uneven," I noticed.

"That's because the liberating soldiers in 1945 chipped off proof they were part of history. I imagine these gray-haired warriors today sitting by the fireside and telling stories of how they helped free a continent while showing the marbled souvenir to their wowed grandchildren."

Again Jesse motioned onward, retracing our steps through the oak-paneled banquet room and into the passage area running in front of the elevator. Just as he said, it wasn't very spacious. There we saw the entrances into the toilets, the kitchen, and the former guards' room.

Outside, Jesse turned right and led us along a narrow walkway, stopping at the L-shaped corner made of granite blocks cemented knee high. Here he pulled out a large picture-book from his daypack and thumbed through a few pages before holding up an image of Hitler.

"Where do you think he's standing in this photo?" Jesse asked.

"Oh...my...gawd!" I gasped.

"He's standing exactly where we are now, isn't he?" Reuben declared.

"Yep." Jesse confirmed.

"You mentioned earlier," I said, "that Hitler was a decorated World War I veteran. What did he do?"

"He was a courier running messages along the front-line trenches. Due to the hazards of the job, couriers were regularly killed in action. But not Hitler...somehow this guy survived. For his bravery on the battlefield, Hitler was awarded Germany's medal of valor, *das Eiserne Kreuz*, the Iron Cross."

Jesse escorted us over to a wooden railing that was the only barrier between a spectacular panorama and a fatal tumble down the mountainside. Reuben took two steps back.

He continued from our new perspective: "Look at Obersalzberg 3,000 feet below. From there, roots nurtured beneath the soil developed into a ravenous tree feeding off its European neighbors. The Nazi regime contaminated an entire continent, and those men we saw earlier on the cemetery wall were the misguided leaves of a generation who fell off that tree in waste...ultimately fighting a war against their own liberation. It was blatantly clear that Hitler had merely given his countrymen guns by which to die with." Our host paused, facing us sincerely.

"Let's forget about Hitler and the Third Reich for a moment. Let's think about the bus ride up here, climbing through an ecosystem that could only be a supreme creation. That alone was worth the journey. Now we stand on top of a mountain and delight in the miracles before us: gently flowing streams, the grandeur of the Alps, blossoming trees that fill the valleys and gallop across the Austrian frontier and beyond. From here, you can see how lucky we are to be born in this generation of peace. The blood of many purchased our freedom...and we should never forget that."

Jesse's speech faded to the silence of the moment. We heard nothing but the wind's whistle and the faint caw of a crow somewhere high above.

How magnificent it is to stand here and savor this unparalleled view of splendor and tranquility. [2]

Reuben was awestruck. He began yodeling, again.

---

[2] Fans of *The Sound of Music* can see this same view at the end of the movie when the von Trapps are "escaping" over the Alps into Switzerland. Now you know, Maria and the gang were actually climbing the mountainside adjacent to Hitler's Eagle's Nest. In essence, they were escaping into Nazi Southern Command. Bad move!

The Letter
(Munich, Germany)

Chapter 7

8 a.m., late June, e-mail to the folks

```
Subject: München

Dear Mom & Dad,
A few days ago I got the royal tour of Berchtes-
gaden. Dad, you would have absolutely loved it!
We saw the Eagle's Nest and what was once Nazi
Southern Command. Today and tommorrow we are
touring Munich, the capital of Bavaria. I'll be
thinking of you both.
Love Syd, your intrepid daughter
P.S. Hi to Alex
```

Reuben and I hauled our backpacks out of the trunk. Jesse walked us over to the train platform, where he handed me an envelope. "Inside are a few things I jotted down that will help you get around town, but don't open it until you arrive at Munich's Hauptbahnhof. Reuben, that means 'main train station.'"

The train blew its horn three times as it came to a screeching halt. I took the envelope, secured it in my bag, and waved goodbye.

"Thanks, man, see ya tomorrow night," Reuben said. "Put a sock on the door if you're busy."

My travel partner and I hopped on board. The train doors closed and we were at once moving in a northerly direction. We hoisted our backpacks onto the storage rack above and claimed two seats facing each other near the door.

"What's in the envelope?" Reuben asked.

"I'm not sure. Jesse only mentioned that he'd written down some stuff to do...and to have fun."

"What about our accommodations?"

"Good question. Let's hope that it's part of the *stuff to do*."

"Fahrscheine, bitte." The train conductor approached and aimed a sinister glare at Reuben's foot resting on the corner of my seat.

"What does he want?"

"He wants our tickets and for you to relocate your foot."

"Tickets?!" Reuben lowered his leg to the floor and felt his pockets while eyeing me with a look of worry. "What tickets?"

The conductor became slightly agitated. "Ven yooz haff no ticket, yooz musst die koal schovel'n'."

I nudged Reuben's knee with mine and muttered under my breath: "Did you hear that?"

"Sure did! What are we gonna do?"

"Buy tickets," I said.

"If you insist."

"Do you have another idea?"

"Yeah, let's run. A movie-like chase from car to car."

"Creative, but somehow I don't think that'll work."

The conductor must have understood Reuben because he widened his stance and blocked any chance of escape via the aisle.

I grabbed my bag from above and delved inside, yanking out my wallet. Jesse's envelope was wedged next to it. I unexpectedly found a pair of train tickets paper-clipped to its back.

"Here you go, sir." I handed over the tickets with a jester's smile.

The conductor validated them and went officiously on his way. "Fahrscheine, bitte."

"That was nice of Jesse," I said.

"Go ahead, while it's in your hand," Reuben pleaded, "open the envelope."

"You heard what Jesse said: Not until we reach Munich."

"Oh, come on. What's it gonna hurt? Plus, we need to know about our sleeping arrangements."

"Well..."

"Go on, Syd!"

I weaseled my index finger under the envelope's corner seal and slithered it partway across, ripping open a small section. "We really shouldn't be doing this. He stressed not until Munich."

"Jesse's my best friend. He won't care."

My finger finished its dance across the seal. The envelope was open and its contents, several neatly folded sheets of paper, stared us passively in the face. I reached in and pulled out a piece of paper that was detached from the main bunch. It shouted: "I THOUGHT I TOLD YOU, NOT UNTIL THE HAUPTBAHNHOF!"

Swiftly, I stuffed the intimidating piece of paper back into the envelope. "I hope you're happy! We're gonna respect his wishes and leave well enough alone. After all, don't you remember Pandora's Box?"

"Hands up...you win," Reuben said, raising his arms pretending to surrender.

Switching gears, I asked him if there were any places he'd like to visit in Munich. He said there was, a traditional beer hall.

"That shouldn't be too hard to find," I told him. "Jesse said that Munich is the beer capital of the world and its name originates from the German word for 'monks,' who in medieval times mastered the art of brewing beer."

"Groovy!" Reuben eloquently articulated.

Suddenly, the conductor materialized and directed his spiel at Reuben and me. "Fahrscheine, bitte."

"He mustn't recognize us," I whispered, nudging Reuben's knee again.

This was a good time to query my quest. "Excuse me, have you heard of *das Bayernkreuz*?"

"Fahrscheine, bitte," he repeated.

Perhaps he didn't hear me. I tugged on his blue jacket and restated my query.

He wasn't concerned. "Fahrscheine, bitte." Keenly he stared us down.

He definitely wasn't a friendly chap. I fished through my bag once more, snagging the tickets. "Here ya go."

"Danke." He punched the tickets as if he'd never seen them before.

Marching down the aisle, he repeated his request to the next passengers in a robotic manner. "Fahrscheine, bitte."

"What's the latest with the cross, anyway?" Reuben asked.

"Good question. Not much new on that front. Jesse figured he'd keep pressing the locals for info while I poked around Munich. I thought I'd ask anybody and everybody."

"Something'll come up," Reuben affirmed.

The train slowed considerably as numerous tracks began converging. On our left we passed a stationary freight train loaded with brand-new Porsches. To our right crawled an endless column of boxcars. Our train slightly jerked from side to side, conceivably changing tracks. On the horizon we approached a massive structure, one that could house a football stadium. It was the main train station.

"Let's open the envelope!" Reuben urged.

Our train tiptoed into its final destination: München Hauptbahnhof. Passengers began to exit. Reuben and I waited for the rush to subside.

We stepped onto the platform and rested our backpacks against a bench. Drawing the envelope from my bag, I handed it over. "You can do the honors."

"My pleasure." However suave Reuben wanted to appear, his actions depicted quite a different perception. He handled the envelope like it was labeled "anthrax." With exaggerated care, he spread the envelope open using his thumb and forefinger. What he'd been craving the previous hour was now within his grasp. We kneeled down to my backpack and Reuben unfolded Jesse's sheets of paper across its nylon surface.

The opening page read:

Rules

1) There are 10 pages in "The Letter"; however, you may only look at one page at a time.

2) When the assignment on that page has been completed, you may then look to the next page.

3) Once you understand these rules, you have the green light to proceed.

We swiveled to each other and nodded in unison. Reuben promptly flipped to the next page.

Page 1

Once off the platform, exit out the right side of the train station to Bayerstrasse. Cross the street with the traffic light to the other side of Bayerstrasse and go left, then make the next right on Senefelderstrasse and proceed to "Wombats" city hostel on the left. This will be your humble abode for the evening. Your reservation is under "Einstein."

The Letter 131

At the hostel's reception desk stood a twentyish brunette writing tomorrow's activities on a large chalkboard.

We set our packs down and Reuben caught her attention. "Hello, we have a reservation under the name...Einstein."

She gave us a welcoming smile then jumped behind the computer to search for our booking. "Hier it is. I found you... Albert und Juliet."

"Err, yeah..." I unconvincingly responded, "that's us."

"You're in a four-bed dorm on the second floor," the receptionist explained, handing us each a card key.

"Excuse me, have you heard of *das Bayernkreuz*?" I asked.

"Ah...the Bavarian Cross," she responded.

This sounds positive. Perhaps she'll provide a clue. My optimism was curtly interrupted.

"Sorry, I'm not familiar with it."

Huh? That was odd. Anyway, she proceeded to teach me how to say my entire request in German, which might speed up the search. Well, that is, until the answer comes buzzing back in German, in which case I'll most likely require a Turing machine to crack the colloquial code. One of these days I need to master the language, otherwise I'll forever be branded a tourist.

Our dorm room had four lockers, one sink, and two steel-framed bunk-bed units pushed against either wall. Reuben threw his pack down next to a bottom bed while simultaneously keeling over onto its mattress. Lying on his back, he completely stretched out his body, resting his feet against the end support frame and interlocking his hands behind his head. He couldn't have looked more comfortable.

After claiming the bed above, I stood anxiously over Reuben. "Let's see what's on Page 2."

His smile reflected my anticipation. I whipped the letter out and moved Page 1 to the back.

Page 2

Congratulations, Albert and Juliet, for achieving the assignment outlined on Page 1. I hope you like the hostel and your new Munich identities. At the reception desk, have staff show you how to get to Marienplatz. Make sure you're there by noon; that's when it starts. Upon completion of the mini-event, turn to the next page.

CHAPTER 7

Affectionately referred to by the locals as their "living room," sprawling Marienplatz, or Mary's Square, is the absolute core of Munich, a bustling plaza in the heart of Old Town brimming with throngs of people buzzing around at a brisk pace.

Staff at our accommodations told us that in medieval times Marienplatz was Munich's commercial and entertainment center, the scene of a lively farmers' market as well as colorful festivals and jousting tournaments featuring knights and nobles.

We arrived two minutes before 12 noon and joined the crowd of camera-toting tourists who were huddled around the Virgin Mary and gazing skyward. The focus of their attention was the ornamental clock tower rising above the neo-Gothic town hall. It was obvious that something of significance was about to take place.

Along the square's perimeter, restaurant workers diligently set up outdoor tables in order to ensnare their lucrative lunchtime prey. In the center of the plaza rose a lofty granite column upon which stood a gilded statue of the Virgin Mary, who appeared to be blessing all of us in her presence.

Loud bells began chiming from the clock tower and all present gaped at the lifeless figurines suspended within. Our hands shielded us from the bright sun as we stood poised for something to happen, but nothing did.

"Maybe we missed the event," Reuben commented as a collective gasp belched from the crowd.

Suddenly, the lifeless figurines became animated as they moved around a king and queen perched upon a pedestal. We learned this recalled the wedding of Duke Wilhelm V and his bride Renata that took place on the square in 1568. At the time the festivities continued for two weeks, including a Ritterturnier, or knights' tournament.

At 12 noon the royal party had begun anew: musicians, jesters, and jousting knights performed past the regal pair. Coming around again, they acted a repeat performance: the musicians played, the jesters juggled, and the jousters dueled. The Bavarian knight, sporting the kingdom's blue-and-white colors, lunged forward with his long lance and stuck the red-striped knight in the chest, thrusting him backwards off his horse. The crowd exhaled an immense moan.

The bells continued while the theatrical program changed to a dozen dancing men in colorful garb twirling like ballerinas on a carousel. These are the coopers, or barrel makers, performing the traditional Schäffler dance to mark the end of pestilence. After enduring a devastating outbreak of plague in the early 16th century, the townsfolk refused to emerge from their dwellings since they did not believe the worst was yet over. The coopers, however, thought otherwise. Resplendent in their traditional costumes, they were the first to come out of their houses, singing and celebrating the end of the deadly epidemic.

After a few minutes, the coopers halted motionless as if they had never begun. The bells continued to chime a few minutes more and the crowd dispersed. Those who remained heard the bells stop and a golden rooster crow three times, frightening nearby pigeons into premature flight.

"Awesome!" Reuben exclaimed. "Time for the next event."

> ### *Page 3*
>
> Cool show, huh? It's the Glockenspiel — literally "bells play" — Germany's largest carillon, having 43 bells (weighing from 20 lbs to 25 tons) and housing 32 life-sized figures, each made of copper, dating from 1908.
>
> (Before we move on, note there are toilets at the neo-Gothic town hall. Use 'em if you need 'em. To get there, go through the archway beneath the Glockenspiel to the inner courtyard and the toilets — costing .60¢ to use — will be to your right.)
>
> When facing the Glockenspiel, head left where the masses are converging. This pedestrian-only drag is Kaufingerstrasse, literally Shopping Street. Window-shop at your leisure — at the 4th giant maple tree (some 250 meters along) is Ettstrasse, and on the corner is St. Michael's church. In its hallowed crypt you'll find Germany's most famous king.

The morning's gray clouds had disappeared to a fine afternoon. As the sun climbed up the sky and intensified, we paused to remove our sweaters. Reuben must have been exceptionally warm in his red velvet pants and Levi's studded shirt.

The crowd flooded en masse down the pedestrian-only shopping street. We drifted along, passing department stores and fashion boutiques. I hadn't yet saved enough money to spoil myself on European threads, but now seemed to be a good time to start that wish list I'd been dreaming about.

"There's the fourth maple tree...and there's Ettstrasse," Reuben reported with letter in hand. "That must be the church."

In front of St. Michael's, I stopped and stared at a street entertainer standing on a wooden box posing as a statue. He was spray-painted silver from his floppy shoes to his top hat. He even held a silver cane. A little boy dropped a coin in his tip jar. The silver man bent over and smiled for a photo before returning to his rigid position.

"Juliet..." Reuben barked, "come on!" He stood at the entrance of the church, holding the door open, anxious to see the crypt and the famous king.

The interior of St. Michael's was enormous and according to the leaflet I picked up upon entering, the high altar at the head of the church is lavishly bedecked in gold and the vaulted ceiling above us is the largest of its kind north of the Alps. Built in Renaissance style and consecrated in the year 1597, St. Michael's was commissioned by Wittelsbach Duke Wilhelm V, the same duke commemorated on the Glockenspiel, ruler of Bavaria for some 20 years from 1579 and founder of the spirituous Hofbräuhaus. Wittelsbachs were staunch supporters of the Roman Catholic Church and the most stalwart among them are honored here within niches on St. Michael's heavenly front facade.

A few people milled around a black-and-white picture exhibition at the back of the church. We walked over for a closer look and saw photos depicting the aftermath of a bombing raid during World War II. Some 75 years ago the church's roof was blown off and where we stood had been reduced to a pile of rubble.

We wandered midway up the central aisle, turning around to see an organ perched high above the main portal. Like the altar, it too was gold-plated. Flanking us, along either side aisle, were private praying areas secured by wrought-iron gates. One gate was open. Inside stood a statuette of the Virgin Mary. Before her blessed eyes burned dozens of white votive candles in memory of loved ones who have departed us.

At the head of the church appeared to be a tomb positioned below a heavenly mural framed by rose-marble pillars. Could this belong to the famous monarch?

Adjacent, wooden doors opened outward from the tiled floor providing passage into a cellar. The posted sign indicated there was an entrance fee.

"Maybe this is where we'll find the king," I said, pointing down the basement passage.

"Let's take a chance," gambled Reuben. "We can at least say we've seen the crypt of an ancient church."

At the bottom of the steps sat a desk and behind it an elderly man, staring intently into the pages of an old book. Without bothering to look up, he announced the entrance fee: "Zwei Euro, bitte."

Here was an excellent opportunity to flaunt my newly learned German. "Entschuldigung, haben Sie schon einmal etwas über *das Bayernkreuz* gehört?"

The man pulled his nose out from behind the tome and ungracefully reached for the pair of spectacles hanging off his shirt pocket. He slipped the glasses over his eyes and tried his best to focus on Reuben and me, squinting. He then, awkwardly, stood up, looked around, held out his hand, and repeated the entrance fee.

Peculiar man. Perhaps his wife forgot to pack his favorite bratwurst for lunch. Regardless, by his curt reply, I had to assume he either wasn't familiar with the cross or he didn't understand a word I said. My money was on the latter.

After handing him four euros between us, we ventured into a hallway filled with stale air that led to a vaulted chamber. Placed along the walls were a series of metal caskets containing the relics of Wittelsbachs, the Bavarian royal family: dukes, princes, princesses, and a king.

"I think we found our famous one." Reuben stated as he led me to a casket that was far more noteworthy than the rest. The large, gilded crown on top was a giveaway.

Yep, he was right. It belonged to King Ludwig II of Bavaria, better known as the slightly unhinged fairy-tale king. Somehow I thought his memorial would be as magnificent as his castles, but it wasn't. I can now say, however, I've seen the last resting place of the legendary monarch.

Having already toured his Herrenchiemsee palace, all that's left for me to complete Ludwig's legacy is to visit his other two fantasy castles — Linderhof and Neuschwanstein, a.k.a. the Disney castle — and, of course, to somehow unearth his jewel-studded crucifix.

By Reuben's body language, I could tell he was ready to move on. I pulled the letter from my daypack and turned to our next assignment.

The Letter   137

> ### Page 4
> Go back the way you came along the Shopping Street and make the second left at the Hunting and Fishing Museum, marked by a giant-sized catfish and wild boar. Shortly thereafter you will come to Frauenplatz — this is for you, Reuben — it translates to Women's Square. Here you'll find Munich's Old Town landmark, the enormous Frauenkirche, or Church of Our Lady, dating from 1488. Go inside to find the devil's footprint.

The museum was a cinch to find. Out front was a hefty bronze figure of a wild boar that I recognized as *Il Porcellino*, a replica taken from the famed Florentine fountain, recreated on the big screen in the Harry Potter fantasy film series.

Around the next bend was Frauenplatz.

"Where are the women?" Reuben asked, curiously.

"It's just the name of the square. It doesn't mean women are standing on corners selling their goods."

"Pity."

"Albert!!" I scolded his Munich alias.

"Oh!" Reuben replied. "I'm sorry, did I say that out loud?"

The exterior of the church was ordinary, comprised of plain red brick devoid of fancy Baroque curves or wicked Gothic gargoyles so common in Germany. Nonetheless, its two landmark clock towers made the building a focal point.

"They look like overflowing beer mugs," Reuben envisioned.

"I think they look phallic."

"Juliet!!" Reuben turned the tables and scolded my Munich identity.

The least I could do was use his material. "I'm sorry, did I say that out loud?"

We entered the holy structure through the main portal and instantly noticed two things: only one stained-glass window, which was set behind the high altar at the opposite end of the church, and directly in front of us stood a small group of tourists huddled around their guide, who was pointing at something on the floor. We were close enough to hear his narration.

"According to legend, Satan left his footprint here more than five centuries ago when he broke in at dawn to inspect the completion and consecration of what he believed to be a one-window church. You see, from this angle, due to an architectural trick, the stained-glass windows along the side walls are not visible when looking to the high altar. The devil was so rapt by the builders' dark and gloomy design rejecting God's light that he decided not to demolish a church that nobody would pray in without windows. During his euphoric spell, Satan mightily stamped his right foot, permanently leaving a size 10 imprint in the floor tile."

Upon hearing this, Reuben backed up and started walking toward the exit.

"Albert," I called out to question his sudden departure.

"Time for Page 5," he insisted.

What's with him? Perhaps he was spooked by the thought of Lucifer. Anyway, it was time to move on.

Page 5

I would assume you're famished by now. Bear with me through this next set of instructions and I'll lead you to a feast.

Face the front of the Frauenkirche, go right then swing left and walk alongside the church to its rear.

During the Middle Ages, a cemetery stood here. It was not uncommon then for the deceased to be buried adjacent to their place of worship in the heart of major cities. However, as settlements grew and space became limited, urban graveyards were promptly relocated. Moreover, mysterious bouts of plague devastated large populations and inner-city cemeteries were hardly vogue on account of hygiene and hysteria.

(Page 5 cont.)

Memorials to these former times are the weathered headstones mounted here on the Frauenkirche's exterior walls that were salvaged from the old church cemetery and remember prominent citizens. One of the last markers features a skull and crossbones symbolic of "memento mori," a Latin reminder of our mortality, that these bones await yours.

Behind the church connect onto Filserbräugasse — roll through this lane to the people-packed Weinstrasse, a reminder that you're in Germany's third largest city.

Skip straight across Weinstrasse and walk the length of Landschaftstrasse. (A park will be to your left and the town hall to your right — other side of town hall is Marienplatz.)

Cross the road and continue straight into the narrow lane, Altenhofstrasse. Near the end of the lane on the right you'll see a plaque dedicated to W.A. Mozart — the condensed version reads: Mozart lived here from November 6, 1780 to March 11, 1781. He completed his opera masterpiece "Idomeneo," premiering in the Old Residenz Theater on January 29, 1781. Remember him and his music as you pass by.

At the end of the lane, make a left. You are now standing at the castle gate of the Alter Hof. Dating from 1253, this was the original Munich residence of the dynastic Wittelsbach family, rulers of Bavaria for more than 700 years. Elite guards were posted here in glorious garb, armed with halberds and swords. Only those in the emperor's court or persons bearing approved wax-sealed documentation were allowed to enter.

But times have changed and you're clear to step through the archway. Look around the peaceful yet contemporary courtyard. The only surviving medieval architecture is to your left. The windowed

> *(Page 5 cont.)*
>
> *oriels climbing up the facade are collectively known as the Monkey Tower. You see, one day the king's pet primate got loose, turning the royal residence into a virtual three-ringed circus until the chamberlain and his staff managed to wrangle the little monkey back to its princely quarters.*
>
> *Ahead, exit the courtyard via the archway at No. 3 in the left corner, passing the fine Alter Hof restaurant and wine cellar. Out the other end is Dienerstrasse — go left. Enter Alois Dallmayr at the fourth portal (through the two narrow swing doors).*
>
> *Inside Dallmayr is a do-it-yourself culinary experience. You don't have to buy your food here; it can be pricey! Another option is to head back to Marienplatz and descend into the subway for a less-expensive selection or stop by the grocery store at No. 13 Tal street (opposite McDonald's). Nevertheless, pick up something, somewhere "to go" — you're in for a picnic. Once you've completed the food mission, return to Dienerstrasse and read Page 6.*

CHAPTER 7

"Famished" was an understatement. Eagerly, we set course for our new destination: Food.

Jesse was right about Weinstrasse being a busy pedestrian thoroughfare. Here we had to dodge, dart, dip, and duck our way across. On the other side we paralleled the neo-Gothic town hall, and in the leafy park to our left we saw a carnival crammed with teeny tots. Traversing our way through a gaggle of kids wielding cotton candy, we navigated the assigned streets and rediscovered Mozart. To trace his whereabouts in Salzburg was fascinating enough; to rendezvous with him in Munich was more than I could imagine.

A few steps farther and we found ourselves facing the castle gate of the Alter Hof, where a modest tin shield denoted the year 1253. This was obviously the place Jesse said elite guards were posted, armed with halberds and swords.

We entered through the archway, wide enough for a pick-up truck, to reach the inner courtyard resplendent in argyle patterning.

Although the Middle Ages are long gone, it was easy to feel the medieval spirit, to imagine the melodic strains of wooden flutes and gut-strung gitterns, falconry and fellowship, rib-tickling monkeys and royal banquets.

Reuben must have been reading into my thoughts of festivities and feasts because he pointed to the exit and declared, "I hope lunch is soon. I'm starving!"

Exiting through the archway at number 3, we left the age-old serenity of the Alter Hof behind and were transported back to 21st-century Munich. The chivalry and knighthood of the courtyard were substituted by the rush of smart-phone toting pedestrians and policemen driving sleek BMWs past Mercedes taxi cabs.

Jesse wasn't kidding about the narrow swing doors. Reuben and I were trying to squeeze into Alois Dallmayr as a team of bulky weight-lifter-types had the same idea. The awkward tussle was rapidly forgotten once inside. The aroma from the food counters was divine, a feast of the senses. Jesse had led us into epicurean heaven.

Food was Dallmayr's game and gourmet its specialty. Numerous white-toqued chefs and neatly dressed shop assistants managed a world of delicacies spread beneath an elaborate cove ceiling supported by marble columns. Each food counter was a boulevard of sumptuous fare, an edible odyssey of Danish pastry and chocolate torte, smoked salmon and cured hams, Dutch cheese and Bavarian sausage, fresh pasta and free-range poultry, goose-liver pâté and Russian caviar, exotic fruits and Champagne truffles, veal schnitzel and quiche Lorraine, vintage wine and Chiemsee schnapps, French breads and petits fours, you name it. The experience was overwhelming. We had to restrain ourselves from buying a sample of everything.

Page 6

I hope you enjoyed your stroll through Alois Dallmayr. It is Munich's oldest and most prestigious deli, thus I included it as one of your assignments. So, with that said and your picnic bags in hand, let's march on.

When facing Dallmayr's, go left and take Dienerstrasse straight into Residenzstrasse — but be careful of the umpteen cyclists who zip through here.

Ahead, at the streetcar tracks, look for the sign-posted corner of Residenzstrasse and Perusastrasse. Walk over to the signpost and stand by it while facing in the direction you've been walking.

From this busy area you can see three noble members of the Bavarian royal family in statue form. You are obviously familiar with the most famous of the Wittelsbachs, King Ludwig II (a.k.a the fairy-tale king, who reigned 1864-86).

To your distant right, at the other end of the boulevard, is his father: King Max II (1848-64).

Now move your eyes left until you see Max Joseph (King Max I, 1806-25) sitting on a throne in his namesake plaza, Max-Joseph-Platz. He is King Ludwig II's great grandfather, and founder of the magnificent neoclassical structure behind him, the Bavarian National Theater. (To MJ's right is the massive Residenz complex, or Residence, where the Wittelsbachs moved to in the 15th-16th century after outgrowing the Alter Hof).

Swing left again and look all the way down Residenzstrasse for a glimpse of the equestrian statue of King Ludwig I (1825-48), the fairy-tale king's grandfather and reason for the Oktoberfest. (Don't worry if he's hard to see; he'll get closer as you forge ahead.)

Continue your original course on Residenzstrasse, passing Max Joseph on the right and

> (Page 6 cont.)
>
> paralleling the Residence itself. Eventually you'll reach the first of four lions. They represent the four seasons and are said to bring good luck when the nose of each lion is rubbed. Make a wish!
>
> It was also here that on November 9, 1923 Hitler's Beer Hall Putsch came to a bloody end with 16 of his followers paying the ultimate price for the young Nazi Party. Opposite the third lion, atop the 10-foot side wall of the Hall of the Field Marshals, locally Feldherrnhalle, a memorial was erected during the Third Reich for those who died that day in the struggle — wreaths were laid, guards were posted, and all passersby had to hail the Nazi salute.

One couldn't miss our first stop. It was an extremely hectic intersection where the main road, bike lanes, pedestrian paths, and tram tracks converged. In the midst of urban pandemonium, we saw the three nobles.

Suddenly, Reuben hollered the approach of an oncoming truck: "Watch out!" Then I heard the blast of a horn followed by the spine-tingling screeches of a tram braking. Reuben grabbed my arm and yanked me clear of the streetcar — straight into a bicyclist! I spun like a top and fell to the ground. The bicyclist lost his balance and rode into a post, leaving poor Reuben at odds for whom to attend to first.

Achtung Tram

CHAPTER 7

"I'll be fine," I insisted. "See if the bicyclist is okay."

Reuben raced over to help. "Are you all right?!"

"Ja, I zink so."

A passerby offered me a hand up. I thanked him and made my way over to Reuben and the shaken bicyclist. "I'm so sorry," I said. "It was my fault this happened and...Albert here saved my life."

The bicyclist brushed off his clothes. "Alles ist ok, don't vurry."

He then adjusted the ball cap he was wearing and his hair fell to her shoulders. He happened to be a she, and she was gorgeous. By the rapturous expression on Reuben's face, you'd think he had just won the lottery.

Reuben, ever melodramatic, tried his best: "Let me buy you a drink to make up for this most unfortunate incident."

"I vould luv zat, but I musst take zee train later zu mein oma's haus in Dresden. How'z about next veek?" she asked, staring Reuben in the face, looking for a positive response.

This was turning out to be quite the love story. I pulled my hair into a ponytail and watched on.

"I... I... fly back home in a few days."

I could see by Reuben's immediate grief that a trip to the dentist to have teeth pulled would have been preferable.

"Vell... I give you mein telefon nummer ins case you stay." She snatched a pen from her bag, scribbled something on a piece of paper and handed it to Reuben. "Hier. It wuz nize meeting you, Albert."

Bicycle Girl maneuvered into the Tour de Munich bike lane and rode off. Reuben wore a vacant stare as she cycled into the distance. He then turned and glared at me. "She thinks my name is Albert!"

He was worried about nothing. But it was clearly my duty to lighten the gloom. "If you play your cards right, you'll get a second chance."

"I can't believe the love of my life just left me and she thinks my name is Albert."

"I think you'll survive. Besides, you've got her number. Why don't you postpone your flight home a week?"

"Yeah...easy for you to say. I start work on Monday."

"You said she was the love of your life; doesn't that count for something?"

"I did say that, didn't I?" He frowned as if contemplating the theory of relativity.

Clearly his fleeting attraction to me had passed and he was on to new conquests, which made things less complicated.

"Hey, Albert, there's Max Joseph." I was trying to garner a change of thought. "Doesn't he look ceremonial?"

"Oh, Joseph, you saw the twinkle in her eye, please offer some advice."

The Letter 145

Well, that idea bit the dust. Reuben was now soliciting statues on his behalf. "Come on," I pleaded. "We've got to catch up with some lions."

"That's right! Jesse did say they brought good luck."

The Residence adjacent to Max Joseph looked quite impressive with its extensive stone-block facade and three levels of arched windows rising to at least 70 feet overhead. Behind Joseph sat a classical structure that could have been mistaken for a newly renovated temple belonging to the Acropolis of Athens. According to Jesse, this was the Bavarian National Theater. Its cornerstone laid in the year 1811.

"Let's go...the lions are waiting!" Reuben squawked. Our previous stroll of leisure became a frantic walk-a-thon.

Reuben had a childish hankering for Bicycle Girl, and it was becoming quite a nuisance. We arrived at Lions' Row and he began furiously rubbing the nose of the first one. "If I ever needed luck, oh dear lion, I need it now! Please let my boss say I can stay a week longer. Please!" He finally looked relieved. But I then reminded him of the legend.

"Don't you remember that the lions represent the seasons, and a wish cannot be cast unless all four noses are rubbed?"

Heeding my counsel, Reuben sprinted to the remaining lions, rubbing each of their noses with passion, until he reached the last lion, which was occupied by a man who appeared to be suffering from a similar surge of anxiety.

Reuben stood behind the man, exhibiting the tolerance of a 5-year-old who had to pee. He bobbed up and down, danced the hokey pokey, and shifted from foot to foot, side to side. From my angle, three lions down, it looked like the makings of a Mr. Bean comedy skit. The man concluded his catharsis and Reuben jumped in, embracing the last lion, rubbing its nose obsessively.

Reuben's infatuation had gone too far. I had to come up with something to get this dog-and-pony show back on track.

"I have this tremendous feeling that your boss will have absolutely no problem with you staying a week longer. Perhaps even two!"

"How can you say that? You don't know my work situation."

"Jesse and I were talking the other day about you, your job, and how lucky you were to have such a nice boss." I was lying through my teeth, hoping he wouldn't call my bluff.

"So Jesse mentioned my boss, huh?"

Oh no, here it comes.

"He's always been one of my biggest supporters, and often had to loan me money when I was earning peanuts as an assistant." It looked as if Reuben might be coming around. "You're right, I'll call my boss later tonight when it'll be early afternoon back home and he's usually done bucketing out lunch to the pod."

"Hey! There's the 10-foot wall." I was fairly confident I could get him to do a 180 with the Feldherrnhalle observation. "This must be where Jesse said 16 of Hitler's followers died in the 1923 Beer Hall Putsch."

"That's right, and all passersby had to hail the Nazi salute," Reuben said on his way over for a closer inspection.

I pulled the letter out of my back pocket to quote Jesse. "A memorial was erected during the Third Reich for those who died that day in the struggle; wreaths were laid and guards posted."

Meanwhile, Reuben had managed to scale the wall like Spider-Man and report on his findings from the top ledge. "Awesome. This must be where the memorial stood."

I made my way up to him via the broad steps around the corner and saw a newer, reworked section that was clearly different from the rest of the stonework. I couldn't imagine having to raise my arm in recognition of Hitler every time I walked by here, saluting what I didn't believe in.

This has to be the memorial my dad told me about. Not all Germans believed in the Nazi way, and those who refused to salute turned left before reaching the memorial, utilizing the lane Viscardigasse to bypass it. In due course, the lane became known as Sidestepper's Alley.

Reuben and I stood in the Hall of the Field Marshals reflecting on the hardships the locals endured during the dark days of Hitler's murderous

Third Reich. Digressing from Nazis and dictators, our stomachs naggingly persuaded us to move on to our banquet of champions.

> ### Page 7
>
> Now that you're doped up on luck, let's settle in the park for a picnic. When eyeing the plaza in front of the Feldherrnhalle, you'll see a considerable archway on the right — venture through this to the Hofgarten, or Royal Gardens, landscaped in 1613 on orders of the king.
>
> Stroll through the garden reserve, past the centrally located Renaissance-style rotunda (named "Diana" temple after the Roman goddess of hunting) and out the back left corner of the gardens. Here, you'll see people heading down a cobbled path and into a darkened tunnel. Follow them through the tunnel — out the other side opens into Germany's largest city park.
>
> Keep to the main trail, which will eventually cross over the picturesque stream. On the other side of the bridge, go left and stick to the left path. After about 200 meters, find a place at the brook's edge for your picnic.
>
> Relax and enjoy the views in the English Garden.

The sun shone brightly attracting throngs of people to the English Garden, where Reuben searched for the perfect picnic place. "What do you think about this spot?"

"Wunderbar!" As hungry as I was, anywhere would've done.

We tore open both bags of food and maneuvered the goodies into strategic positions. Reuben began cutting the bread rolls while I unwrapped the Emmenthaler cheese and slices of ham. Our surroundings were ultra conducive to a picnic as we sat on the edge of a crystal-clear stream in the middle of the park.

Opposite us, on the other side of the stream, were a few shrubs and umpteen sun worshippers spread out on an extensive grassy field staking a piece of prime Munich real estate for the afternoon.

Reuben peeled back the lid on the potato salad while bobbing his head and addressing his self-made sandwich: "You look sooo good... mmm, I'm gonna eat you all up!"

I shoved two plastic forks into the potato salad and dug in before Hungry Boy inhaled it all.

"Cowabunga!" Reuben's eyes bulged and his jaw dropped as he stared past me.

"What?!" I shrieked. "What?" Reuben had me worried.

I turned to see what he was spying: two girls graceful like swans wading in the water — wearing only their birthday suits! A naked guy followed their lead.

Perfect Picnic Place

It appears Jesse sent us on a "clothing optional" picnic.

Reuben sat motionless, gawking, mouth open. "Wake up. Wake up," I repeated, accompanied by aggressive finger snapping. "Earth to Albert."

"Errr, yeah...looks awesome. I mean, what a tasty bread roll."

"Sure is," I said, slapping another sandwich together and rearranging the deli items out of the charring sun.

"Do you want to jump in and cool off?" Reuben asked, spontaneously.

I double blinked.

"What do you mean?" I said, giving him a guarded look.

"I mean, it's awfully warm sitting here in the sun."

"We don't have towels."

"I dare you!"

"You dare me?" I scoffed at his challenge. "What do I get in return for this *dare*?"

"I'll buy ya dinner."

"No thanks. I'd rather stay dry and take in the scenery."

"Okay, fine. Suit yourself. I'm going in anyway."

Reuben leapt to his feet and sprinted to the stream, leaving a trail of clothes on his way.

Waist high in water, Reuben, grinning, turned to me and sang: "The water's refreshing! Ya sure you don't want that free dinner?"

I dismissed his offer with a phony smile and a friendly wave.

At that moment, the Birthday-Suit Girls began wading in his direction. Reuben ogled their every move, seemingly captivated by their bare bodies only feet away from his gangly frame. I wanted to remind him that nudity wasn't such a big deal in Europe, as I discovered after visiting the Friedrichsbad in Baden-Baden.

The Birthday-Suit Girls reached his watery domain and he couldn't help himself. "Hi! Are you two from around here?"

They waded past him with only a faint upwards bend of the lip as a sign of acknowledgement. Reuben's telling eyes scanned their bodies like a barcode. His feelings had obviously veered from Bicycle Girl and his lucky lions.

Dejected, Reuben made a quick exit from the water and gathered his clothes on the way back to our picnic place. He was a sorry sight in his sopping Bugs Bunny boxer shorts, head hung low from striking out with the ladies.

I felt awful for my traveling companion, but all I could do was hand him a sandwich as consolation.

Reuben plopped his dripping body next to me, took the roll, and sensibly suggested we move on.

Page 8

Wasn't that an eye-opener? I thought it might liven up your lunch. Nude bathing is broadly accepted in Germany, and one of the nation's prime settings for this bare-all get-together is Munich's beloved English Garden.

Now, continue along the brook via the asphalt path; make your first left and cross over the bridge. Follow the path straight for about 5 minutes leading you out of the park and to a large fountain at the end of Veterinärstrasse, ultimately arriving at the 50,000-student University of Munich.

Here, you'll meet up with Ludwigstrasse — jump to the other side of the boulevard via the crosswalk on the right.

You are now on the side of the main university building with its striking Romanesque-style facade. Go left (being careful of bicyclists) then immediately right and follow the asphalt lane towards the building's entrance. Another fountain will be to your left, and the eight columns supporting the university's front facade will be getting closer in front of you. Take a seat on one of the first benches in front of the entrance and face the fountain. Once you're cozy, read Page 9.

As per Jesse's directions, we ambled through the park and over to the university, where we made ourselves comfortable on a bench in front of the entrance with Page 9 in hand.

Brett pictured in front of university

Page 9

I do apologize for the uncomfortable seats, but the following narrative will more than make up for it.

The square you are now in is Geschwister-Scholl-Platz — a strange name, I know, but not so strange once you understand its origin. The word Geschwister means "siblings," and the tragic story below dates to the nation's hellish past.

Hans and Sophie Scholl were exemplary students who lived defiant lifestyles. They attended studies at the university and walked the same cobblestones where your feet now rest. Both in their early twenties, Hans was a soldier and a medical student, while his sister Sophie explored courses in philosophy and biology.

It was the early 1940s. Germany was at war and Hans had seen conflict on both fronts, the Western and Russian. Hans returned to Munich disturbed by the atrocities he had witnessed and began to doubt the policies of his government.

Through social circles at the university he came in contact with fellow students and a member of faculty, Professor Kurt Huber, who had equal reservations about the Nazis.

With their mantra "We will not be silent," the newly formed alliance composed leaflets denouncing Hitler's regime, hoping to gain support for a popular uprising. Each new flyer was circulated a few thousand at a time, reaching all points in Germany, and some even found their way abroad.

Around this time (summer 1942), Sophie found out about the clandestine operation and demanded to join its ranks.

To make the resistance movement appear larger than it really was, they arranged for flyers to be distributed from other cities in Germany, which would also divert attention from their center of operations.

(Page 9 cont.)

For nearly a year the fledgling movement defied the system with impassioned words composed to incite insurrection against Nazi oppression. With the recurring waves of Allied bombers devastating German cities and the increasing setbacks on the Russian front, the nation's love affair with Hitler began to cool. The time was ripe to call the public to immediate action. Hans and another activist, Alexander Schmorell, set out with paintbrushes in hand and over the course of three nights graffitied anti-Nazi slogans on dozens of walls along main avenues. The resistance movement seemed to be gaining momentum, particularly after the shocking defeat of Germany's Sixth Army at Stalingrad (February 2, 1943).

Early on the morning of February 18, 1943, the labors of Hans and Sophie turned exceedingly audacious. For unknown reasons, perhaps out of desperation, they openly distributed the movement's leaflets (its sixth edition) in the very building behind you, leaving them on windowsills, along corridors, and in front of lecture room doors. As if it were a final gesture, they fervently tossed what remained of their flyers over the balconies like confetti. The spirited words of the movement gently cascaded through the air, decorating the floor below with neatly trimmed pieces of paper.

Among the curious students bending down to inspect the leaflets was the janitor, a Nazi sympathizer. Within minutes the university was in lockdown and the Gestapo (Secret State Police) were called to arrest the Scholl siblings. At first, the Gestapo felt they'd apprehended the wrong people, for Hans was a soldier in the Reich's army and Sophie was his younger sister. Nevertheless, the siblings stood defiant and admitted to their revolutionary actions. Four days later, after a bogus.

> (Page 9 cont.)
>
> trial, Hans and Sophie were found guilty of treason. That same afternoon they were beheaded by guillotine!
>
> Now you know the meaning of the square in which you sit, and in Germany today there are numerous cities and towns with streets and schools named in memoriam of the "Siblings Scholl." The resistance movement was called the "White Rose," and by your feet, embedded between the cobblestones, are replicas of the White Rose flyers and the heroic faces of its authors.
>
> Inside the university is a plaque dedicated to the principal members of the White Rose who, mournfully, were all put to death (listed here in order of execution date):
> - Hans Scholl: Sept. 22, 1918 † Feb. 22, 1943
> - Sophie Scholl: May 9, 1921 † Feb. 22, 1943
> - Christoph Probst: Nov. 6, 1919 † Feb. 22, 1943
> - Prof Kurt Huber: Oct. 24, 1893 † July 13, 1943
> - Alex Schmorell: Sept. 16, 1917 † July 13, 1943
> - Willi Graf: Jan. 2, 1918 † Oct. 12, 1943
> - Hans Leipelt: July 18, 1921 † Jan. 29, 1945

We got up immediately to investigate. Sure enough, the White Rose flyers were mere meters from our feet.

Reuben lowered to one knee for a closer look. I suggested we explore the interior of the university. He nodded and we made our way between the massive columns supporting the building's entrance and past billboards pinned to the brim with various advertisements for guitar lessons, shared accommodations, items for sale, cocktail party next Thursday.

On the other side of the entrance portal, the youthful scene of college students kicking around a hacky sack and playing bongo drums by the fountain yielded to an inspiring atmosphere of academia and antiquity. The staircase before us climbed to prominent statues of scholarly elders; their sculpted eyes kept watch over the structure's interior that was highlighted by more stylistic arches and bold pillars. Rays of sun beamed through sizeable windows that lit the central hall and surrounding balconies. Then we saw it: a plaque flush with flowers adorned the wall in front of us.

Steps cascaded from our plateau to the main floor, which was inlaid with cream and ash-gray ceramic tiles similar to those used by ancient civilizations to create patterns and designs. Reuben and I walked over slithering snakes, half-moon arches, even a freaky-headed Medusa before we reached the memorial.

On the wall were seven engraved names — I brushed the indentations with my forefinger — the last two were that of brother and sister Scholl.

Reuben and I gazed around the premises in reflection. I imagined Hans and Sophie hastily tossing the leaflets from the balcony above and watching them gently fall to the very floor on which we stood. Perhaps it was also here that the Gestapo apprehended the siblings before hauling them off to their brutal deaths.

"These seven young fighters are heroes in the name of humanity," I said, breaking the stillness while pointing to the memorial.

"My sentiments exactly. Hopefully in our next assignment we'll have time to drink a toast to Geschwister Scholl and company."

"Cheers to that!"

Page 10

Whew...what an emotional story. I'm glad you had the chance to experience the courageous actions of the White Rose.

Congratulations for reaching the last page in your 'Letter' escapade. I anticipate that you've enjoyed your jaunt through Bavaria's capital thus far. For your next installment of adventure, you'll be throwing on your research hat.

Exit Geschwister-Scholl-Platz right and head back into Old Town via Ludwigstrasse — you'll recognize the Feldherrnhalle ahead in the distance.

At the next traffic light go left, crossing over to the other side of the boulevard, then go right — you'll soon reach the Bavarian State Library (fronted by 4 Greek scholars), founded in the year 1558, which ranks among the most important repositories of knowledge on Earth with its astonishing collection of more than 10 million books, 50,000 periodicals, and the world's largest collected works of incunabula. Within this colossal building you're bound to find some info on the Bavarian Cross.

Lastly, after perusing the library, saunter over to the most famous beer hall in the world to experience some German culture. No doubt you deserve it! The tavern is called the Hofbräuhaus — just ask anyone where it is — locals and tourists alike can point the way. Enjoy your evening and have a stein for me.

Cheers, Jesse

The library, indeed, had a tremendous collection of knowledge. While I researched the crucifix, Reuben kept busy by thumbing through a provocative array of German fashion magazines.

Jesse was right. I did find some info on the Bavarian Cross. In fact, I found much more than I had anticipated. The crucifix doesn't date from the 19th century, as previously thought. It dates back to the 14th century! It was hard to fathom. My object of pursuit increased from precious to priceless in an afternoon.

In the year 1328, much of Central Europe had banded together to form the so-called Holy Roman Empire, which stretched from the North Sea to the Mediterranean. At this time the newly elected emperor to rule this vast territory was none other than Ludwig the Bavarian, the fairy-tale king's medieval ancestor.

Apparently, Ludwig the Bavarian was an extremely pious individual who believed the prosperity of his empire lay with a particular bejeweled crucifix made of gold given to him by Augustinian monks upon his coronation.

Ludwig referred to the cross as "das Bayernkreuz" and traveled with it everywhere while his kingdom flourished. One day Ludwig went on a hunting trip outside Munich without the crucifix and mysteriously dropped dead. Consequently, *das Bayernkreuz* vanished for some 550 years until it reappeared at Chiemsee in the 19th century. By that time the Holy Roman Empire had gone the way of the dodo bird and the ruler of the Bavarian kingdom was Ludwig II, better known as Mad King Ludwig, or the fairy-tale king.

Ludwig II somehow found *das Bayernkreuz* but then for whatever reason gifted it to the wine merchant's son, just as ShoSho had initially said. A month later, the king died. The official record of his death was "drowning." But after doing more research, it didn't add up.

When it was Ludwig's turn to wear the Bavarian crown in 1864, he did a rather sloppy job, as ruling a kingdom did not come naturally. Ludwig first sided with the Austrians against the Prussians, or northern Germans, in the Seven Weeks' War, then he sided with the Prussians against the French in the Franco-Prussian War. Ludwig was more of a romantic, a pacifist, and a lover of the arts than a warmonger. Instead of riding high on a horse and heroically leading armies into battle, Ludwig built castles. The most magnificent and luxurious in the land. Ludwig furnished them with colorful murals of Wagnerian operas and medieval themes, showpiece bedrooms and glitzy thrones, gaudy chandeliers and intimate grottos. However, this weird and wonderful lifestyle bankrupted the Bavarian economy. Add Ludwig's inept mode of leadership to the mix and you've got a motive for murder.

Behind his back, Ludwig's cabinet conspired against him. On June

12, 1886, they declared the king clinically insane and exiled him to Schloss Berg at Lake Starnberg, 25 kilometers southwest of Munich. The following day Ludwig drowned in knee-deep water in the lake, together with the psychiatrist who had certified him as insane. Not only did it seem amazing that two grown men simultaneously drowned in shallow water, but even more amazing for Ludwig, who was 6 feet 5 inches tall!

There had to be more to the story than accidental drowning. And why did Ludwig hastily give away the crucifix? Perhaps he knew someone was after him, or more precisely: after the Bavarian Cross!

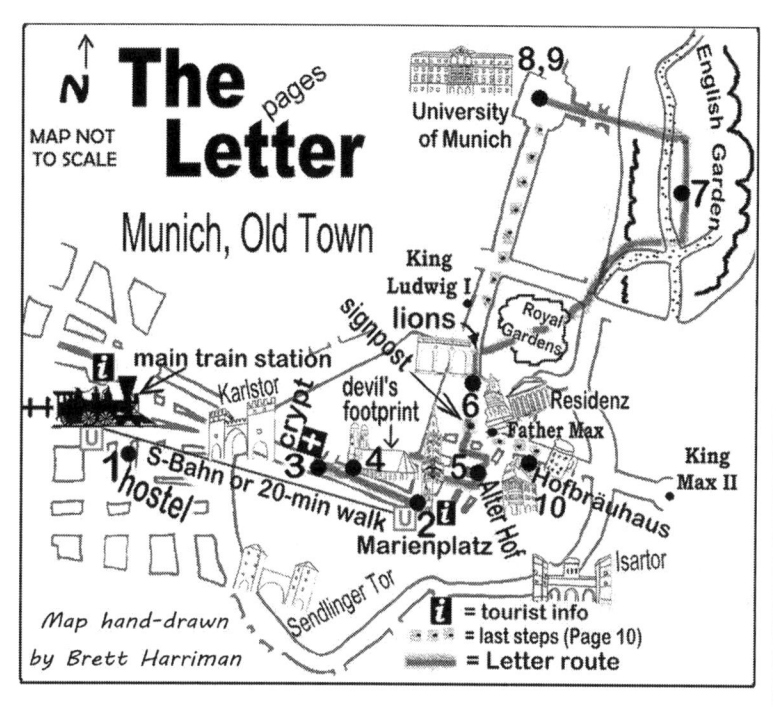

∞

Reuben stood idle as he scanned the cobbled lane. "There's the Hard Rock Cafe," he observed; his head swiveled like a periscope, "and... there's the Hofbräuhaus, the world's most famous beer hall."

The scene inside the cavernous hall was lively, and noisy! The steady sound of clinking glasses and the chatter of voices emanated from hundreds of people sitting elbow to elbow at long, picnic-style tables busily conversing while quaffing tankards of golden-colored beer.

Flanking the main aisle before us were four pillars rising to a ceiling splashed with colorful murals, and in the center of it all was a small stage laden with musical instruments that left hardly any room for their owners to play.

The only seats available were at a nearby table occupied by six people gleefully attending to their large, liter-sized beer mugs.

"Excuse me, are these seats available?" I asked no one in particular, gesturing to the vacancy either side of the table.

"Jawohl!" said the closest guy with a rosy-cheeked grin.

We weren't quite sure what "jawohl" meant, but by his friendly demeanor the answer had to be "yes."

While we were settling in, a buxom dirndl-clad waitress clutching fistfuls of frothy beers promptly marched over to our end of the table. "Was möchten Sie, bitte? Wir empfehlen Bier!" She delivered her spiel like bullets from a machine gun.

We must have looked perplexed, because our waitress rephrased her question: "Vhut you vant zu trink, pleez?"

"Zwei Bier, bitte," I replied, holding up two fingers to make sure my German translated. She lowered the beer to the table and released a pair of dimpled steins dripping with suds.

"Oh my gawd...so much love!" wailed the funky Californian.

"Good cheer by the liter," I noted. Although, I wondered whether Reuben's euphoric mood had anything to do with his eyes being buried in our waitress' cleavage.

First things first, we elevated our gargantuan mugs in a toast to the others at the table. "Prost," meaning cheers, we roared.

It took both my hands and stark concentration not to chip a tooth or drop the mug on my lap. Afterwards, through introductions totaling almost a liter of beer, we met Andreas and Kurt from Berlin; Verena and Marietta from Innsbruck, Austria; along with Gemma and Catherine from Australia.

Now was the time to have that drink in honor of the White Rose. Reuben and I faced one another and hoisted our steins once again. "Prost... to the White Rose!"

Andreas, Kurt, Verena, Marietta, Gemma and Catherine must have been listening, because they too raised their mugs and roared: "To the White Rose!"

The amber brew was undeniably making itself felt; things got nuttier by the hour. The Berliner boys were getting better acquainted with the Austrians and some guy from another table obnoxiously made himself comfortable next to Catherine. As for bonhomie Reuben, he made a play for her pretty pal.

"Hey, Gemma, where do you come from in Australia?"

She got up and moved next to Reuben, who began to sparkle with delight. "Byron Bay, two hours south of Brisbane," Gemma replied, emphasizing her harmonious accent.

"I think I've heard of that place."

"You have?!" She sounded thrilled.

"Yep, they have kangaroos there, right?"

Uh oh. Surely that didn't score him any points. He'll be lucky to get the rebound.

"We have a lot of wallabies in my area..."

Reuben unknowingly cut her off. "What's a wallaby?"

"They're ferocious creatures!" Gemma responded, sarcastically. "They have a tubby, long tail with monstrous hind legs, nimble feet and vicious forepaws."

"Wow!" he exhaled with startled eyes.

"Excuse me, I've got to go to the loo," Gemma said before getting up and venturing in the direction of the toilet.

Reuben eyed me, glumly. "She's not interested," he said.

"How can you tell?"

"Oh, I can tell...and she's not interested!"

"She'll be back," I reassured him.

"Girls don't like me," he woefully claimed.

"What do you mean...'girls don't like me'?"

"Exactly that."

"That's ridiculous!"

Interrupting our discourse, a folk band took the stage and began to play. I watched as rows of people locked arms and rocked back and forth. Others stood, swaying their mugs to the beat of the oompah-pah. An elderly gentleman with a green felt hat and handlebar moustache bought a pretzel from the mobile vendor to complement his beer. The frothy stuff flowed copiously and the mood was carefree. Some in the crowd decided to use the tabletop as a disco dance floor. Reuben McJiggy was soon waved down by security.

"Prost!" Another round of cheers shook the table.

"Albert, look," I happily announced, "Gemma's back!"

"Yeah, with a player in tow," Reuben stated, jumping to conclusions. "I bet that guy gets more ass than a toilet seat."

He was clearly disappointed, and intoxicated.

"Girls just don't like me. I've tried everything from brushing my hair in the opposite direction to an assortment of deodorants."

"Don't be so hard on yourself," I said. "If it's any consolation, when we first met, I saw you as a type of...Reubeniser."

This statement seemed to boost his spirits.

"Really!" he said, excitedly. "You mean like a guy the chicks dig?"

I nodded.

His eyeballs ballooned, ready to initiate liftoff. "I guess you're right, this isn't my first rodeo."

I wrapped my arm around Reuben's shoulders. "You see that pretty redhead over there?" I said, pointing to a girl sitting alone at a table full of revelers ignoring her company. He nodded. "Go over and cheer her up."

Reuben greeted the idea by jiggling his hand as if he'd burned his fingers on the flames of love. "Oh, baaaby!"

My suggestion took hold as he rose to his feet with the look of sheer confidence. Perhaps I had come to know my traveling companion almost too well, because as I watched his next move, I swore I could *hear* his drunken thoughts:

Mmm, Sydney was correct, this chick's the cat's meow. Here comes the Reubeniser to hand out some sweetness. "You mind if I sit here?"

"No, please do."

I situated myself next to her and began my spiel, "So..."

Not more than two nanoseconds had transpired when the game was visibly over. A guy approached, took her hand, and whisked her away. Just my luck, she was probably waiting for him to come out of the toilet.

Refreshingly, I was plucked from anonymity. A girl from the next table must have noticed the Reubeniser because she made an effort to lean my way and pierce the rhythmic clamor. "Hey. What's your name?"

"Albert Einstein. What's yours?"

"Sarah."

"What?" I couldn't hear her because the folk band suddenly got louder. I tried to explain with a wealth of words and a variety of hand expressions that I wasn't receiving her transmission.

She leaned over some more, reaching the vicinity of my ear and shouted: "My name is SARAH! Why don't you move over to my table?"

As she spat out the last sentence, the music stopped and a nosy few craned their necks in our direction with mischievous grins as if to say, 'Someone's gonna get lucky tonight!'

I nodded in response and redeployed to her table with brew in hand. We lifted our mugs in recognition of a newly formed friendship.

"Cheers!"

Sarah seemed the talkative type; an English chick from Cornwall, not one to set the world on fire, but hip just the same. We had a spirited conversation picking on each other's accents, my name, and peculiar British jargon. I must have really impressed her; before she left for the loo she kept referring to me as King Wanker. I was flattered to be associated with royalty.

Sydney appeared with a liquored smile. "Oh there you are, Albert. So, how ya doing with the ladies?"

"Sensational. I'm feelin' love in the air."

"Of course you are, you're a groovy guy." She put her arm around me again. You know what we haven't done yet?"

"What?"

"Had a toast on behalf of our thoughtful guide."

Without moving from our spot next to the souvenir stand selling Hofbräuhaus T-shirts and other logoed thingamabobs, Sydney hoisted her mug to offer a toast.

"Dear Jesse, thanks for the Letter, nothing could have been better. This is for you. Prost!"

There was one last thing to do: call my boss. Sydney and I belly laughed our way over to a pay phone, traversing through a gaggle of tipsy patrons doing the Chicken Dance to the beat of the oompah-pah. It was exactly how I imagined walking through the cafeteria of a mental hospital.

The phone ate sickening amounts of coinage before I heard my boss' voice. "Marine mammal care, this is Delphinus, the head trainer, how can I help you?"

"Del...it's Ruby!"

"Ruby, how are ya?"

"Good, Del. Good. Look, I gotta make this quick. I've got three Bavarian babes tugging at my lederhosen. I can't come to work on Monday. I'll see ya the following week, auf Wiederseh'n!" Click!

I hung up the phone and glanced at Sydney. "How was I?"

"Terrific! Now let's get outta here." She grabbed me and we whizzed out the door.

Back at the hostel, we tried to be as quiet as church mice — but to no avail. Sydney kept imitating the train conductor to an unfair advantage. In no way do I remember him having glistening hair that ceaselessly brushed against his breasts and a horrendously bad German accent with a beer-induced slur.

Before heading down the hallway in search of the john, I promised a swift return. When I came back, Sydney was fast asleep, tucked in like a baby. She looked prettier than ever.

∞

"Albert. Wake up. Albert!" His snoring was brutal, chasing away the other hostelers hours earlier.

"Huh, wha... leave me alone." Reuben pulled the covers over his head and continued snoring.

"Albert, we've overslept!" I shook him until a catastrophic 9 registered on the Californian's Richter scale.

The cleaning lady walked in, reminding me that it was 12:30 in the afternoon and, "If he doesn't get out of that bed in the next five minutes, management will have no choice but to drag him out onto the street by his schnitzel."

Then, as if smelling salts had been administered, there was life in the West Coast party animal. Reuben tiredly lifted himself up to his elbows and peeled open his sensitive, bloodshot eyes, resembling a vampire registering first light.

He then fell backwards onto the mattress as gracelessly as he'd raised himself up. "Oh, my pounding head." Reuben massaged his brow. Pillow creases defined his face.

"Are you okay?" I asked.

"My head's killing me."

Reuben tried desperately a second time to lift himself up. He succeeded, groggily exited the room, and headed along the hallway to the bathroom. He looked quite the sight with his beach-blonde hair standing on end, mouth wide open, yawning, wearing his Bugs Bunny boxer shorts.

A minute later there was a light knock at the door. Then it slowly opened. I figured it was the cleaning lady returning to make good on her schnitzel crusade.

A frail, elderly man with thin gray hair stepped into the room. His sagging face projected an unsettling, grim picture. I could only hope he was lost.

Without breaking eye contact, the frail man reached into the pocket of his woven sweater and pulled out a small piece of paper that had been folded in half. His hands trembled with every movement.

The man lifted up the piece of paper and held it in front of his wrinkly face. "Zis ist für you," he said.

I anxiously swiveled my head around to see who he was talking to, but I was the only one in the room. Of all the times for Reuben to be in the toilet, why now? Where was the cleaning lady?!

The man slowly extended his shaking hand outwards and gave me the paper. I warily opened it and read the contents:

> What you can't see can easily be found.

I didn't understand. What could this mean? I read it again. By the time I looked up, the man was gone. I charged out the door to try to catch him, but the hallway was empty. He had vanished!

Bulwarks and Mysteries
(Rothenburg ob der Tauber, Germany)

Chapter 8

*I*n some way, the Frail Man's note has to be connected to the Bavarian Cross. But how? Or maybe it's just me wanting to believe they're connected. I do know one thing for sure: this quest is beginning to drive me crazy. Totally crazy! I've paged through a mountain of old books, questioned what seems like half of Germany, worn fresh grooves into the cobbled lanes of nearby villages, burned the midnight oil surfing the Web, and I have nothing to show for it except strained eyes, sore feet, and a cleavage-enhancing Bavarian dress called a *dirndl* that Sep, a local fisherman, gave me because he thinks I'll look "wunderschön" in it at next week's yodeling and costume festival. Well, at least my German is improving.

What you can't see can easily be found ... What you can't see can easily be found ... I must have run those words through my head ten thousand times or more. And then, suddenly, it hit me. I dashed over to a neighbor's room who I knew had what I was looking for. She switched it on and, sure enough, the blacklight illuminated what could easily be found:

> What you can't see can easily be found.
> Dearest Investigators: Before a Brook and Forest
> Calculate Adventure 1010347000

The Frail Man's note was a clue within a clue. The second part was written with a special ultraviolet pen, whose marks are fluorescent and transparent. Now I knew it had something to do with the Bavarian Cross. The whole episode was too mysterious yet calculating to be otherwise. But why would the Frail Man want to help me? Maybe he didn't. Maybe it was a ruse. Maybe there are others involved. Enough gibberish. I've come too far to be talking nonsense.

Just when I thought all leads had dead-ended, a riddle and some numbers appear. Now I had something to really sink my teeth into. Wait till Jesse sees this. He'll be ecstatic. Good thing Reuben's not here. He would've flipped out.

Reuben has been gone for almost a month. Although, I'm sure he'll be back sometime soon. Indeed he chased up that dream date with Bicycle Girl, or the love of his life, whichever you prefer. Jesse and I didn't see him until two days after the big rendezvous. We began to get worried and planned a full-scale search of Munich, precisely when Reuben walked through the door grinning from ear to ear.

The day came when he had to fly home — and that was, to say the least, not a pretty sight. I thought my departure from Mom was a difficult one, but this airport episode proved to be even more draining. Reuben had fallen ass-over-tea-kettle in love, all right. Jesse, Bicycle Girl, and I bid farewell to him under a hail of hugs and kisses. Reuben wept virtually the entire time in the arms of his love, while Jesse and I received periodic attention. I figured corralling a band of wild horses would have been easier than saying goodbye to someone who could be "The One." When I told Jesse how they met, he smiled and sagely affirmed: "That's how you know it was meant to be."

We knew Reuben would've loved to have hit the road with us. However, going in spirit would have to suffice. Jesse asked me if I wanted to take a drive up north with him for a few days. His girlfriend, for some reason, wasn't going. Reuben had mentioned something about "trouble in paradise." I could only hope. There was no way I was going to pass up such a serendipitous opportunity.

The trip was research for one of the chapters in his travel book, with emphasis on the Valley of the Loreley. This is the castle-studded stretch of the Middle Rhine River from Bingen to Koblenz that recently joined the ranks of such unique and diverse places as the ancient pyramids of Giza and the Great Barrier Reef as an esteemed member of UNESCO's World Heritage List. Here we'd encounter picturesque hamlets and juicy vineyards adorning the riverbanks, as well as the famous Cat and Mouse castles, the bewitching legend of a maiden named Loreley, and a boat cruise likened to a mythical ride at Disneyland. I was especially looking forward to the latter, cruising back to a time when petty kings and ruthless robber barons occupied the magnificently medieval castles that crowned the unassailable bluffs. I even packed my bikini for the sundeck.

Then, despite the lure of the Loreley, our plans changed. The night before our departure I was dissecting the new clue, as usual, but this time I felt confident that I had flipped the numbers just the right way and possibly had solved the riddle. The only problem was that I wouldn't know for sure whether I had cracked the code unless I went to where the clue pointed.

I immediately ran to Jesse's room and briefed him on my discovery. I didn't go into specifics. We'd have plenty of time for that on the road. Moreover, I was too anxious to think clearly. With what information I did impart, Jesse was convinced my findings carried enough weight to warrant a change in plans.

Courtesy of the Frail Man, the Rhine River got relegated to another day and our next installment of adventure led Jesse and me to a new destination: Rothenburg ob der Tauber, a walled community dating from the Middle Ages situated on Germany's Romantic Road.

Jesse calculated our drive to Rothenburg would take about four hours. We decided to leave early to get a full day's sightseeing in along the way. Our first stop: Augsburg, 60 kilometers northwest of Munich.

∞

It was a sunny and warm day in August with few clouds in a blue sky. The once snow-capped Alps revealed their solid-rock crests. Balmy summer gusts ruffled the tea-green grass carpeting the velvety pastures. Due to the proximity of Augsburg, the camera-friendly backdrop gradually changed from delightfully rustic to densely urban. Golden fields of wheat yielded to endless lengths of sagging power lines supported by monstrous steel structures crisscrossing the landscape.

Commercialism prevailed over rural harmony while automobiles clashed at intersections. All northbound traffic merged onto the city streets. We knew the old town was close, but exactly where remained unclear. The dizzying array of directional signs ultimately brought us to the periphery.

Jesse couldn't contain his enthusiasm. "Augsburg, a settlement that rings loudly in the history books. It's one of the three oldest cities in Germany and was named after its founding father, Roman Emperor Augustus, in 15 B.C."

How appropriate it was to be in Augsburg in August, since both were christened after the gallivanting Augustus. No doubt I wanted to know more. I could see Jesse waiting for the call. "What else can ya tell me?"

"Since you asked...Augsburg in the late 15th century, already having a population of 50,000, became a center for high finance. Nowadays we hear about the European Central Bank; then it was the Fuggers."

Here I had to giggle. The name sounded corny.

The traffic light turned green and Jesse motored ahead. Thick metropolitan air circulated through the car.

"The Fugger family was a dynastic authority commanding the wealth of an empire, financing the Habsburgs themselves. The Habsburgs frequently held the throne of the Holy Roman Empire, influencing power over Western Europe. In those days, imperial diets, or assemblies, of the kingdom were held here...for example, the Augsburg Confession and the Augsburg Peace."

I recall Jesse identifying the First Reich as being the Holy Roman Empire founded by Charlemagne, but the Augsburg something or other was news to me. "What were the latter two?"

"You've heard of Martin Luther and the Reformation, right?"

"Right, but not in detail."

"Well, late in the Middle Ages, scholars began assessing translations of the Bible along with other documentation that shaped the foundations of church doctrine and ritual. In the mid-15th century, Johannes Gutenberg revolutionized publishing with the invention of the printing press, giving innovators a new mass media to work with to spread ideas quicker. One such innovator was Martin Luther, a theologian who popularized the theory of religious freedom when he nailed his Ninety-Five Theses to the door of the Castle Church in Wittenberg. To cut a long story short, the Church of Rome held a monopoly on the Christian faith. But Luther believed that it was the Bible, God's words...rather than the church...that should be the source of religious authority." Jesse turned to me for a split-second to see if I was paying attention before fixing his eyes back on the road and continuing.

"Luther's liberal philosophy of guidance by faith alone struck a powerful chord with commoners, and in the thousands they began to sever their allegiance to the Church of Rome, which in turn spread rebellion across the northern parts of the empire. The rulers unsuccessfully tried to quell the people's uprising and the Augsburg Confession, a summary of the new Lutheran faith, was presented here in the year 1530 to German nobility. The convention was a landmark event. While nobles conferred within their posh chambers, Luther's followers were protesting on the streets demanding freedom of religion. For this reason, Lutherans also became known as Protestants. Nevertheless, the emperor rejected Lutheranism as a legitimate faith, and consequently their struggles raged on." Jesse paused and I seized the opportunity for a question.

"Does that mean the battle for religious freedom was fought here?"

"No, that battle was fought throughout the land. In fact, it wasn't until some 25 years later that the emperor, due to diminishing support, felt obliged to end the religious civil war by supporting the Augsburg Peace. This meant that Protestants finally gained official status and the concept of a solitary Christian community in Western Europe under the supreme authority of the Pope...was over, whereby the ruler of a territory now determined the religion of his subjects."

"Is it possible to see the signing chambers?"

"I read that they don't exist anymore..." he double blinked, "but we'll investigate."

"I wish my parents were here to witness the history." I eyed Jesse with a childish grin. "Do you think we could stop so I can pick up a postcard to send the folks?"

He must have been reading my mind, because at that moment Jesse pulled in front of a souvenir shop. Its windows displayed molded Martin Luther figurines, beer steins with pewter lids, and rigid mannequins modeling T-shirts featuring rotund monks with slogans such as *Stay away from the friars — the Augsburg Diet, since 1530.*

Out front tourists were busily thumbing through the revolving postcard stands, giving each a few squeaky twirls. Walking past, a vivid illustration caught my roving eye. "Hey! Check this out."

"Oh, yeah...that's right," Jesse confirmed. "Mozart's father, Leopold, was born here in Augsburg."

This was excellent. I had found a postcard showing Leopold as a youngster playing violin on the market square. I knew Mom would be thrilled to receive it. The shop lady, noticing our interest in the history of her city, provided us with directions to sites uptown, downtown, and all around. The Fuggerei was one of those sites, and the closest.

The architecture of the immediate area was indicative of contemporary design until we reached a gated community called the Fuggerei, which I learned dated to the year 1521 when Fugger the Rich founded a welfare district to house the poor. With its 67 ivy-covered row houses nestled on quaint lanes, the Fuggerei is the oldest existing social housing complex in the world. Amazing, for sure, but probably more so is the fact that its residents still pay the same rent today as set in the 16th century, the equivalent to one Rheinischer Gulden, or 88 cents, per year.

Our few hours tooling around Augsburg proved fruitful. Other than the Fuggerei — which by the way cost Jesse and me four euros each for admission, essentially more than four times the annual rent for residents — we discovered original documentation pertaining to the Reformation in St. Anna's Church as well as a plaque near the cathedral commemorating the spot where the Augsburg Confession was proclaimed.

During our travels we noticed that Augsburg had triple the amount of parking-enforcement officers than any normal city, but our passing observation couldn't compare to the scrumptious food stand that our noses led us to dishing up the Fugger lunch special: bratwurst smothered in sauerkraut, topped with mittelscharf mustard.

Upon our return to the car, we became aware that the city, to express its deepest appreciation for our visit, had left us a 30-euro parking ticket, payable at any police station. There, we learned why Augsburg had so many traffic wardens. The darned "academy" is located here!

Tickets and enforcement officers aside, it was time to concentrate on our destination: Rothenburg. On our way out of town, Jesse expressed concern. "I'm sorry we didn't have time to track down Leopold Mozart."

"That's okay. I'll be back. Besides, I'm already more than grateful for everything you're showing me."

"It's my pleasure," Jesse replied, turning my way with his megawatt smile. "Say, did someone teach you that flattery will get you everywhere?"

"Sure did." I relish any chance for a memory of my sweet grandmother, who has since passed. "Speak of angels and they shall enlighten your path."

We respectfully left the time-honored city of Augsburg behind us. Our northerly route opened to a four-lane highway that wasn't much different from one back home. This continued until we crossed the Danube at Donauwörth. The river flowed with moderate strength and its width was unremarkable. If you weren't paying attention, you'd easily miss one of the three great waterways of Europe.

The highway began to climb above Donauwörth, providing us with hurried glimpses of a community clinging to the banks of its commercial lifeline.

As we descended from the ridge, Donauwörth's pitched terracotta roofs and soaring church steeple gradually disappeared and the four-lane highway narrowed into a popular country excursion. The geography ahead presented a delightful portrait of green rolling hills sprinkled lily white with sheep. The world of modern conveniences fell centuries to our rear and the Romantic Road was beginning to make sense.

Around the following bend, we saw an intimidating fortress perched upon the hill. It was a stark reminder of the Middle Ages, when this road was a major trade route. Below its ramparts rested a picturesque hamlet split by a gently flowing stream. We motored up the hill and were met at the summit by a yellow sign marking the village limits of Harburg.

Townships napping in the afternoon sun flanked us. To our right, a meandering rivulet cut a channel through the shallow marshland. On the horizon came the village of Hoppingen and beyond it a land formation Jesse dubbed Peak Peppermint Patty, a distinctive knoll sporadically tattooed with stumpy pine trees.

I couldn't imagine why Jesse picked that name for the knoll, so I asked him.

He replied, "Doesn't it remind you of the freckle-faced character in the *Peanuts* comic strip?"

"No doubt you have an active imagination."

The next sight along our route required little imagination. The conspicuous bell tower soaring above the walled community of Nördlingen was visible from several miles away. Jesse told me the 90-meter-tall tower is named "Daniel" and from its lofty perch a whopping 110 villages can be counted on a clear day. He continued to say that from this vantage point Nördlingen's resident night watchman, the last full-time civil position of its kind in Germany, howls "So G'sell so" every evening from 10 p.m. till midnight on the hour and half hour.

This didn't mean a whole lot to me until he emphasized the legendary call dated from the year 1440 when the gatekeepers of the Löpsinger Tor were bribed by the powerful Count von Oettingen to leave the Tor, or gate, unlocked so he could return later with his troops and pillage Nördlingen. In the dark of the night, while the count quietly approached with his army, a passerby noticed the gate was unlocked and shrieked *So G'sell so,* meaning: 'Ah ha, you've been caught!'

The citizen guard was rallied and defensive positions were bolstered. Hence, the pending invasion was thwarted and the gatekeepers executed. From this incident forward, *So G'sell so* has been sounded through the ages by local night watchmen as a caution to gatekeepers and tower sentries to be vigilant on their watch, as well as a reminder that traitors pay with their lives.

At closer inspection, Nördlingen seemed to be a throwback from the Dark Ages, Asian style. Massive pagoda-like watchtowers with upward-curving roofs jutted into the baby-blue sky. Imperial eagle crests were plastered onto the thick, ashlar stone. We paralleled the town's fortifications, moat, and modern sprawl until tranquil green fields again bound our path.

Interestingly, Ries county in which Nördlingen is located is widely known by geologists and meteoriticists alike because of a terrestrial impact. According to a reliable source, the region was struck some 15 million years ago by a blazing meteorite thought to be traveling at 20 kilometers per second and discharging a massive amount of energy equal to 1 million Hiroshima-type atomic bombs, which penetrated a depth of three football fields and created a prehistoric crater 25 kilometers in diameter. In medieval times, residents of Nördlingen mined the crater and built many of the town's original structures with the extraterrestrial material known as *Suevit*.

Although hardly noticeable to the general tourist, the vast Ries impression is regarded as one of the best-preserved craters on Earth. For this reason, NASA sent astronauts from the Apollo space program to the Ries in 1970 on field exercises. As a "thank you" for the generous hospitality offered by the locals, the Apollo 14 team donated a moon rock to the town of Nördlingen.

We didn't have time to visit the town museum exhibiting the lunar rock but I knew I'd be back, soon. For now, Rothenburg was calling.

Our route took us through the next village, where a column stood in the middle of the road, almost as an obstruction. Jesse explained it was a remembrance of plague. Many townships vowed to commemorate their deliverance from the deadly epidemic by erecting something of stature.

That was Wallerstein, another traditional hamlet we left behind in favor of a breathtaking vista. Farmers were active in these parts; adequate time had passed for them to safely go beyond their walled communities and cultivate the surrounding land.

The smell of recently mowed grass lingered in the air. A slick tractor with rotary arms dispersed the young hay for drying, while in the neighboring pasture a man wearing black

Bulwarks and Mysteries

rubber boots, shabby jeans, and a plaid shirt with rolled-up sleeves stood bent over, raking the grass into piles by hand.

Farther ahead a fertilizer truck spewed its contents onto the fields, reminiscent of a skunk dousing its victim. I was a tad worried Jesse might lose consciousness from the ghastly odor leaving us in the precarious position of a pilotless vehicle. This was the perfect time to fill Jesse in on the details of my findings regarding the Frail Man's code. His cryptic language had been tough to crack.

> What you can't see can easily be found.
> Dearest Investigators: Before a Brook and Forest Calculate Adventure 1010347000

At first I explored the numbers as a possible telephone sequence, but that went nowhere. Then, I scrutinized the numbers as a probable credit card or bank account. Still nothing, but I couldn't be sure. I had to delve further, so I put the digits aside and concentrated on the riddle, which appeared to be a pretty straightforward message. Wherever the clue pointed was likely to be near a brook and forest. But how did the rest translate?

Another option was to convert the riddle into digits, such as A equals 1, B equals 2, or the reverse sequence Z equals 1, Y equals 2, and so forth. Since there were so many alphanumeric combinations, I had to put emphasis on the capital letters, which seemed to be a logical call. When starting with the front-end of the alphabet, I got the configuration: 4922631. So I thought, great, more numbers to add to the ones I already have and don't know what to do with.

After fiddling with corkscrew reasoning that induced umpteen bouts of brain strain, I came up with something that seemed to make sense. However, in a blur of sleepless nights, nothing made sense.

Anyhow, I scoured numerous puzzle Web sites. All contributed bits of useful information. Although, one site stood out concerning geocaching. These folks found hidden treasures via Global Positioning System, or GPS, which is a satellite-based navigation system maintained by the U.S. government. In essence, some 12,000 miles above Earth, there are upwards of 31 operational satellites that orbit us twice daily and are used for determining precise points on a map. To lock into these satellites all that is required is a handheld GPS receiver, which essentially acts as a high-tech compass.

When comparing the digits I now had with those used for GPS, I still had nothing. Unless, I dropped the last three zeros. Then the enigmatic sequence became explicit coordinates to four worldwide locations, depending on the directions used. For example, if the numbers were married with a point south of the equator and east of the prime meridian, the coordinates point to somewhere around South Africa. Digits wedded to south and west drown in the Atlantic Ocean, north and west land in Ireland, but when the Frail Man's digits were coupled with north and east, they point to not-so-far-away Rothenburg: N49 22.631 E10 10.347.

I had two options: treat the whole GPS coordinates mumbo-jumbo as a coincidence and continue to decipher the code, or get off my duff and head north to possibly solve this mind-numbing quest. I had to consider that not only did the digits jibe, so did the riddle: Dearest could be likened to romantic, as in road, and Calculate to coordinates. What's more, Rothenburg's complete name is "ob der Tauber," meaning on the Tauber River, which could represent the Brook. In the end, all the telltale signs seemed convincing enough — thus the last thing I did before we hit the road was swing by the hotel's engineering department to borrow a GPS receiver.

According to our map, the next community was Dinkelsbühl. The town's posted boundaries whizzed by, in addition to the 'reduce your speed' sign. Jesse slowed the car and we were instantly awestruck by Dinkelsbühl's dramatic movie-set feel. Authentic to its roots, this castle town was no doubt the embodiment of medieval drama and intrigue. Perhaps there was a damsel in distress waving a white hanky from one of the towers, or was it home to the Holy Grail? We decided to take a closer look.

High sentry towers — solid bastions outfitted with strategically placed loopholes for sharpshooters — sat menacingly above Dinkelsbühl's fortified walls. Some defense positions were backed up by even thicker walls, creating a daunting No Man's Land in between.

Tucked within the fortifications was an impressive Gothic cathedral whose steeple towered above a sea of red-roofed dwellings that cluttered the skyline like ill-managed dominoes. Inside, the cathedral was vast and awe inspiring. Midway along its right aisle, we discovered the encased relics of St. Aurelius, executed because of his Christian faith nearly 2,000 years ago in Rome at the command of Emperor Nero.

Although the cathedral sat at the confluence of four quaint lanes, Jesse told me streets like these in medieval times were hardly charming. Rubbish, sewage, muck and debris from both humans and farm animals, like chickens and goats, littered the cobbles. When it rained, water would wash the filth away. But if there was even a brief drought, or say a string of hot sunny days in summer, a foul stench would permeate the town. The rich folks residing in their patrician houses had the luxury of moving out to their country estates to escape figurative asphyxiation.

While the retched odor and swarming flies weren't lethal, the thousands of rodents — for example rats attracted by the unsanitary conditions — were. Since towns across Europe dealt with their sewage in a similar manner, most everyone was affected when diseased fleas carried by these rodents transferred to humans, kick-starting a killing machine that accounted for scores of the population in what incurably became known as the Black Death.

On a cheerier note, Jesse bought me two scoops of homemade strawberry ice cream in a cone from a nearby parlor. That concluded our history-drenched tour of Dinkelsbühl. We exited town via its bumpy cobbles leading through the longstanding Wörnitz gate.

Today, the battlements of Dinkelsbühl are at peace. Well, almost. The only unfolding struggle was that of three ducks squawking over what appeared to be mating rights in the otherwise stagnant moat that brushed against the fortified walls, shielding the populace from savage armies and, evidently, horny ducks.

We were to encounter two more towns before reaching our overnight destination. The first was called Feuchtwangen, which Jesse said translated to "moist cheeks." This made me wonder whether the town had themed street names, like Perspiration Avenue or Lustrous Lipstick Lane.

The next town had a less imaginative name: Schillingsfürst, or Prince Schilling. No wonder Dinkelsbühl had such prominent fortifications. With the likes of a crowned head and the Moist Cheeks as neighbors, it would undeniably be a wise decision to keep one's guard up.

Jesse laughed at my determination to make sense of all the oddities and then imparted a fast-food analogy. "How about the northern German city of Hamburg? Imagine the names of its streets: Mustard Road, Pickle Place, Veggie Burger Drive."

Damn, his voice was starting to make me melt like the cheese on a grilled sandwich. My focus returned to the road when the car suddenly jerked. I gripped the armrest as Jesse steered through a swarm of locust just outside Moist Cheeks.

Prince Schilling was somewhat kinder; there we only mingled with misfortune when a fox ran in front of the car causing Jesse to momentarily swerve onto an adjacent pasture. Otherwise, the times and troubles on Route 25 were simply *wunderbar*.

It was a delight meandering through a countryside standing firm against the greedy desires of would-be property developers seeking to profit from shopping malls and apartment complexes.

Picture-perfect villages accentuated the cinematic landscape, each having something unique to offer: a thin bell tower rising above an ancient church, a charming collection of wood-beamed houses, a muscle-flexing castle. More churches, more walled towns, more green fields — anywhere else and it could have been construed as an overdose of culture, but not here — this was the Romantic Road.

"Do you think you'll renew your work contract after the 13 months are up?" asked Mister Curious.

"I've been wondering that myself lately," I said. "No doubt I've enjoyed my overseas break, and being a chambermaid certainly has had its moments, but I'm thinking about going back to school."

"In the States?" Jesse asked, looking stricken.

"No, I'm toying with the idea of attending a study abroad program over here. That way I can kill two birds with one stone. Dad will be happy that I'm back in college...and I can stay in Europe!"

Jesse's grin returned. "That would be perfect. How about the University of Gibraltar?"

"Gibraltar." I raised an eyebrow. "Why Gibraltar?"

"Well...you can go to Morocco whenever you want."

"Morocco. What's in Morocco?"

"Snake charmers in Marrakech."

"That's it, sold!"

"Really?!" He sounded surprised.

Bulwarks and Mysteries

I was kidding, of course. So far, Vienna's academic program topped my list of prospects.

Out the window I was distracted by a curious sight that I've been confronted with way more than I'd like since arriving in Europe. "There's another one," I uttered under my breath.

Rows of cornstalks in the sun-drenched field were at least 6 feet tall, but there was no confusing the figure I saw before them: a guy tactfully peeing at the road's edge, which wasn't very tactful at all.

"Another one what?" Jesse asked, his bionic hearing tuned in.

"Another guy with a bursting bladder."

"Oh, that." Jesse laughed at my alien view of the local custom before explaining: "It's legal, as long as your back is against traffic."

"Hmm."

Upon our approach to Rothenburg, images of peeing men were replaced by sprawling crop fields, grazing cows, and a string of tourist buses congesting the road. This was a popular town to say the least. I'd never seen so many buses in one location. If German fortresses were royalty, I would have to say Rothenburg was king.

We paralleled the town's extensive fortified wall before making a left turn at a junction with a quirky name, Vorm Würzburger Tor. Here we parked outside the main gate and agreed to sightsee Rothenburg on foot.

On the other side of the fortified wall, Jesse and I witnessed the Middle Ages magically preserved in the midst of a modern world. At any moment we half expected to find villagers queuing to pay their tithes, costumed acrobats performing gymnastic feats for titled heads, or blacksmiths hammering iron by their charcoal-fired forges.

We wandered along cobblestone thoroughfares and crooked lanes flanked by flower boxes, bay windows and wrought-iron signs extending from lopsided, half-timbered houses. If one could realistically walk through a postcard, this was it.

In this quaint must-see community, pedestrians were king of the road. Cars were either parked or driving very slowly. Jesse and I couldn't believe our eyes; it was like being in an open-air museum, a thriving medieval settlement inside turreted walls. I walked in wonderment, just one in a procession of awed visitors.

It was getting late and our first goal was to find lodging. The steady flow of vacationers anxious to spend their money led us past a gazillion shops to the main square, where we noticed a sign pointing to tourist information.

Jesse entered through an archway and I followed. The door to the tourism office was locked. On it a sign read, *Closed 6 p.m.*

Jesse glanced at his watch. It read 6:05.

Thoughtfully for us latecomers, fixed to the opposite wall was a large town map having an accommodations directory with hotel information, prices, and availability.

We skimmed the list of room rates that ranged from 60 to 200 euros per night.

"How about this place, Gästehaus Raidel?" Jesse asked, referring to a bed-and-breakfast situated in the middle of Rothenburg.

I gave Jesse the thumbs-up and we sped off. In search of what we hoped to be our night's lodging, my sidekick and I made our way past the market square and down the main drag, Obere Schmiedgasse. Here we saw a succession of shops selling a plethora of wares: artwork, souvenirs, T-shirts, chocolate pastries, Erich Trumpp's Franconian sausages, mock medieval weaponry, even a suit of armor. And did I mention souvenirs?

Farther down, we swung left on Wenggasse and through the arched doorway of the handsome half-timbered gasthaus. The innkeeper, Herr Raidel, a reserved man in his late-60s who spoke softly in broken English, offered to show us a room upstairs.

The staircase creaked with every step. Herr Raidel told us his house was built some six centuries ago. It was hard to fathom a place so old, and still standing. But no doubt this historic residence looked adorable, exuding cartloads of character and old-world charm. We passed common areas delightfully furnished with antiques and paintings on the way up to the second floor that held the last available room, a clean and comfy twin with polished wood-framed beds and fixtures that Herr Raidel himself said he had crafted by hand.

We pivoted to our skillful host and told him we were sold. He smiled, and handed us the key. Jesse asked Herr Raidel about parking and if he had any recommendations for dinner. He responded by spreading out a town map across an antique table and showing us a nearby place to park, his favorite restaurant, and a few local attractions, including where to meet the Night Watchman's tour.

Since it was getting late and the tourist to-do list sounded appealing, we decided to postpone our search for the Bavarian Cross until first thing in the morning. Moreover, our GPS receiver pointed the Frail Man's coordinates to a location in a non-populated, forested area outside Rothenburg's defense walls, which could be a tad spooky at night.

We offered Herr Raidel our thanks and left to pick up the car. En route, Jesse spotted a Vinothek and suggested he buy us a bottle of wine for later.

I didn't pay much attention to his proposal because I thought I'd noticed something peculiar: a person trailing our every move, peering from street corners.

"Jesse, look!" I pointed. "There...that person by the bakery."

Confused, Jesse whipped his head around to eye the direction in which my finger pointed.

The mystery man disappeared. I ran to the bakery, scanned the adjacent lane but it was empty, as were the other side streets. When I returned, Jesse wore a perplexed look. He asked me if everything was okay.

I reassured him I was fine and that perhaps I was just seeing things.

Jesse nodded, then repeated his previous suggestion. "How 'bout a bottle of wine? That'll remedy strained eyes."

"If it's a red...you've got a deal." I reached out my hand to shake on our agreement.

Jesse and I got a little medievally lost on the way back to the car, not remembering which parapet we parked near. We must have looked pretty funny bouncing between bulwarks, bastions and battlements while brandishing a bottle of Burgundy.

We got in the car, but this time our drive was to take us through the main gate and onto Rothenburg's antiquated streets. Regardless of Herr Raidel's assurance, it was still rather strange to cruise cobbled lanes that were once trod by Teutonic knights.

Maneuvering through the droves of dawdling tourists wasn't easy. At times it seemed as if we were herding cattle. Dozens retreated to the sidewalks while the occasional disgruntled sightseer gave us a dirty look for the inconvenience. But what else could we do except drive slowly, and smile.

In addition to umpteen pedestrians, I noticed there were an inordinate amount of fountains in Rothenburg. Jesse emphasized that because most sizeable communities in the Middle Ages consisted of narrow streets lined by wood-framed houses, fire posed a constant threat. In order to keep the blazing danger in check, as well as to maintain a running water supply for residents, numerous fountains were constructed.

Jesse then pointed through the windshield to a tall house coming up on the right. He instructed me to eye the wooden beam jutting from its gable. The beam and attached wheel, he said, is part of a pulley system to hoist grain up from the street to be stored in the loft. Interestingly, these beam-and-wheel winch contraptions were installed throughout Rothenburg during medieval times because each household was required to store at least a year's supply of grain in case of an enemy siege. That certainly sounded more arduous than a trip to Costco.

Finding a parking space was relatively easy compared with reaching it. Jesse stopped briefly in front of the gasthaus to unload our bags; he then continued up the road to chase a space. He was soon back and I had our belongings situated in the room. Jesse suggested food and I couldn't have agreed more. I was famished.

One of Herr Raidel's recommendations was the local Franconian wine house tucked away on a quaint lane. The restaurant's facade was unmistakable, creeping with ivy and having a wrought-iron sign hanging over the door publicizing its trade. The interior was engagingly rustic and bordered on hopelessly romantic, glowing with candlelit tables for two. Light strains of Vivaldi danced through the air.

The hand-prepared entrées and Franconian wine were delectable. We finished our meals as the time struck 7:45 and dusk began its course.

The Night Watchman's tour kicked off on the hour in the Market Square and we didn't want to be late. By the time we arrived, numerous people in cliques of twos and threes were already patiently waiting for the English-speaking tour to begin.

At the stroke of 8, the Night Watchman appeared. Jesse nudged me with his elbow. "Get a load of this guy."

A lantern swayed from his fingertips as he approached, causing the flame to flicker with every footstep. The palm of his other hand clutched a deadly hatchet-head lance. His dark and mysterious guise was enhanced by an all-black uniform: pants, boots, long-sleeved shirt, floor-length cape — a medallion and an ebony horn hung from his neck. He was of average build about 6 feet tall with a full, dark-brown beard and shoulder length, tousled hair that was partially covered by his pilgrim hat.

He introduced himself as the Night Watchman and explained that only the gravedigger and village executioner were lower on the community social scale than he was.

Beneath the town hall are dark and clammy dungeons, he said, where lawbreakers were tortured until they confessed, at which point they were brought up to the Market Square, locked in stocks and pelted with rotten tomatoes, or worse. The Night Watchman then pointed to the two open windows on the clock tower displaying unremarkable wooden figures reenacting the so-called "Master Draft." This is the Protestant story of Rothenburg's deliverance from total ruin in 1631 during the Thirty Years' War, when the magnanimous general of the invading Catholic army offered to spare the stronghold if a town councilor could chug a gallon of wine.

The mayor accepted the challenge and miraculously drank the tankard dry. With tipsy success, Rothenburg was saved and the legend of the Master Draft was born. Hearsay suggested the mayor was seen later that evening at Hell wine tavern hitting on the "iron maiden" before passing out on the torture rack while the gravedigger danced his way past elated merchants, clerics, blacksmiths, tanners, bell ringers, rope makers, seamstresses, fortune tellers, potters, stone masons, wenches, and humble street cleaners feasting and celebrating their newly won independence.

The Night Watchman's tour traversed darkened streets, marched across a drawbridge, paralleled bulwarks, and strolled past half-timbered houses standing side by side like books on a chock-full shelf. Our discoveries included a medieval manhole, a Gothic doorbell, and a sinister stone mask chiseled high on the tower gate designed to inform would-be invaders that their evil actions will be rewarded with a cleansing river of hot oil raining down upon them courtesy of the local neighborhood watch association.

The hour whizzed by faster than a full-throttled Porsche on the autobahn. We wrapped up the tour at the entrance to Hell, a historic wine tavern. The majority of the crowd dispersed while a few lingered to chat with the black-caped raconteur.

Jesse had other ideas. "What do you say we take care of that bottle of red?"

I agreed, and we retraced the Night Watchman's route down Herrngasse and into the Castle Garden. Along the way we politely asked a restaurateur if he could open our bottle of wine. We didn't have the nerve to ask for paper cups as well.

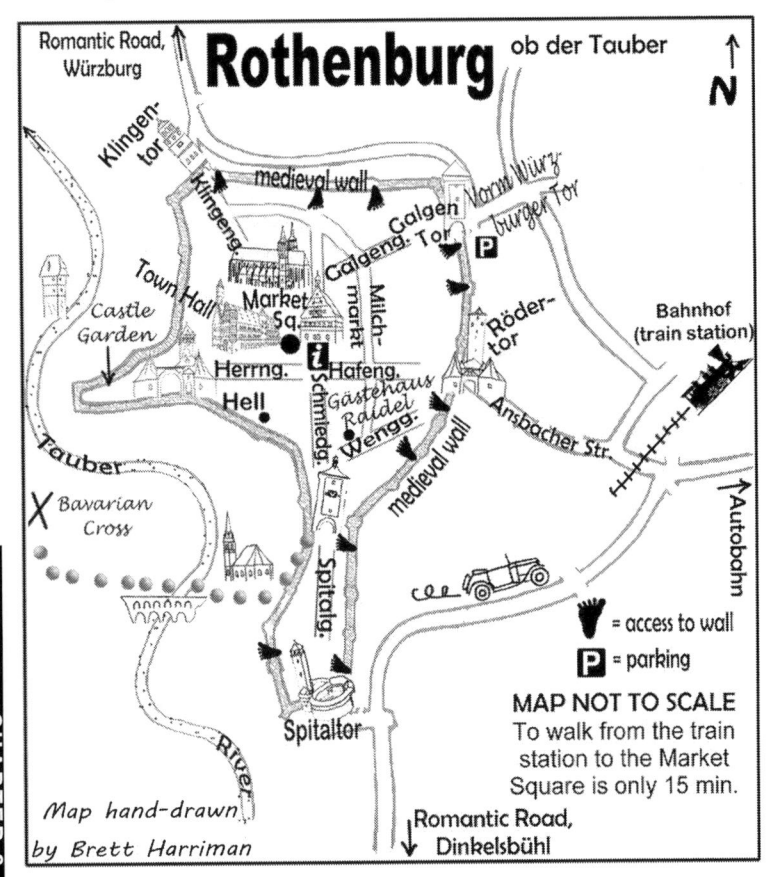

If you think of Rothenburg as shaped like a pork chop, the Castle Garden sat on the western tip of its mid-section and overlooked the handle of the bone.

Gazing south at the handle yielded a breathtaking view of Rothenburg. It was the quintessential storybook setting with its silhouetted collage of turrets and towers and tilted roofs against the twilight sky.

Rothenburg was arguably the capital of medieval highlights — most I'd never heard of, but I certainly won't forget them any time soon.

To take best advantage of the view, we hoisted ourselves onto a waist-high stone wall that was half a meter in width. We watched Germany's version of Camelot twinkle under a canopy of stars from our enchanting location.

I wished I could capture the magic of this moment in a photograph to mail home, but that would be impossible. One has to experience it for themselves.

I sneaked a peek at Jesse and wondered if Mom would approve of him. Stupid notion; of course she would.

"I'd like to propose a toast," I said.

"Please do."

"I'd like to drink to Dolores and Sid, my thoughtful parents. How can I convey to you, Mom and Dad, what I saw today in an e-mail or over the phone? Encountering millennium-old castles and towns that look more like digitally created location sets for the movie 'Braveheart' than tangible reality."

Jesse expressed the rest. "To Mr. and Mrs. Endicott," he raised the Burgundy, "may your health allow you to be as spunky and spirited as your daughter so you, too, may come here one day and delight in your own magical moments."

Jesse handed me the bottle, smiling. The moon shone full, accentuating his alluring presence.

Beneath us, in the ravine, the Tauber River snaked a path around Rothenburg. The town was partly built on a plateau and the ledge upon which the fortifications rested fell sharply into the watercourse below.

Jesse lifted his head from staring into the river's current. He asked me a question. "What's big on your to-do list...I mean, besides the quest for the Bavarian Cross, do you have any other pursuits?"

"Yeah. I'd love to travel all over Europe. I'm especially looking forward to visiting Berlin."

"Ah...the capital of Germany," he stated, reacting as if it were a revelation, bobbing his head and gazing at the stars.

"I've heard the city is fascinating, constantly reinventing itself," I said, "a place where you don't just see the history, it's happening before your very eyes. They say if you stand still long enough, you'll miss the latest changes."

"Yes. True." Jesse was still profoundly absorbed in thought.

A pleasant summer breeze patted the leaves of nearby trees.

Enjoying another sip of Burgundy, my handsome friend became animated again. Pointing past our feet, which were dangling over the wall's edge, Jesse commented: "Hey, doesn't that look like one of those Roman-style viaducts?"

I saw that a double-arched stone bridge crossed the Tauber, but I didn't hear all of what he said because I had something on my mind.

"I'd like to propose another toast."

He handed the bottle over. "The stage is yours."

I took the wine, raised the bottle, and solemnly summed up my last six months: "Here's to you, Jesse. You've made Germany a very special place for me and I really want to thank you for all the amazing new experiences. I couldn't have done it without you."

Jesse's aura was magnetic as he took his acceptance drink. His pheromones were tingling my innermost senses, making my heart thump.

He replied with an announcement of his own. "I guess you heard that my girlfriend and I broke up."

"Yes, Reuben mentioned it. You must be very sad."

"No. Not really," Jesse said, sincerely. "In fact, it was my idea. The truth is, I've fallen for someone else...a certain chambermaid."

Then, as I looked into his eyes, he took my hand. In the glowing moonlight, our eager lips drew closer and locked passionately. I dissolved in his arms. At that moment, the patter of leaves fell silent and the river ran still.

∞

The next morning, my fellow adventurer and I powered up the GPS receiver and exited Rothenburg in the direction it pointed through the Kobolzeller gate. According to our high-tech compass, we were less than one kilometer from either realizing that I needed to re-examine the Frail Man's clue or unearthing a 600-year-old relic that could pay off in a lifetime of dreams.

The palm of my hand began to sweat as I gripped the receiver. It now indicated .63 kilometers as we walked over an ancient stone bridge spanning the Tauber. Off to the right were more tremendous views of Rothenburg.

Our rural route led us past picturesque farmhouses, horses trotting in paddocks, green meadows, and a Gothic church. As we got closer, our scenic path paralleled the river, which was more like a babbling brook, one that matched perfectly with the Frail Man's clue. Ahead, a wood-covered footbridge straddled the Tauber, where the receiver pointed to the opposite bank, estimating 100 meters farther to Pay Day.

We traversed the bridge and were directed left across a lush field dripping with dewdrops that had accumulated overnight. Jesse and I stared at the compass like two kids transfixed on a new video game as the distance lessened with every pace: 30 meters, then 20, 10, 5, until it zeroed-out near a cluster of trees and bushes. Jesse looked at me with nervous anticipation. I began to tremble.

The engineering department told us that GPS receivers were accurate to within 10 to 100 feet, depending on signal strength with orbiting satellites. Therefore, we still had our work cut out for us.

Nearby, I heard rustling noises coming from the bushes. I snapped my head in the direction of the sound but didn't see anything.

"Did you hear that?!" I asked, anxiously. Jesse was too busy surveying the ground for unusual formations to notice. Perhaps my nerves were getting the better of me.

The cluster of trees hugged the riverbank and extended some 20 feet into the lush field. I concentrated on the task at hand and began kicking over leaves and branches looking for anything odd. We painstakingly combed every inch of the area, but nothing appeared out of the ordinary.

Every now and then we did spot a few suspect patches of earth, which brought us to our knees like archaeologists hunched over and scratching at the dirt for that illusive find. Alas, our efforts always ended in disappointment and nursing sore fingers. Perhaps we were going about it wrong; maybe it was hidden up, and not down. Therefore, we scoured the limbs and boughs of the trees. Still nothing.

Things weren't looking so good. I was beginning to feel like the dim-witted student banished to the corner of the classroom. Nearly an hour had passed and all we'd accomplished was to successfully transform the once pristine area into a grid of deep cavities and heaped piles of leaves and twigs as if a band of gophers high on amphetamines had blown through.

It was obvious: I had failed at solving the clue and had led Jesse on the proverbial wild-goose chase. We hung our heads low and began hoofing it back to Rothenburg. That's when Jesse detected an unnatural soil arrangement under his foot.

"Wait...this doesn't quite feel right," he said, somewhat anxious.

We dropped to our hands and knees once again, clawing at the earth with the tips of our fingers. Dirt piled up at our side as we dug deeper and deeper, until our elbows were lost in the hollow. Suddenly, my fingers touched metal. I yelped in excitement!

We impatiently brushed the dirt away and scraped around the sides of the object. It appeared to be an old lockbox.

Jesse lifted the heavy container from its earthen grave to ground level. We struggled with the latch and then, without warning, it burst open. A box full of newspaper clippings and hand-written notes stared us in the face, and beneath them was a layer of coarse fabric. Neither Jesse nor I had the faintest idea of what to make of it.

After separating the contents, we found an exquisite jewelry box made of wood, hand-carved and big enough to hold a pair of sneakers.

Behind us, more rustling noises came from the bushes. This time Jesse heard them, too. As we turned around, a faceless figure darted from the dense shrubbery and snatched the jewelry box.

Jesse leapt to his feet and pursued the thief up a steep path that disappeared into a shadowy forest. I grabbed the lockbox and followed.

The path climbed steeply in the direction of Rothenburg's fortified walls. Jesse was somewhere up ahead, but nowhere to be seen. I jogged frantically to keep pace. My leg muscles started to tighten, but I couldn't stop. I had to keep moving. I was alone, breathless, in a dark forest. With the lockbox securely tucked under my arm, I rushed forward like a football player running with the ball.

"Sydney!" Jesse hollered from a distance. "Are you all right?"

I cranked my head around and saw Jesse stomping out from a veil of trees. I've never been happier to see my faithful friend.

"I'm fine," I insisted. "How 'bout you?!"

Jesse looked relieved. Beads of sweat slid down his face and onto the brown soil below. He held up the jewelry box with both hands.

"I was within an arm's length of the thief..." he puffed, "and as I reached out to grab his shirt, he tripped over a log and the box flew from his hand as he tumbled down the embankment."

"Did you get a look at him?"

"No. Once he got back on his feet, he took off running."

On that note, we refocused our attention on the mysterious jewelry box. Kneeling to the ground, Jesse placed the box before us and gently levered it open with a pocketknife.

I doubled blinked, not believing my eyes. Inside sat a golden cross studded with jewels that glinted in a rainbow of colors. It had to be *das Bayernkreuz*.

Jesse reached in to pick up the sacred relic. As he did, he shifted his deep brown eyes to me and smiled that infectious smile.

"I think this belongs to you," he said, placing the cross carefully in my hands.

I cradled its weighty frame and rose to my feet.

Seemingly mesmerized by the relic, Jesse gently brushed the jewels with his forefinger. We looked at each other, soberly, then began to giggle. I cried tears of joy.

Jesse wrapped his arms around me — and the Bavarian Cross — and lifted me a foot off the ground, laughing.

I could not believe that I held an object that was centuries old and certainly worth a fortune. I was thrilled, elated, tense, and nervous as all heck. We had to make tracks, fast, before the thief returned with backup.

Jesse gave me a soft kiss. "What now?" he asked.

"I don't know," I replied. "I really don't know. I never thought we'd actually find it. Maybe we can locate its rightful owner. Maybe there's a reward?"

I felt confused, and sad. A river of emotions washed over me. "I guess it's over. The adventure is over."

"Oh shit!" Jesse cursed, grabbing my shirt and towing me to the ground. He pointed into the trees. "Someone's coming."

We crouched behind a bush, hidden from view. Jesse held my hand. His grip was tight. He turned to me, looking anxiously into my eyes. "Maybe the adventure is just beginning?"

THE END

meet the author
brett harriman

Brett Harriman grew up in the seaside town of Dana Point, California, and was fortunate enough to have parents who dragged their kids with them everywhere they went, including on overseas vacations. Thus, the travel bug kicked in early.

Brett's writings are inspired by his love of travel, to which he has driven across America, trekked around Australia, and explored Europe extensively. Brett lived in Australia for a decade and in Europe for five years, where he was an official tour guide for the U.S. Armed Forces in Germany. In that role, Brett led more than 10,000 servicemen and women and their families through many historically rich cities, towns, villages and Alpine hamlets.

Brett continues to spend some three months every year in Europe leading tours and updating his guidebooks (trekking across cities and towns knocking on doors and asking a zillion questions, inspecting hotel rooms and looking under mattresses, double checking prices and opening times and transportation schedules, sampling schnitzel and beer and strudel...).

In 2011, for all his hard work, Brett was selected by the president of Oktoberfest to represent the USA during the world-famous festival in Munich, Germany.

When he is not in Europe sleuthing out the latest travel information or on tour, Brett spends his time in Pahrump (55 miles west of Las Vegas), Nevada, where his parents have retired and he finds serene sanctuary to compile and compose his travel book series, tour packages, and publishing business.

Brett enjoying the Austrian Alps high above Innsbruck

D-Day Beaches & Beyond tour

Join Brett in Normandy, France
— September 3-6, 2019

This year (2019) marks the 75th anniversary of the D-Day landings

A history lesson you will never forget!

Belgium Beer & Battlefields tour

Join Brett in Belgium— September 7-13, 2019

Bruges to Dunkirk via Bastogne
& Battle of the Bulge

Germany & Austria Highlights tour

Join Brett on his adventure novel tour "Quest for the Bavarian Cross" that takes in wowing highlights from both Germany and Austria

Join Brett in Europe —
September 14-21, 2019

Frankfurt to Munich via Ludwig's Castles & The Sound of Music

...the Eagle's Nest, too

The best of Oktoberfest

Join Brett in Munich, Germany — Oktoberfest dates (2019): September 20 thru October 7

Experience Oktoberfest like a local on one of Brett's inexpensive packages

OktoberfestPackage.com

Complement this guide with other Brett books and resources

Every year Brett's brand recognition increases across the world together with his array of destination guides and tour programs.

This year, if you're headed to Germany, Austria, Belgium, or Normandy in France, join Brett for a cornucopia of culture and feasts of fun.

So come along, and travel like a local. *Your journey begins now!*

In the works — Munich & Ludwig's Castles, Hitler's Eagle's Nest

In the works — Vienna & Innsbruck

Available — Salzburg & The Sound of Music

Free on our site — American Military Lest We Forget Cemeteries in Europe

47

HILLS

Brewing Co.

☆ SSF,Ca ☆ Est.2012 ☆

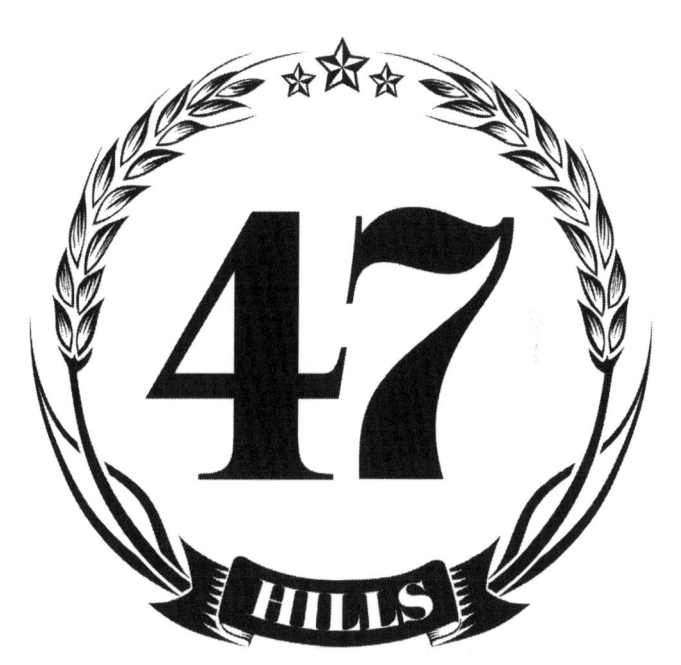

Printed in Great Britain
by Amazon